MW00563476

WE WALKED INTO RIP'S APARTMENT. You wouldn't think a single guy, an ex-bouncer to be so immaculately neat. Rip didn't own a lot of possessions, but what he had was clean and orderly. A stack of dinner plates sat on the kitchen counter next to two coffee cups in perfect alignment. Clean silverware stood in a drinking glass. The toaster, minus crumbs, shone like a beacon. Two spotless sauce pans and a skillet were arranged on top of the icebox. What little space he had in the kitchenette he made good use of. The cabinet held a can of sardines, a can of pinto beans, and a box of Wheaties. On the top shelf inside the icebox, sat a package of bacon, carton of eggs, and a stick of butter. The lower shelf held a case of Falstaff beer cans, also aligned with each label showing out. I looked over to find Dixon was staring off into space.

"What is it?"

"Betsy's lying. She knows more than she's telling."

"She's scared. You should have pushed her harder."

"Let her stew for now. Was Rip in the military?"

"Not that I know of. Why?"

"I can't find one wrinkle in his bed sheets. His pillow case smells freshly laundered. There's no dust on the floor under the bed. His dresser contains the usual undershirts, socks, underwear, and handkerchiefs."

Dixon opened the closet door. Two dress shirts, a pair of slacks, a sport coat hung neatly, each in their proper category. "Look at this. A pair of scuffed cowboy boots."

"Don't sound surprised. Any self-respecting Texan has scuffed cowboy boots, even me." I looked down at his wingtips.

"What?"

"This entire time I thought you were perfect, but I just realized you're not."

Dixon straightened his tie. "You're questioning your assessment of me?"

I held up Rip's boots.

"Wait. I'm not ever going to wear cowboy boots. I don't have to, I'm not a Texan."

"You will soon be one by marriage. I suggest black boots, slightly rounded toes, modicum amount of stitchery. I'll shop around."

"No."

"At least you can wear them around the house."

"No."

"Wearing nothing else, just your boots."

"Well, maybe."

"Look at this," Dixon said. He held up a photo that had been sitting on the end table. A younger Rip and a middle-aged woman wearing a light-colored dress and white gloves.

"Probably his mother. He talked about her a few times."

"He's a big guy."

"He made a great bouncer at the Keyhole Club. He could be mean when he needed to, but he has the heart of a lamb. For a few moments, he fell for Ruth."

"I can understand that. A lot of men fall for your zany cousin. But what happened after just a few moments?"

"I dissuaded him."

"What else can you tell me about him?"

"Honestly, he's not the smartest guy in the room, but he's likeable, loyal."

"He sounds like a golden retriever. This guy plans to make it as a detective?"

"One who finds lost souls."

"Oh, that fits. There's nothing else here to see. Let's lock up and have another go at Betsy."

On the way out the phone rang. "You answer it," I said.

"Hello, Rip Thigbee's residence."

"Who's this?" I heard the caller shout.

"You first," Dixon said. After a few seconds of silence, Dixon threw down the receiver and flew downstairs into Rip's office. "Betsy!" Dixon shouted. "Damn!" He darted out the door into the street.

"What's happened?" I asked.

"Someone's nabbed Betsy."

Welcome to
Kathleen Kaska's

MURDER at the PONTCHARTRAIN

What is it like reading a Sydney Lockhart Mystery? Picture if you will, Carl Hiaasen writing a classic film noir featuring the zany, red-haired reporter Sydney Lockhart who somehow gets herself into more tight situations than Lucille Ball did in a whole season of I Love Lucy.

—*Bruce Rolfe, author of the Chip Hale Handyman Mystery*

"Sydney Lockhart is one of the feistiest, funniest P.I.'s in Texas-or anywhere else! '50s pop culture and a crowd of quirky characters make Kaska's latest mystery a killer read."

—*Sheila Webster Boneham, author of Catwalk and the other Animals in Focus mysteries*

MURDER AT
THE PONTCHARTRAIN

Also by Kathleen Kaska

The Sydney Lockhart Mystery Series
Murder at the Arlington
Murder at the Luther
Murder at the Galvez
Murder at the Driskill
Murder at the Menger
Murder at the Ponchartrain

The Man Who Saved the Whooping Crane:
The Robert Porter Allen Story

The Kate Caraway Mystery Series
Run Dog Run
A Two Horse Town
Eagle Crossing

The Classic Mystery TriviographyTM Series
The Sherlock Holmes Quiz Book
The Agatha Christie Triviography and Quiz Book
The Alfred Hitchcock Triviography and Quiz Book

Do You Have a Catharsis Handy? Five-Minute Writing Tips

MURDER AT

THE PONTCHARTRAIN

Kathleen Kaska

Anamcara Press LLC

Published in 2023 by Anamcara Press LLC
Author © 2023 by Kathleen Kaska
Cover and Book design by Maureen Carroll
Arial, Tomarik, Lato, Professor Minty
Printed in the United States of America.

Book description: Sydney Lockhart is at it again, trying to solve a murder in another famous hotel while avoiding being locked up for the very crime she's investigating. Bribes, fixed races, dirty money and unkempt places. She'll get to the bottom of this case in her own determined style.

This is a work of fiction. Names, characters, and incidents are products of the author's imagination or are used fictitiously and are not to be construed as real. Any resemblance to actual events, locales, organizations or persons, living or dead, is entirely coincidental.

All rights reserved. No part of this publication may be reproduced, distributed, or transmitted in any form or by any means, including photocopying, recording, or other electronic or mechanical methods, without the prior written permission of the publisher, except in the case of brief quotations embodied in critical reviews and certain other noncommercial uses permitted by copyright law. For permission requests, write to the publisher, addressed "Attention: Permissions Coordinator," at the address below.

ANAMCARA PRESS LLC
P.O. Box 442072, Lawrence, KS 66044
https://anamcara-press.com

Ordering Information:
Quantity sales. Special discounts are available on quantity purchases by corporations, associations, and others. For details, contact the publisher at the address above. Orders by U.S. trade bookstores and wholesalers. Please contact Ingram Distribution.

ISBN-13: Murder at the Menger, 978-1-941237-94-6 (Paperback)
ISBN-13: Murder at the Menger,   978-1-941237-96-0 (EBook)
ISBN-13: Murder at the Menger, 978-1-941237-95-3 (Hardcover)
FIC022040   FICTION / Mystery & Detective / Women Sleuths
FIC022070   FICTION / Mystery & Detective / Cozy / General
FIC027250   FICTION / Romance / Romantic Comedy

Library of Congress Control Number: 2023935245

To Chase & Kim

who have their own inspirational story to tell.

ADRIAN DISTRICT LIBRARY
143 E. Maumee Street
Adrian, MI 49221

CHAPTER ONE

Danny Pistow tried to hang himself three times and still couldn't get it right. I know, I was there. Most women my age have had three kids. I've had three careers, each one more bizarre than the last; add to that the colorful characters I've attracted, and you'll get the idea of what my life has been like.

I'm Sydney Lockhart. PI Ralph Dixon, my partner and soon-to-be husband, and I own the Dixon, Lockhart, and Ludlow Detective Agency. The name Ludlow belongs to our young, handsome partner Billy Ludlow who used to work as a deputy for the Palacios Police Department. He helped me solve a murder case, one in which I was the main suspect. Actually, we opened our agency because most of the murders we'd been involved in, I was the main suspect. There's not much on the books right now, so here I sit in a decrepit old theater watching a potential hanging.

Yesterday, I got roped into helping Lydia LaBeau—colorful character doesn't even begin to describe Lydia—set up a gallows on stage at the Next to Nothing Theater in Austin. The production company was staging a new play—*Madame Butterfly Seeks Revenge*. Danny Pistow was playing Pinkerton, a character who deserved a good lashing for what he did to Butterfly, but I have yet to understand how his hanging fits into the story. I've learned to keep my mouth shut. Only age twelve, Lydia seemed to know what she was doing, even though it appeared as if the pint-size playwright made it up as she went along. Since her father, Serge, owned the theater, Lydia could pretty much do whatever she wanted, which was good for business because Serge's I.Q hovered just above lukewarm.

My job was to make sure the trapdoor worked properly, an important task I know, however, my heart was not in it. Two weeks ago, Ralph Dixon, the sexiest guy south of the Mason-Dixon line, and I were eloping to New Orleans when we made a U-turn outside Beaumont and headed back to Austin. We'd been discussing our previous case, a murder at the Menger Hotel in San Antonio. I'd been working the case from the Menger while Dixon was doing his thing in Austin. I was telling him more about Nora Jasper, a key player in that case who fled before I could bring her in. The more we talked, the more we realized we'd screwed up by not pursuing Nora, who scammed several people out of a lot of cash and almost killed me. There was no way we were getting married with the boondoggle hanging over us. So, Dixon was on his way to Hot Springs, Arkansas to find out more about Nora, who, as it turned out was really his sister, Loretta.

"Sydney, will you stop daydreaming and get up there and check the trapdoor?" Lydia was going toe-to-toe with actor Danny Pistow. He had threatened to walk off the stage and not return. I wanted to join him.

"Trapdoors are not my field of expertise," I said, "but I'll take a look." A seven-foot-tall wooden box-like structure with a ladder leaning next to it had caused Pistow, aka Pinkerton, some issues. He was supposed to climb up with his hands tied behind his back. Being acrophobic, he was more concerned about falling off the ladder than dropping from the trapdoor. Lydia's response to his concern was to assign him a series of balancing exercises.

The stagehand operating the trapdoor was crouched inside the structure, checking the release mechanism. The mechanism worked, but the door only opened halfway. Inside the structure, and directly under the door, was a platform on which Pistow was supposed to land, preventing a real hanging. It appeared to me that the trapdoor was not clearing the platform.

But I detected another complication. Danny is about six feet tall. Add his height to the height of the platform on which he stood, and the audience would have to crane their necks to see what was going on. I climbed up the ladder and looked down.

I couldn't see all the theater seats, which also meant that a good part of the audience couldn't see me above my knees. I called down to Lydia, telling her she had bigger problems than the trapdoor. My pronouncement caused all chatter and noise in the theater to stop. Everyone turned to Lydia. Opening night was only two weeks away, and redesigning the structure would be no small task.

A light breeze blew in from the back door, and I detected the unmistakable scent of Jungle Gardenia. *Please, God, don't let it be her.* I've always heard that if you don't pray when life is good, you shouldn't pray when it's not—an idiom I could never remember. I focused on becoming invisible. It didn't work.

"Sydney Jean Lockhart, what the hell are you doing here in this trashy theater? I found out the truth about what you're up to, and I will have none of it. You've pulled this antic before, and you will not, do you hear me, not pull it again."

"Mom? It's so good to see you."

"Oh, shut up and get down from there before you break your neck."

"I'm busy, Mom."

"Too busy to tell me you were engaged? Too busy to tell me you were eloping? Too busy to tell me why you are not married yet?"

"Something like that, yes."

"You get your sarcasm from your father. Why didn't you tell me you were back in Austin? As far as that goes, why didn't you tell me you were in San Antonio? I could have driven up. We could have talked wedding plans. That looks like a gallows. What are you doing up there anyway?"

The only answer to the first two questions was, "None of your business," which I didn't bother verbalizing. The last one was reasonable to assume since I've often thought of hanging myself when my mother was around.

Lydia had turned her attention away from Danny and was watching the mother/daughter scene unfold. Having heard, I'm sure, the words, "trashy theater," she shot Mom a death stare.

"More importantly, what are you doing here?" I said.

"I'm your mother. I know I've allowed you to go about your life how you see fit, but enough is enough. You're going to settle down. I will not let you ruin another chance at marriage."

"I'm thirty, Mom." Since giving birth to me, my mother's had one goal: to see me married and settled down to a traditional life. Forget reminding her that this is 1953, not the Victorian Era. Forget reminding her that before she settled down, she sought an acting career in Hollywood during the silent film era. She once vied for the role of the shop girl in the movie "It" but lost out to Clara Bow. Mom came back to Texas, met dad, married him, and started a family. She never forgave Clara for, as Mom often says, "ruining her life."

"My point exactly. Excuse me, young lady, but your clock is ticking." Mom turned her attention to Lydia. Being a kind-hearted person, I would have thrown myself between them to protect Lydia, but she could manage on her own. I quietly eased down the ladder and nodded to the side theater door. Lydia got my message.

"Is that really a gallows you have on stage?" Mom said to Lydia. "I dabble in community theater. You should set it farther back. If you have it too close, the audience will see too much. Let me take a look."

With my mother now focused on the hanging platform, I took the opportunity to disappear. The last thing I heard was the door clicking shut behind me. I dashed across the street to Jelly Bluesteen's club, the Blue Mist, the best blues club in Austin, Texas. Jelly took a liking to me when I solved a case involving one of his bartenders who had sticky fingers. I used to think of his place as seedy, but it's become like a second home—a place to go when I don't want to be found.

"Hey, Jelly, mind if I use your phone?"

"Use the one in the back. It's good to have you back in town, Syd. Oh, and I heard what happened to your agency's office yesterday. Is anything salvageable?"

"Luckily, the fire was in the outer office only, and most of the files are readable. Some are charred, and they all smell like smoke. All the furniture has to be replaced, but we're insured, thank goodness."

"Any idea what happened?"

"The fire department thinks it was a bad wall circuit."

"Those old buildings." He shook his head as if old buildings were a natural disaster. "I'll clean out the junk in the back room. You're welcome to use it until you are up and running again."

"Thanks, Jelly. We might take you up on that. Billy and Phoebe have most of the mess cleaned out. I'm about to go over there now to see for myself."

"I also heard about what happened on your last case in San Antonio. You should stick closer to home."

"I doubt that would help."

I placed a collect call to Galveston. My dad accepted the charges.

"As much as I love hearing from you, I'm going to have to go back to work to afford these calls."

"I'll make it short. Mom's here."

"Wonderful. Is she staying? Please tell me she is."

"You really wouldn't wish that on me."

"You're right. Maybe she'll move in with your brother. They still like each other."

"I'll work on it. How did Mom know I was back in Austin? You didn't tell her, did you?"

"Of course not. I told her you and Dixon moved to Ecuador. I guess she didn't buy it. So, if you're in Austin, that means you decided to put off the honeymoon."

"Actually, we put off the wedding." The gasp was strong enough to suck me through the phone lines. My dad and Dixon hit it off, and although my dad loves that I have an independent streak, he would also love to see me married. "Don't worry. We had to return to take care of some urgent business first."

"Your mother is still planning a big wedding for you."

"Good, let her. Just make sure she doesn't put down any deposits."

"She won't. I've hidden the checkbook. My advice, not that you asked for it, is to elope as soon as possible."

"That's still the plan. Dixon should be back tomorrow, and then we leave for New Orleans—again."

"In the meantime, what about your mother? How are you

going to make your escape without her knowing?"

"I think she found something to occupy her time."

"She's going to remodel the capitol building? If so, that should take, how long? Ten years?"

"Funny. Love you."

CHAPTER TWO

I heard Billy and Phoebe Sullivan, our secretary, giggling when I got off the elevator. They are hot and heavy into a romance. I wonder how much work gets done when Dixon and I aren't around. I walked in. "Ahem." Phoebe buttoned her blouse and winked at me. She no longer ran for the closet when caught in a romantic embrace with Billy. He wiped the lipstick from his mouth and had the decency to blush.

"The insurance adjuster will be by this afternoon," Phoebe said.

The wall was charred where the faulty circuit was located. Most of the water from the sprinkler system was mopped up, thanks to the building's cleaning crew.

"Dixon called and said he'd be back early in the morning," Billy said.

"The phone is working?"

"He called the accountant's office next door, and the guy relayed the message. Good news though, despite the fire, we took on two new clients today. A cheating wife case and a missing person case."

"The cheating wife case will be easy. The missing person could take time. Maybe Dixon and I should postpone our trip. New Orleans isn't going anywhere."

"I can handle both," Billy said. "Besides, you two need a vacation."

"Jelly said we could use his back office if we need it."

"I think we're good," Billy said. "An electrician's coming tomorrow, and the outer office won't take long to repaint. We should also have phone service this afternoon. We were lucky, you know. The entire office or even the building could have been destroyed."

"I'm ducking out to the furniture store to see what's on hand," Phoebe said. "I'll find something similar to what we had. Want to come along, Syd?"

"No thanks. I want to hear about this missing person."

"Lawrence Earl Nash went fishing on the river below Tom Miller Dam on Saturday," Billy said. "When he didn't return home the next morning, his wife called the police. They found his boat on the shoreline about half a mile away from the boat launch, but no Nash. They dragged the area, no Nash. According to the wife, he was a devoted husband and father, pillar of the community, usher at the 10:00 Mass at Saint Mary's every Sunday morning. She was certain something bad happened to him."

"Do you know the guy?" Billy's a devoted Catholic and a member of St. Mary's Parish.

"Nope, I usually attend the earlier Mass. But here's the thing. Mrs. Nash didn't hire us. His girlfriend did."

"The two women became too much for the guy to handle, so he bailed?"

"Not quite. The story gets more interesting. I just came from Sears, where the devoted husband and pillar of the community works as the automotive department manager. Last week, he was fired for *adjusting* the books to a tune of eighteen thousand dollars. His secretary was in tears and swears that it was all a big mistake. She seemed very attached to her boss. I took the poor girl for a cup of coffee, and she spilled. She and Larry were getting married as soon as he divorced his wife. And guess what? The secretary wasn't the girlfriend who hired us."

"Girl number three."

"Girl number three."

"I love this job. Are all three women in the dark?"

"Looks like it. I'll break the news to the woman who hired us. Then I'll call the cops and tell them not to bother searching for Nash's body. Quick case, solved."

I LEFT BILLY AND PHOEBE to take care of business and stopped by my newly renovated apartment where I've lived for five years. Dixon and I hadn't had time to discuss our living situation once we tied the knot. The small cottage that he rented from Lester and Carolyn Granger was once a carriage house, and much nicer than my apartment. It made sense for me and my pets to move into the cottage since the Grangers had become like a second family to us.

I've lived alone since I graduated from UT, and the thought of giving that up scared me. True, Dixon and I spent most nights together, but having my own place meant I could have privacy if I wanted. I looked down at my new engagement ring—a gold band with a small, sweet, solitary diamond. Dixon and I picked it out together. We wanted something that would look nice snuggled up against his grandmother's wedding ring, which would be mine soon. It looked odd on my finger. Mrs. Ralph Dixon. Sydney Dixon. I don't think I could ever get used to not being called Lockhart. Few people called Dixon by his first name. And they do so without being told. He's a solid Dixon, not a Ralph. My mother is the only one who calls him by his first name. That should tell you something. It's become trendy now for women, once they marry, to hyphenate their name, but to me, that shows a lack of decisiveness. I am not Dixon. Dixon is Dixon. I'm Sydney. Jeez, I'm insane. Thankfully, my poodle Monroe scratched at the back door, putting an end to my crazy thoughts. Sunset was fast approaching, and my dog and I both needed a walk along the lake.

Some people referred to it as a waterway, others as a river. The Colorado River's flow is dammed up northwest of Austin. The Tom Miller Dam is located right before the river begins to flow through the middle of the city, creating Lake Austin. I live a five-minute walk from the boat dock. This is my backyard, and I love it.

I let Monroe off the leash. She jumped in the water and sent a flock of mallards into flight. Her favorite thing to do. To keep her from swimming after them, I distracted her with a tennis ball. Otherwise I feared she'd follow them all the way upstream to the dam. We played toss and splash until my arm gave out. I took off my shoes and dangled my feet in the water. A pleasant breeze blew across the lake. Monroe stood over me, repeatedly dropping the dirty ball into my lap. After a few minutes, she gave up and flopped down next to me. We watched the sky turn from a smoky blue as streaks of magenta and purple ushered in another lovely evening in the capital city. When the mosquitoes came out, we made our way back to the apartment.

I HOSED THE NOW DRIED MUD off of Monroe and watched my crazy dog dry herself on my lawn. We went inside, where she claimed the sofa. My ornery cat, Mealworm, had come out from under the bed only once since I'd been home from San Antonio. While I was gone, Lydia and Carolyn Granger saw to my four-legged family. Although I rescued Mealworm from the pound, I've never been her favorite person. I could go as far as saying I'm her least favorite person. My poodle, on the other hand, adores me. Lydia's father, Serge, claims that Mealworm hates her name and is punishing me. I gave Monroe a biscuit, and she smiled. The cat got a fresh saucer of milk, not that she cared.

I was eager to speak to Dixon. To make the phone ring, I made a cheese sandwich, poured a glass of wine, and started a bubble bath. It worked every time. I accepted the collect call.

"Did I interrupt your bath?"

"It's ready and waiting. Find out anything?"

"Not much. My grandmother hasn't heard from Loretta in at least three years, neither have any of her friends."

"I haven't met your grandmother. I'd like to."

"My grandmother will love you. We'll pay her a visit after we get hitched."

"How about your mother? Did you ask her about Loretta?"

"I didn't bother. My mother is wackier than Loretta."

I filled Dixon in on the Nash case and the state of the office.

"Do you think we should stick around?" he asked.

"I thought about it until my mother showed up today."

"Oops."

"She managed to track me down at the theater. I think she suspects we'll elope, and she's here to try and prevent it. I managed to avoid her, but I fear she'll be around later. I thought I'd take the dog and cat and stay in your cottage tonight."

"Good plan. We'll deal with the fallout later. I'll be home in the morning."

"You're going to drive all night?"

"That's my plan. Have your bags packed. We'll leave as soon as I get there. If I hadn't overreacted, we'd be married now and lounging in our room at the Pontchartrain Hotel. You can do the driving tomorrow. I'll sleep. We'll be in the Big Easy tomorrow night. Does that answer your question?"

"It does."

"Good. Take one suitcase, a small one. You won't need a lot of clothes. Don't let your bath get cold. Oh, one more thing. My car's engine has been missing a lot lately. I don't want to drive it to New Orleans. Why don't we take yours?"

"I told Phoebe she could use it while we were gone. With all that's happened, she needed wheels. I'll see about renting a car first thing in the morning. We can turn it in when we get to New Orleans since we won't need it there, and we can fly home."

"Sounds good."

I hung up. Before I could put a toe in the water, the phone rang again.

"Syd, I tried to call you several times," Billy said. "But your phone's been busy. I wanted to warn you. Your mother is on her way over to your apartment as we speak."

I pulled the plug in the bathtub, threw a few clothes in a suitcase, and had the animals in the car in less than two minutes. We made ourselves at home in Dixon's cottage. After another glass of wine, I set the alarm. Within moments, the aroma of beignets and chicory coffee made their way into my dreams.

CHAPTER THREE

I thought I'd died and gone to Tara. I woke to see luscious green-print brocade drapery covering the floor to ceiling windows. I wanted to rip them down and do what Scarlett did in *Gone With the Wind*, except I don't sew. I rubbed the sleep from my eyes and when I looked again, the drapes were still there, open to an early morning. I was not in Georgia or my little apartment on Enfield Road in Austin. I was not dreaming. I was in New Orleans in a two-room suite at the Pontchartrain Hotel with a warm pillow beside me and rumpled sheets twisted around my legs.

Light from the window cast a soft glow over the body of an Adonis with messy hair, wearing only a towel. He lifted the silver cover off of a gleaming white china platter and smiled at me. Detective Ralph Dixon, my Detective Ralph Dixon, poured me a cup of coffee and offered me a croissant.

"We're really here," I said.

"We are, hon. I hope I didn't get you up too early. You drove like a demon yesterday while I slept."

"Once my head hit this pillow, I was out."

"If you don't mind getting married in your work clothes—I assume you don't want a gown—we can get the licenses and make it official before noon."

"No flowers?"

"We can pick up some at the French Market." He handed me my coffee.

"We're really going to do this?"

"You changed your mind?"

"No, absolutely no. Well, no."

He smiled. My heart melted. "Was that 'hell no,' or 'well, no?'"

"Last thing I remember thinking about before falling asleep was my name. I like the sound of Sydney Lockhart."

"Oops. This doesn't sound good. We can wait."

"No, no. I'm ready with the 'I do.' But Sydney Dixon sounds so odd."

"Don't change your last name. Leave it. I met Sydney Lockhart and you will always be Sydney Lockhart. Anything else bothering you?"

"I don't have a ring for you."

"We'll stop at a jewelry store, or I'll use a rubber band."

"You make things so easy."

"They are. Sit up." He fluffed my pillows and brought the breakfast tray and placed it between us. "I'm glad we decided to come here. I've only been to New Orleans twice. The first time was with some of my college buddies. As you might expect, we had a raucous weekend."

"You?"

"Wasn't my thing, but yeah, we partied, or they did most of the partying. I made sure we got back to the place where we were staying without being arrested. Years later, when I was in the police department in Hot Springs, I came here by myself on vacation mainly to fish and enjoy the food. It was a completely different world compared to Hot Springs. We had our gangsters and thugs, sure, and so did New Orleans, but here the atmosphere felt raw, jovial, more carefree and not so notorious. When I was a kid growing up in Hot Springs, you never knew who was going to get gunned down on the streets. Crazy times. Anyway, back then I often thought of bringing my future wife here."

I turned and looked at my future husband, and realized I knew so little about his past. He's the type who's always in the present. Maybe that comes from being in law enforcement.

"I have another connection to this place. My parents met here. My father had a brief stint in the Merchant Marines. My mother was here visiting a friend. They met at some afternoon soiree, as she told it. She was eighteen and he was twenty seven."

"Love at first sight?"

"Hardly. My father was smitten, but my mother wasn't too impressed by his shyness. But by the end of the month, they decided to get married."

"Your father must have turned on the charm."

"That, and it was 1917, WWI was in full swing. Who knew what the outcome would be? It was one of those, let's get married now because the world might end tomorrow romances. They put up with each other until my sister, Loretta came along sixteen years after me. Want this other croissant?"

"It's yours. You've hardly ever talked about your childhood or your family."

"Not much else to tell. My mother was young and unsure of herself in a manic sort of way when she married dad. Even as a kid, I thought she was wacko."

"Not unlike my mother."

"You're wrong there. Your mother may be a bit dramatic, but your parents are still married. And your dad is a saint. I spent most of my time with my grandmother who I've already told you about. My mother would up and leave sometimes, not say where she was going or when she'd be back. After a while my dad didn't even ask and I didn't care. I left for college when Loretta was two. We never bonded. She was with my mother most of the time while I was with my grandmother. My dad died when I was a freshman at the University of Arkansas, and I rarely saw my mother after that, nor my sister, except to drop by on birthdays and once in a while for Thanksgiving. Considering my mother's shenanigans, I wouldn't be surprise if Loretta was my half-sister. We look nothing alike."

"If you're trying to scare me out of marrying you, it isn't working."

"Good, but I woke up this morning thinking that I knew a lot about your family, spent a bit of time with them when they celebrated their thirtieth anniversary, and you knew next to nothing about mine. Also, with Loretta coming out of the woodwork and almost getting you killed and scamming a bunch of people out of a bunch of money, I thought you needed to know what you're getting into."

"I'm in if you're in."

"The courthouse isn't open yet. Let's unpack, then go for a walk and enjoy this lovely morning. Are you sure you're ready?"

"Pour me another cup of coffee and I'll think about it while you get dressed."

"You can also think about this." He sat my cup aside and removed the tray. The towel was gone and I was in sensual heaven.

We strolled down to Bourbon Street. Bars and nightclubs were airing out, sweeping away last night's merriment. Juke boxes still spilled out zydeco music, a few musicians still played their instruments on street corners. While we slept, the Big Easy was squeezing out every last drop of life from the previous evening.

Dixon and I held hands and talked. Something we didn't do often enough. It's been a mad rush since the day we met less than a year ago—solving cases, opening the agency, solving more cases, dealing with the crazy people in our lives. They seemed to wriggle out of the woodwork and latch on to us, resulting in conversations that always centered around our work. Life savers of the insane, we were. Finally, the chance came for us to be together and enjoy one another's company. We drove all day arriving at the hotel in time for a late meal. The plan, when we left Austin yesterday morning, was to get married, have fun in New Orleans for a few days, and return to work. In the business we're in you can't assume what the next day will bring. You have to grab downtime before it slides away. You have to get up early before the crazies show up.

The owner of the jewelry store on Jackson Square placed his open sign in the window and we walked in. I bought Dixon a plain 14 karat gold band. I decided flowers weren't necessary. Our next stop, the courthouse.

Even this early in the morning, the courthouse was already stifling. Stale air hung thick, the ceiling fans merely churning a vapor soup. The clerk in charge of marriage licenses was a woman. At least I think she was. Her face was hidden by a halo of cigarette smoke. Her voice sounded raspier then a barking seal. She handed us the papers we needed to fill out.

"I need to make sure you are who you say you are. A copy of your driver's licenses and birth certificates will certify this. I hope you brought them."

"We did," Dixon said.

"If you've been married before, you need to show a certified copy of the divorce degree," she said.

"No divorces," Dixon said.

"If widowed, you need to show a copy of your deceased spouse's death certificate."

"Neither one of us has been married before," I said. She looked as if she didn't believe either of us.

"You have to know your social security number."

I reached for my purse, Dixon for his wallet.

"I don't need to see them. Just wanted to make sure you had them. Fill it in where the form indicates. I hope you didn't plan on getting married right now because we have a twenty-four-hour waiting period."

"We're here for a few days," Dixon said. "We'll be back tomorrow."

"A lot of people think they can waltz in here and tie the knot immediately. We don't allow that."

"Understood," Dixon said.

"This is New Orleans. People go to Pat O'Brien's, have a few Hurricanes, get friendly with strangers, wind up spending the night together, and think they're in love. They fill out the form, waltz out of here, and I never see them again."

"We've known each other for a few months," Dixon said. "We haven't had any Hurricanes, nor have we been to Pat O'Brien's."

"You're not from here, then?"

"Texas."

She looked down from her perch. "Where are your boots?"

"My fiancée's from Texas, I'm from Arkansas."

"Close enough. Like I said, you have twenty-four hours to think about it."

I wanted to tell the headless, nosy woman that we started sleeping together shortly after we met, but she'd probably ask for certification, so I kept my mouth shut and we waltzed out.

"That went well," I said.

"I should have realized there'd be a waiting period."

"No problem. Tomorrow is fine. Hey, since we're here, let's stop in to see how Rip Thigbee is doing," I said.

"The ghost detective. I haven't yet had the honor of meeting the guy. I want to shake his hand for pulling you out of the San Antonio River. We should take him to Pat O'Brien's so I can buy him a drink. For some reason, I have an urge for a Hurricane. Lead the way."

"Rip's place is next to Marie Laveau's House of Voodoo. Up ahead, there, Thigbee's Finder of Lost Souls." A closed sign hung crooked on the door. I peeked in through the front window. The room, unlike the House of Voodoo with its over abundant paraphernalia that seemed ready to ooze out onto the street, was sparsely furnished and uncluttered. Long and narrow, no more than ten feet by twenty, the room faded in the dark the farther back it went into the building. Dim light coming through the front windows showed two posters on one wall: the St. Louis Cemetery near here, and the Lafayette Cemetery in the Garden District. The opposite wall held framed photographs of headstones and monuments. I guess this was Rip's attempt to give his office an eerie atmosphere. Other than a small desk and two chairs, I didn't see much else. "Doesn't look good," I said.

"Maybe he has limited hours. How busy can he be?"

I stepped into the House of Voodoo. A young wisp of a woman was having an emotional conversation with an older woman wearing a turban who was seated behind the counter. A deck of tarot cards spread out on the counter. They jerked around when we walked in. You'd think customers coming through the front door was the last thing they expected.

"Excuse me," said the woman in the turban. "Come back later. We're in the middle of something right now. Besides, I'm not actually open yet. I like to keep the door open in case a breeze wanders by."

"We're looking for Rip Thigbee," I said. "Do you know when his office will be open?"

The young woman burst into tears. "You know Rip?" she said. It was more of an accusation, than a question.

"Friends from Texas," I said. "Is everything okay?"

The two women exchanged looks. "I'm Frida Mae. This is my shop. This is Betsy Radley. She works for Rip. We're worried. He hasn't been in for more than a week. We're afraid something has happened to him."

"Perhaps we should have a look," Dixon said, flashing his PI license. "Do you have a key to his office." He had a way of making his voice sound smooth and soothing—warm, rich chocolate sliding down his throat. He could have held the two women at gunpoint and demanded they empty the register, and they would have been delighted to do so.

Betsy reached into her skirt pocket. "I'll let you in. I have a key."

"After you're finished next door," said Frida Mae, "come back in. I have some wonderful love potions you might like."

CHAPTER FOUR

Betsy inserted the key and pushed open the door. "You'll have to excuse Frida Mae. She gets too friendly sometimes. Look around. Rip was so excited about his new business. He was here every morning when I came to work and often stayed late."

"A lot of business?" I asked.

"No, hardly any, but that didn't get him down. He knew sooner or later, things would pick up."

"Do you mind?" Dixon asked, pointing to the desk.

"Clues? You're looking for clues? I've already looked around, but go ahead. I might have missed something."

"Sydney, you're better at this than I am. Take a look, will you?"

I was not better than Dixon in uncovering evidence, but I knew his motive for passing the search over to me. Betsy was already putty in his hands. I'm surprised she wasn't drooling. I sat down and began my meticulous perusal of the drawers and files on Rip's desk.

"Has anything happened recently?" Dixon asked.

Betsy's faced reddened and her eyes widened. "What do you mean?" Dixon's question must have sent the girl's thoughts to something other than investigating the souls of dead people.

"Like a case, I mean. Something that would cause him to leave town."

"Oh, I see." I suspected Betsy was clearly relieved from having to admit to a crush or budding romance with her boss. "I don't know if I should talk about clients."

"You don't have to name names," Dixon said.

"Oh, that's true. There was this one woman who came in a few days before Rip disappeared. She said someone was vandalizing her husband's tomb. He's buried in the St. Louis Cemetery." She pointed to one of the posters hanging on the wall.

"Would that be a Mrs. Frank Threadgill?" I said, looking down at the notes Rip made on his calendar.

"Oh!"

"It's okay, Miss Radley. I'm also a detective," I said. "Rip worked with me on a case not long ago."

"Oh, you're the one from Austin. Rip told me about you."

"I'm Sydney Lockhart and this is Ralph Dixon."

"Rip couldn't stop talking about you, Miss Lockhart. He said you were the one who inspired him to become a detective."

"If he's in trouble, maybe we can help," I said.

"Yes, okay. The wife's name is Mildred Threadgill. She was spitting mad about someone messing around with her husband's tomb. Said the police wouldn't do anything, said that vandals had always been a problem in the cemeteries."

Dixon held back a chuckle. "Did Rip say he'd look into it?"

"At first, no, but the woman was insistent. Finally, Rip agreed to go with Mrs. Threadgill and check it out. That's the last I saw of him." Tears slid down her face.

"We could have a quick look, I suppose," Dixon said.

"I've always wanted to see the historic cemetery," I said. "Would you like to come with us, Betsy?"

"Oh no! Not me. That's the most haunted cemetery in New Orleans. I wouldn't go within a mile of it."

"Can you tell us anything else about Mrs. Threadgill?" Dixon asked.

"All I know is her husband died about a month ago. I just got a funny feeling about Mrs. Threadgill when she was here. Frida Mae said it was bad juju. If you don't deal with it, it gets worse."

"I'll trust you on that one," Dixon said. "Can you think of any place Mr. Thigbee would go for any reason?"

Her eyes darted to the desk, the door, and the ceiling. She shook her head.

"If Mr. Thigbee returns, tell him we're staying at the Pontchartrain Hotel for a few days," Dixon said. "We'll let you know what we find out at the cemetery. In the meantime, why don't you keep the office open."

"I will, yes." The blush returned. "Thank you, Mr. Dixon." One would have thought I wasn't even in the room.

THE MORNING HAD TURNED MUGGY and a fog had rolled in from the river, but St. Louis Cemetery felt eerily cool. "This place is huge. It will take us all day to find Frank Threadgill's tomb."

"There's the cemetery attendant's building. Let's see if we can find a map."

The place was no bigger than a closet. Dixon waited on the front step while I went inside.

"Threadgill tomb?" he said. "Are you family or friends?"

"Acquaintances."

The attendant hesitated but marked the map, showing the location of Threadgill's tomb. "The quickest way to get there is to take the path on the left." He pointed out the window to a narrow path overgrown with weeds that led between a long row of vaults. I thanked him and left.

"According to the map, Frank Threadgill was laid to rest in the non-Catholic section."

"This place is ancient," Dixon said. "Look at some of these vault markers—1789, 1803. I could easily spend an entire day wandering around here."

"It's eerie seeing all these above-ground tombs."

"Hey, look. Here's a legend showing the tombs of famous people, one of them being Marie Laveau, the original Voodoo Queen. We should also find her tomb since Rip is so enamored with the deceased woman."

"I can hear it now. 'What did you do on your honeymoon?' 'We toured the cemeteries in New Orleans.'"

"Those who know us wouldn't be surprised," Dixon said.

I looked at the map. "This way. Not far."

The Cornelius family mausoleum overshadowed Frank Threadgill's tomb on the western edge of the cemetery. I doubted we would have found it without the map. Threadgill's tomb was more than a little disturbed. The lid of the vault containing the coffin had been recently chipped away on one corner and red paint splattered over it. One of the cement flower vases had been smashed to pieces. Flowers torn up and strewn next to the grave. It looked as if someone had tried to stomp them into the ground.

Dixon knelt down and picked up some of the crumbled concrete, then ran his hand over the paint splatters. "I can still smell the paint."

"Looks like someone was angry. This isn't the work of pranksters."

Dixon stood and realized he'd muddied his slacks. "Damn, I'll have to change and send these out to be cleaned." *Did I mention my fiancé was obsessively neat?* "I'll also call the police. They need to have another look at Frank Threadgill's tomb. Then we can head back to Rip's office."

UNFORTUNATELY, OUR RETURN TO RIP'S office was delayed, thanks to the commotion we found in our hotel room—a covey of cops, and a dead body slumped in a chair, a dead body wearing a blood soaked blouse caused by what appeared to be a stab wound.

CHAPTER FIVE

Dixon and I were sitting in the interrogation room in the downtown police station when we got word that the dead woman was Mildred Threadgill. Dixon explained our interest in Mrs. Threadgill, as well as the damage done to her husband's tomb, and that our friend Rip Thigbee was missing and last seen with Mrs. Threadgill. None of which made a rat's ass difference to Detective Bergeron who was questioning us. Luckily, our alibi checked out. The people staying in the room next to ours said they heard a commotion and then a scream at the time we were talking to the attendant at the cemetery. Nevertheless, the woman was killed in our room. There was a knife missing from our breakfast tray, possibly the murder weapon. The only person in New Orleans who knew we were staying here was Betsy Radley. We were released, but told to stick around.

"Are we on a case?" I asked.

"We're on a case. What choice do we have? Deal with a murder today. Get married tomorrow."

"Does that marriage license have an expiration date?" I asked.

"It's good for two weeks. Maybe we should have kept the rental car."

BETSY WAS A LITTLE MORE forth coming with information when we returned to Rip's office to tell her that Mildred Threadgill had been murdered.

"Oh, my," Betsy said. "Mrs. Threadgill was here after you left, demanding to see Rip. I told her I didn't know where he was and that the last time I saw him he was with her. She became livid.

She said he was supposed to call her a couple of days ago."

"And you sent her to us?" Dixon asked.

"She wouldn't leave," Betsy said. "I didn't know what else to do. You said you'd help, so I told her where you were staying."

"Any idea who would kill her?" Dixon asked, adding a hardness to his voice. When he did that, I knew he was losing his patience.

"I . . . I don't know," Betsy stammered.

"I'll look through Rip's notes again," I said.

"So the last time you saw Rip he was headed to the cemetery with Mildred Threadgill, and you haven't seen or heard from him since?"

"Yes, yes that's right," Betsy whispered.

"You've been here all week and you haven't heard from anyone? No one's called or come in? Just Mrs. Threadgill after we left?"

Betsy began blubbering, which turned to sobs, then to hiccups. Finally, she managed a vigorous shake of her head.

"I want Rip's home address," Dixon said.

"He lives upstairs in the apartment on the left. I don't have a key, but Frida Mae is the landlady. She has one. Wait here. I'll get it."

WE WALKED INTO RIP'S APARTMENT. You wouldn't think a single guy, an ex-bouncer to be so immaculately neat. Rip didn't own a lot of possessions, but what he had was clean and orderly. A stack of dinner plates sat on the kitchen counter next to two coffee cups in perfect alignment. Clean silverware stood in a drinking glass. The toaster, minus crumbs, shone like a beacon. Two spotless sauce pans and a skillet were arranged on top of the icebox. What little space he had in the kitchenette he made good use of. The cabinet held a can of sardines, a can of pinto beans, and a box of Wheaties. On the top shelf inside the icebox, sat a package of bacon, carton of eggs, and a stick of butter. The lower shelf held a case of Falstaff beer cans, also aligned with each label showing out. I looked over to find Dixon staring off into space.

"What is it?"

"Betsy's lying. She knows more than she's telling."

"She's scared. You should have pushed her harder."

"Let her stew for now. Was Rip in the military?"

"Not that I know of. Why?"

"I can't find one wrinkle in his bed sheets. His pillow case smells freshly laundered. There's no dust on the floor under the bed. His dresser contains the usual undershirts, socks, underwear, and handkerchiefs."

Dixon opened the closet door. Two dress shirts, a pair of slacks, a sport coat hung neatly, each in their proper category. "Look at this. A pair of scuffed cowboy boots."

"Don't sound surprised. Any self-respecting Texan has scuffed cowboy boots, even me." I looked down at his wingtips.

"What?"

"This entire time I thought you were perfect, but I just realized you're not."

Dixon straightened his tie. "You're questioning your assessment of me?"

I held up Rip's boots.

"Wait. I'm not ever going to wear cowboy boots. I don't have to, I'm not a Texan."

"You will soon be one by marriage. I suggest black boots, slightly rounded toes, modicum amount of stitchery. I'll shop around."

"No."

"At least you can wear them around the house."

"No."

"Wearing nothing else, just your boots."

"Well, maybe."

"Look at this," Dixon said. He held up a photo that had been sitting on the end table. A younger Rip and a middle-aged woman wearing a light-colored dress and white gloves.

"Probably his mother. He talked about her a few times."

"He's a big guy."

"He made a great bouncer at the Keyhole Club. He could be mean when he needed to, but he has the heart of a lamb. For a few moments, he fell for Ruth."

"I can understand that. A lot of men fall for your zany cousin. But what happened after just a few moments?"

"I dissuaded him."

"What else can you tell me about him?"

"Honestly, he's not the smartest guy in the room, but he's likeable, loyal."

"He sounds like a golden retriever. This guy plans to make it as a detective?"

"One who finds lost souls."

"Oh, that fits. There's nothing else here to see. Let's lock up and have another go at Betsy."

On the way out the phone rang. "You answer it," I said.

"Hello, Rip Thigbee's residence."

"Who's this?" I heard the caller shout.

"You first," Dixon said. After a few seconds of silence, Dixon threw down the receiver and flew downstairs into Rip's office. "Betsy!" Dixon shouted. "Damn!" He darted out the door into the street.

"What's happened?" I asked.

"Someone's nabbed Betsy."

"Just now?"

"Looks like it. It couldn't have been more than five minutes ago. Someone knew we were here. The caller said, 'Tell Mr. Thigbee that if he wants to see that little mousy woman again, to lay off nosing around the cemetery.'"

"Looks like Rip is involved in a nasty case," I said. "But the threatening caller doesn't know that Rip is missing, otherwise he wouldn't have called with a message for him. And what is he planning on doing? Holding Betsy until Rip calls and promises to be a good boy? How does that sound to you?"

"Lame," Dixon said. "The office looks the same. There's no sign of a struggle."

"Look at this." I picked up a note tab from the telephone table. "A phone number. It's underlined twice."

"See if Frida Mae saw something. I'll call the number."

I WALKED INTO THE SHOP to find Frida Mae had a line of customers, some loaded up with voodoo trappings, some curious seekers wanting information on the famous Marie Laveau. Frida Mae was taking her time giving her spiel, explaining how the position of Voodoo Queen had eventually been passed down to her since Laveau's death in 1881.

Dixon walked in. "I called the phone number. No answer." Frida Mae continued to talk while shooting glances at us. Dixon paced up and down the aisle until he lost his patience, went behind the counter, and slammed the register shut. The lady waiting to pay threw her armload of voodoo stuff on the counter and scurried out, followed by the other customers.

"What do you think you're doing?" Frida Mae said.

"Betsy's gone."

"Well, who could blame her? She came in again after she got the key for you. She couldn't stop crying. I told her to go home."

"I'm pretty sure she didn't go off by herself," Dixon said. "Someone came in the office a few minutes ago and took Betsy against her will."

"How do you know?"

"I answered Rip's apartment phone while we were up there. The guy calling said to tell Mr. Thigbee that if he wanted to see Betsy again, he needed to stop nosing around Frank Threadgill's tomb. I ran downstairs and she was gone."

"Oh, no," Frida Mae said. "Poor Betsy."

"Are you sure you didn't see anyone lurking around outside, watching the office?" Dixon said.

"This is New Orleans. This is Bourbon Street. Who doesn't lurk? Besides, it's been busy in here."

"Listen," I said. "Betsy's holding something back and so are you. She told Mildred Threadgill where to find us. Soon after, we find Mrs. Threadgill's body in our hotel room."

Frida May turned white. "Body, as in dead?"

"Body, as in murdered while we were at the cemetery," I said. "And now Betsy is gone, and I'm suspicious about the entire course of events."

"What's that supposed to mean?" Frida Mae asked.

"Betsy sending Mildred Threadgill to the hotel."

"You think Betsy did it?" Frida Mae said. "She wouldn't hurt a fly. Besides she was here the entire time."

"How would you know since you were busy? Listen, we're not saying Betsy killed Mrs. Threadgill," Dixon said. "However, she does look guilty. The police will think so too."

"I can't help you." Frida Mae hugged her arms tight across her ample bosom and stuck her chin in the air.

"Can't or won't?" I said. "Betsy might be in trouble. You're her friend. She confides in you. She's more than just Rip's employee."

"Rip's a stupid ass," Frida Mae said. "He doesn't know a great girl when she's right under his nose. Betsy's got it bad. She fell for the guy right away, and now he's gotten her mixed up in something shady. If I knew anything, I'd tell you. Betsy doesn't deserve this."

"Where does Betsy live?"

"Not far. A few blocks off Bourbon on Toulouse. I don't know the exact address. Now if you don't mind, I have more customers coming in."

We went back to Rip's office and found Betsy's address in the phone book. A ten-minute walk had us on her door step. We knocked. No answer. The curtains covering the windows were pulled tight not allowing even a slit of light inside. Dixon knocked louder.

"Miss Radley," Dixon said. "It's Ralph Dixon and Sydney Lockhart. We need to talk to you."

A neighbor lady stepped out onto her front porch. "Betsy's not home. She left not long ago. What do you want?"

I let Dixon do the talking. "We spoke to her this morning. She asked for our help in regard to a situation at work. Any idea when she'll be back?"

"I don't keep tabs on her. She threw a suitcase in the back seat and left about an hour ago."

"Was anyone with her?" I asked. "Anyone following her?"

"No." The woman went back inside, slamming the door behind her.

"So, sounds like Betsy left on her own accord," I said.

"Or the neighbor wanted to get rid of us," Dixon said.

"While we were upstairs, Betsy left the office, came home,

packed a suitcase, left, then got kidnapped? Something about that call doesn't sit well."

The neighbor was still watching us from her parted curtains. "Think she's telling the truth?" I nodded to the neighbor.

"Despite claiming she doesn't keep tabs on Betsy, I'm sure the nosy neighbor is aware of every movement Betsy Radley makes. If there was someone with Betsy, I'm sure she would have been glad to tell us."

CHAPTER SIX

We hailed a cab to take us back to the hotel. I wanted to share my thoughts on the matter with Dixon, but our cabbie was the talkative sort.

"You two having a good time in NOLA?" the driver said.

"How did you know we were tourists?" I asked.

The guy laughed. "Because you're in the heart of the French Quarter and you hailed a cab. Locals walk. I can give you a tour of the Garden District, the historic cemeteries, haunted houses, and all the hidden places locals like to go."

I wanted to tell the guy we've been here less than twenty-four hours and we've had our fill of cemeteries.

"Maybe another day, buddy," Dixon said. "Take us to the Pontchartrain Hotel."

"If Mildred Threadgill came to the hotel in a fit, how did she get into our room?" I softened my voice so the cabbie wouldn't hear.

"Maybe she bullied the desk clerk into giving out our room number, but that's highly unlikely. The police thought so too, otherwise we wouldn't have spent a lovely two hours being questioned," Dixon said. "We're their main suspects. Our alibi is not that strong. Do we look suspicious?"

"I always do. You, never. There's one way to find out how she got into our room. *We* bully the desk clerk."

UNFORTUNATELY, THE DESK CLERK referred us to the hotel manager.

"The police have already asked that question," the hotel manager said. "We do not, I repeat, do not give out room numbers to people who ask to see a guest. We offer to call the rooms to let guests know someone is asking about them, we take messages, and explain why we can't give out room numbers. Our entire staff knows that, and they know they would be fired if they gave out room numbers."

"But someone got into our room and killed a woman who also wasn't registered at this hotel."

"Maybe you left the door unlocked. Here." He handed us a key. "We've put you in a different room and have moved your luggage for you. What happened was unfortunate, but try to enjoy your stay. Excuse me. I have to get back to work."

The room was on the same floor, but in a separate wing.

"Impressive," Dixon said. "He gave us another double-room suite with a spectacular view. And a basket of fruit."

"He's being nice," I said. "Doesn't want us asking any more questions."

"We need to figure out how Mildred Threadgill got in. Room service has to have keys. See what you can find out from them. I'll talk to the housemaids assigned to this floor. Come here." Before I could protest, his fingers were in my hair and his tongue in my mouth.

"We're still not married."

"As if that ever stopped us. Cowboy boots, huh?"

"Black, scruffy. We have work to do."

"Work, right."

Dixon left to find the maids and I was on the phone with room service. It didn't take long. I used the excuse of questioning the champagne we'd ordered last night. "We ordered a bottle of Monet Chardon," I lied. "You delivered a less expensive brand. I hope you will adjust the charge."

"Ma'am, I assure you we delivered what you ordered and charged you correctly."

"To be sure, could you please go over everything that was delivered to our room since we checked in? I want to make sure no other bogus charges were made."

"We only charged you for the champagne since you cancelled the meals. You did cancel, didn't you?"

"We didn't order meals."

I could hear the discomfort coming through the telephone line. "Were you the ones staying in that room?

"Yes, but—?"

She slammed the receiver down.

While I waited for Dixon to return, I unpacked the second time since our arrival. The day was half over and we had applied for a marriage license, found out Rip had disappeared, studied a damaged tomb, found that a murder had been committed in our room, spent two hours at the police station, searched Rip's apartment and learned that his girlfriend/office assistant had disappeared. Except for lounging in bed and applying for a marriage license, the rest sounded like a typical work day for us. But we didn't come here for a typical work day. We came here to get married, have a honeymoon, spend some much needed vacation time together.

I pulled the drapes apart. Our room faced St. Charles Street. Streetcars rocked and rattled by, shops and cafés were open, a flower shop displayed buckets of gladiolas and irises for sale, couples strolled down the streets arm-in-arm. I could picture Dixon and me enjoying a meal and sipping wine in that café across the street. We'd talked about having a light lunch so we could indulge ourselves tonight at Commander's Palace, starting off with a dozen raw oysters, followed by softshell crab and grits, and top it off with Bananas Foster. He'd buy me a gladiola, snip off the stem and place the bloom behind my ear. We'd walk to the streetcar stop, anticipating our tour of the city.

"Hey."

I jumped, almost tripping over the lamp cord. "I didn't hear you come in."

"I know. I've been watching you for the last minute. What's going on out there?" Dixon walked over and put his arms around my waist.

"It's not what's going on, it's what's not going on—you and me relaxing without a care in the world. This morning was perfect, we should have stayed in bed all day."

"I promise we'll have a real honeymoon as soon as this is wrapped up." He looked out the window, and picked up the phone. "Hello, this is Ralph Dixon. I'm staying in room 702 at the Pontchartrain. Can you deliver a dozen of those yellow flowers? Yes, glads. That's great. Thanks."

"You're the best."

"Did you learn anything more from room service?"

"You bet I did. I'm pretty sure how Mildred Threadgill got our room number. She was crafty. She ordered a meal and then gave room service a bogus room number, which they noticed and to be sure, they gave her the correct number to confirm. Then she called back immediately and cancelled the order. This is conjecture, but I plan to find out for sure. The woman whom I spoke to hung up on me when she realized I was the one staying in the room where a murder was committed this morning."

"Good work, hon. Mildred Threadgill got our room number, but how did she get in?"

"That I don't know. Picked the lock maybe?"

"That's possible. But why the subterfuge? If Mrs. Threadgill wanted to see us, why not just leave a message at the front desk?"

"Maybe she didn't want to see us. Maybe she thought we had something that she desperately wanted."

"I doubt that. We dropped in to see Rip unannounced, he wasn't there, and we spoke to Betsy. We had nothing Mildred Threadgill would want. She was angry because someone vandalized her husband's tomb. She came to Rip's office this morning right after we left. Betsy told her Rip was missing, but two friends were here and were going to check out her husband's tomb. Betsy also told her we are staying at the Pontchartrain. She rushed over, finagled our room number out of room service and managed to get into our room."

"She must have been with someone, and that someone killed her. It's convoluted, but it's the only thing that makes sense right now. How did you do with the housemaid?"

"Lavine Rose, she's the one assigned to our floor. The police rattled her pretty well, and I couldn't get much out of her. She claims she didn't see or hear anything. Another liar. She might be willing to talk after she calms down and thinks things over."

"I'm going down to the kitchen to see if I can find out how

Mildred got access to our room. I want to have another talk with the room service woman who hung up on me."

"I'll make another trip to the voodoo shop. Meet you back here in an hour."

MOST OF THE IMPORTANT LESSONS in my life were taught to me by my dad or my grandfather: hot wiring a car, picking a lock, playing poker like a pro, but I hated to admit I had also learned a few things from my mother. She had no compunction when it came to confronting people who'd pissed her off. One of her favorite things to do was march directly into a restaurant kitchen and complain about an unsatisfactory meal she'd been served. Why bother the waiter when you can go directly to the source of the problem? Many cooks have torn their hair out trying to appease my mother over a bowl of cold soup. Some of her audacity wore off on me.

Acting like I owned the place, I pushed through the swinging doors into the kitchen of the Caribbean Room restaurant. At first, no one paid me any attention. Waiters, busboys, and dishwashers, scuttled about in what first appeared to be a mass frenzy, but upon closer observation the activity was more like a well-oiled machine. Waiters loaded trays with steaming dishes onto their shoulders, darting through the melee with confidence, then flying out the swinging doors into the dining room. Busboys flying through the same door, exiting the dining room carrying tubs of dirty dishes, then scraping off the scraps, and sending everything onto a conveyor belt. Dishwashers dunking plates, glasses, silverware, and cutlery into a huge sink of steaming soapy water. No one got bumped, no one tripped, everyone shouted obscenities, but no one seemed to take offense. Everyone knew their jobs and went about their tasks with uncanny precision like what I imagined goes on in a beehive.

I moved out of the way and watched a line cook removing the skin from a chicken with a knife sharp enough to sever bone. A sous chef was sautéing mushrooms and garlic in a butter sauce. In the middle stood who I assumed was the head chef, judging by his clean, starched chef's hat and smock and his shouting directions. He caught my eye and pointed to the door.

"Guests are not allowed in the kitchen! You must get out before a terrible accident happens," he said in an accent I recognized as French. He turned to fuss at a line cook who had plated the wrong garnish. The chicken-skinning guy made as if to cut his throat and pointed his knife at me. The dishwasher sent me a facial message that said, "be afraid, be very afraid." Finally the chef came over and stood inches away. His angry look turned to one of interest and then to one I can only describe as lustful. The name stitched on his smock was Pascal La Duc. "Are you lost? I told you to get out."

"I need to speak to the person in charge of taking room-service orders."

"You have a complaint?"

"A woman sent a bogus order to my room."

"A mistake. Unfortunately that happens sometimes."

"Mistakes happen often, murders don't." Except in my case, I thought. "Whoever placed the order came into my room when I was gone. I need to find out how she got in. Her name was Mildred Threadgill."

"Ah, the lady with the knife in her heart. The authorities have already been here making a nuisance of themselves. That's why we're behind on getting orders out. As you can see, we are very busy. We cannot help you."

"How did you know she was stabbed in the heart with a knife?

He leaned a little closer. "I told you the cop people were here."

"Is that beef stroganoff I smell, Chef Pascal?" I went over to the stove, picked up a wooden spoon, stirred the thick sauce bubbling in a skillet, then tasted it.

"If you tell me it needs more salt, I'll stab you in the jugular."

"Like you stabbed the woman in the heart?"

He smiled. His eyebrows bounced up and down. Chef Pascal was clearly enjoying the banter. I kept it going.

"Actually, it's perfect. What kind of sherry do you use?"

His face softened. "The good stuff from the Spanish province of Cádiz, of course."

"The Frontera."

Now his eyes grew wide, and he managed to fight back a lecherous grin. "If you stay you'll need a hair net." He moved even closer and his voice turned soft and sultry. "I love long, curly red hair, but not in my stroganoff. It will sully my reputation, Mademoiselle." He kissed the fingers of my right hand.

I stuck my left hand, which now sported an engagement ring, in my pocket and gave him my most shameless smile. "Lockhart. Sydney Lockhart. You don't have a net large enough to cover all this hair. Will the stroganoff be the main course on the menu tonight?"

"The question is, Mademoiselle Lockhart, will *you* be the main course on *my* menu tonight?"

"Ah, I need a room service name."

"Lily Morton, talk to her. I get off soon. Come back and we can get to know one another, yes?"

I wished I spoke French, but a wink would have to suffice. Was I flirting with a French chef? No, definitely not. But then . . .

CHAPTER SEVEN

Lily Morton was tucked away in a tiny, stifling alcove off the kitchen. Order forms covered her desk. She jerked around as I approached. Her face was tear stained. The skin around her eyes sagged and her hair looked as if it hadn't been brushed in a week. She was clearly not happy. "What do you want?"

I opened the back door to let in fresh air. "How do you know Mildred Threadgill?"

"Who are you?"

"I'm the guest who called you about the bogus room service order that was cancelled, the guest staying in the room where the woman was murdered. Why did you tell her my room number? I'm sure if your boss knew, he'd fire you in an instant."

"I've already talked to the police. I have to get back to work. I have room service orders to fill."

"They can wait a little longer. We need to talk now."

"Let's go—outside. We have too many ears in the kitchen."

She stepped out and I followed. "Was Mildred a friend of yours?"

"She was my cousin." Lily began to sob. "I got her killed."

"I'm sorry, Miss Morton. Maybe I can help."

"There's nothing you can do."

"My name is Sydney Lockhart. I'm a private detective. My partner and I happened to be in New Orleans and we looked up a friend of mine who it turns out has recently disappeared." Mentioning that Rip was a detective of the dead wasn't a good idea so I stayed mute on that point. "He had some dealings with Mildred Threadgill concerning her dead husband, Frank. Did Mrs. Threadgill say why she wanted in our room?"

"She told me she wanted to see you about a problem. She didn't say what."

"If that were true, she could have waited in the lobby until we returned or left a message at the front desk. Getting into our room while we were gone simply doesn't fit, does it? How did she act when she came to see you?"

"She was upset. Panicky. I've never seen her like that. She's never come to the hotel before. But—

"But what?"

"I don't like to speak ill of the dead, but Mildred was odd."

"In what way?"

"She didn't mingle with the family. Kind of stayed to herself, secretive. She wasn't always that way. It was that husband of hers. He was bossy. Always telling her what she could and couldn't do. When I heard he had died, I thought, 'good riddance.'"

"You didn't like Frank Threadgill?"

"Who did?"

"Did you let Mildred into our room?"

"No. I don't know how she got in."

"She placed the room service order, so she could get the correct room number. Why didn't she ask you?"

"She did. But I wouldn't give it to her, and she left. Then the room service call came in. She disguised her voice. She must have called from the lobby phone. So I guess I did give it to her, but not on purpose. Mildred could be sneaky."

"But you didn't let her in?"

"I already told you I didn't."

"She didn't give you any hint as to what she was distressed over?"

"No. The way she was acting, I just wanted to get rid of her. I thought it probably had something to do with Frank."

"What can you tell me about Frank Threadgill?"

"Frank—a piece of work." Lilly rolled her eyes. "He moved to New Orleans a little more than a year ago and bought a retail store. He was an immigrant. Anyway, he met Mildred and they married rather quickly. The family thought that maybe she was pregnant. But in time, we realized she wasn't."

"How did they meet?"

"At church. He had just moved here and came to a service and stayed after for one of our picnics. I didn't like him from the beginning. My aunt, Mildred's mother, sort of pushed Frank and Mildred together. She sensed he had a promising future, owning his own business and all. And Mildred wasn't getting any younger. She wasn't the most attractive woman either. We gave her up as a spinster. I think she agreed to marry Frank because she believed he was her only prospect."

"What business did Frank own?"

"He owned Threadgill Appliances. Mildred worked in the office. But he sold it about a month ago. From what I heard, he made a killing, for all the good that did him. He died a few days later."

"He didn't own it very long to have made a killing."

"The previous owner was going bankrupt and Frank bought it for a song. I guess he was able to turn the business around and sell it for a good profit. I'm not really sure."

"Where's the store located?"

"West of the downtown area on Claiborne Avenue and Burgundy Street. I've got to get back to work. If you find out anything, please let me know."

"I'd like to talk to your aunt, Mildred's mother."

Lily turned white and grasped her throat. "When?" she cried.

"As soon as possible."

"Her daughter was murdered this morning."

"I understand, but the longer we wait the harder it will be to find the killer."

"The police will do that."

"Did you tell them you were Mildred's cousin?"

The flush rose from the bottom of her neck and shot up to her hairline.

"I didn't think so. Now, where does your aunt live?"

"She's in the phone book under Jonathan Ivy. Look it up yourself."

Lily Morton turned and left.

I used the directory in the lobby phone booth and looked up the addresses for both the appliance store and the Ivy residence as Dixon walked in.

"Did you have any luck with the room service lady?" he asked.

"Some. She's Mildred Threadgill's cousin, Lily Morton, in charge of room service orders. Mildred went to her to get the key to our room. Morton claims she didn't give Mildred the key. But she did say that Mildred was in a panic over something. Morton also told me a little about Mildred's family. I think we should go see them and pay a visit to Threadgill's appliance store."

"Good idea. I've got the city map, but let's grab a quick bite at the hotel before we go. It'll give us a chance to compare notes, and I can't think on an empty stomach. We skipped lunch. I'm starving."

"You? I've seen you go all day without food."

"True, but this is New Orleans. The entire city smells like gumbo." Dixon laughed.

OVER LUNCH I TOLD DIXON everything I learned about the Threadgills. He told me a more fascinating story. Before Mildred Threadgill hired Rip to investigate the vandalism of her husband's tomb, she came to see Frida Mae for help. Mildred claimed to have had several visits from her dead husband and she wanted Frida Mae to provide a protection potion. When that didn't work, she returned to the voodoo shop and demanded her money back. Instead of returning her money, Frida Mae talked Mildred into investing in more powerful potions. Frida Mae went on to say that Mildred was convinced her husband was coming back to life. She wanted to make sure he stayed dead because she hated the bastard. She purchased another potion made to pour over Frank's tomb. She also hired Frida Mae to perform a ritual over it. The event took place about two weeks ago at midnight when the moon was full. The next night Frank made another ghostly appearance and this time he told his widow that he planned to drag her to hell with him. More angry than frightened, Mildred showed up again at Marie Laveau's the next morning.

"I love persistent women." I couldn't help but laugh.

"So do I," Dixon said.

"Was Frida Mae able to help the poor woman?"

"Frida Mae told her she had some bad juju hanging over her and before they could get rid of Frank, Mildred had to get rid of the juju. More money changed hands, more were potions used, and more incantations learned, these at Mildred's home. Finally, Frida Mae pulled out her most powerful voodoo tool. Having received the required tokens, Frida Mae made a voodoo doll in Frank's image and threw in a complete set of voodoo pins for free. But Mildred reported that the more she stabbed the Frank-doll, the more he visited. Finally, Frida Mae threw up her hands and sent her to see Rip."

"We're dealing with a crazy woman," I said.

"You mean crazy women."

"Yes, but the one I'm most concerned about was murdered in our room."

"Hard to forget that."

"Miss Lockhart?"

I turned to see a bellboy looking around the restaurant. I raised my hand.

"You have a telegram at the front desk."

"Oh, thank you. Can you bring it to the table?"

"I'm afraid with what has happened, I mean with your room number and all, you need to go to the desk and claim it."

"It must be from Lydia," I said to Dixon. "She's the only one I told where we are staying. This can't be good."

"Billy and Phoebe know too. I had to tell them. They promised not to mentioned it to anyone. Oh, and your father. Uh, yep, I screwed up."

"We should have put a full-page ad in the *Austin American*."

I followed the clerk to the front desk and signed for the telegram. It was from Lydia all right and the news was not good. I shoved it in my pocket and joined Dixon. He had a bottle of wine on the table and was perusing the menu. "How about something Cajun? I have a hankering for seafood gumbo, hushpuppies, and a side of cornbread."

"Sounds good. Pour the wine and I'll read Lydia's telegram, or maybe we should save the telegram for dessert."

"You're my dessert. Read."

Wow. I'm now on two menus; Pascal's entrée and Dixon's dessert. "Okay, here goes. 'SYDNEY, I HATE YOU—STOP— YOUR MOTHER IS RUINING MY LIFE—STOP— SHE TRIED TO TAKE OVER MY THEATER PRODUCTION—STOP— SHE FIRED THE ACTRESS ASSIGNED TO PLAY MADAME BUTTERFLY—STOP—SHE PLANS TO PLAY MADAME BUTTERFLY—STOP—SHE'S BOSSING ME AROUND— STOP—HOW LONG IS A HONEYMOON SUPPOSED TO LAST?—STOP'"

"You didn't tell me your mother was in Austin," Dixon said. "She's never visited before."

"I didn't know she was coming until she walked in on rehearsals at the theater. The reason she came was to arrange for an appropriate wedding for her only daughter. I would have told you, but I didn't wanted you to pack your bags and move to New Zealand."

"She's really not that bad, Syd. But there's an easy solution to the wedding planning. Send her a telegram and tell her we eloped."

"We haven't yet."

"After gumbo and wine and dessert up in our room, we'll see if Lavine Rose is still around, and then we can head over to the Ivy house. We'll be married in the morning."

CHAPTER EIGHT

We didn't have to search for the maid. We opened the door to leave and found Lavine Rose about to knock.

"Oh, sorry," she said. Your slacks have been cleaned, Mr. Dixon. I was going to put them in your room."

"Thank you, Miss Rose." Dixon smiled. "We were just coming to look for you." She handed Dixon his slacks and attempted a quick getaway.

"Please come in."

"I have work to do."

"This won't take long."

"I told you everything I know."

"I thought you might have remembered something since this morning," Dixon said. "You were fairly upset after talking to the police. I can understand. They can be so accusatory."

"What do you mean?"

"Make people feel guilty when they're not."

"Oh, yes." Lavine relaxed a little. "But I didn't remember anything. I swear."

"Come in and have a seat. We'll talk," Dixon said.

"I can't do that. I'll get in trouble."

"We'll have our chat out here in the hall then." Dixon raised his voice.

"Okay," Lavine said. "Just a few minutes."

I pulled out the desk chair for Lavine, and told her to sit. She perched on the edge in escape mode.

"Miss Lockhart and I are private detectives. We're trying to locate a missing friend who has ties to the woman who was killed in our room. She came here looking for us. Kicked up quite a scene from what we've been told. Since you're the maid assigned to this floor, surely you heard the ruckus."

"I don't know anything."

I flung open the curtain to let some light into the room. It was all I could do not to fling something at Lavine. Dixon glanced at me. His look said, "take it easy." He pulled out the other chair and sat across from her, folded his hands over his knees, and looked directly at her. "With all due respect, Miss Rose, you are lying to us." His soft, silky voice did the trick.

"I . . . I saw the woman knock on your door." Tears flooded down her face. I handed her a tissue. "She went into your room."

"How? Did she have a key?"

"Key?"

"Yes, a key. We weren't there to let her in. So, she must have had a key, right?"

"Oh, yes, yes. A key. I was at the other end of the hall, so I couldn't see much. I thought you let her in, but since you weren't there, I guess she did have a key."

"Where would she have gotten it?"

"I don't know."

"Did you let her in?"

"No! I did not. I swear."

Dixon did his silent thing. He leaned back in his chair. Looked out the window. Smiled at me, checked his watch, then turned back to Lavine.

"You saw her go in, then what?"

"I went to clean another room at the other end of the hall. I stripped the sheets and collected the towels. I was in the linen closet putting them down the laundry shoot when I heard someone scream. I ran into the hall and down to your room. The door was open. The people in the room next to yours came out into the hall. We looked in and saw the woman covered in blood. I ran down the stairs. I heard the man say he was calling the police."

"And you told all of this to the police?"

"Yes."

Dixon rose and went to the credenza. He removed a glass and added a splash of scotch. He handed it to Lavine. "Go ahead, Miss Rose, you look like you could use it."

Lavine sipped her drink and coughed.

"Miss Rose, thanks again for bringing up my suit. That was nice of you."

"That's my job," she mumbled.

"What would have happened had we not been here?"

"I would have just laid it on the bed."

"You would have used your pass key, then?"

"Yes." She dropped her glass in her lap.

Dixon pulled out his handkerchief and handed it to her. I went into the bathroom for a washcloth.

"Miss Rose, may I see your pass key?"

"I, I left it downstairs."

"But it's not downstairs, Miss Rose. It's in an evidence envelope at the police station because Mrs. Threadgill had the key and dropped it when she was attacked. She had the key because you gave it to her. How much did she pay you?"

Lavine Rose looked as if she were about to pass out.

"Did you think to wipe your fingerprints off the key?"

Dixon caught her before she hit the floor. When she came to, he handed her another shot of scotch. This one she gulped. "You cannot tell the police. They will send me away. I am not a citizen. I have an Alien Registration Card only."

"I'll keep your secret for now, but I won't promise anything. But you have to stop lying to us."

She shook her head. "She paid me fifty dollars. She promised to bring the key back to me in a few minutes, but she was murdered. I couldn't look for the key because the guests next door came running out. I don't want anything to do with this." She stood up. "I want to forget everything. I will have nightmares." With that she was gone.

"Great move," I told Dixon. "The police don't have the key because they would have mentioned it when we were at the station this morning. The killer must have taken it. It's probably in the Mississippi River now."

"You're probably right. Unfortunately, knowing this doesn't give us a lead to who the killer is, except that he came in right after Mrs. Threadgill. He stabbed her, and ran."

WE ARRIVED AT THE HOME of Mildred Threadgill's mother's house, and found that a small group of relatives and friends had gathered on the lawn. Instead of quiet grieving and hushed voices, we heard angry shouts. Within the few moments of our arrival, the accusations had grown to a crescendo and turned into a finger pointing fiasco. Someone was blaming Mrs. Ivy for coddling her daughter while another person was complaining that the deceased Mr. Ivy was too strict with Mildred. Getting a moment to talk to Mrs. Ivy was not going to be easy. I spotted Lily and was about to ask her if she could be our conduit to Mrs. Ivy when a man came over and introduced himself.

Elliott Ivy, Mildred's brother, assumed we had been friends of Frank's since he'd never seen us before. I held my breath while Dixon explained in a few words who we were and our connection with Rip.

"How did you know to come here and start asking questions?"

"Your cousin Lily Morton works at the hotel," I said. "I spoke to her earlier today."

"Lily," he called. "Come over here."

Lily didn't look too happy to see us.

"Did you tell these people to come over here, Lily?" Elliott Ivy said.

"Don't start with me, Elliott. I told her this was not the right time to see Aunt Alma, but they came anyway." She turned on her heel and left.

"You will have to leave before I call the police," he told us.

"Mr. Ivy. We know this is a difficult time," Dixon said. "We'd like to find out what happened to your sister as much as you would. We spoke to the police today and told them about our missing friend and they didn't seem interested. We're certain his disappearance and your sister's murder are connected. Miss Lockhart and I are good at what we do. I'm sure we can help find out who was responsible for this."

"Let's talk somewhere else." He led us to the other side of the yard away from the others. "I'm sorry about my rudeness, but I'm sure you can understand."

"We can," Dixon said. "Anything you can tell us about your sister would be helpful."

What I've learned in my short time as a detective is when to push and when to wait. What I also learned is that talking to strangers can, at times, be easier than talking to people you know. Elliott Ivy seemed relieved we weren't part of the melee that was going on behind us. It didn't take long for him to open up, and when he did, he started with his deceased brother-in-law. Elliott Ivy didn't much care for Frank Threadgill. The word he used several times to describe Threadgill was arrogant. Ivy also criticized Mildred for being so naïve.

"At first, he seemed okay," Elliott said. "He had just moved to New Orleans shortly before he met Mildred. He didn't know many people, so I even invited him to join a community organization I belong to. I was hesitant at first, but he eventually joined and started to come to meetings, which was great. Mildred should not have married him."

"Why?" I said.

"Frank Threadgill was not a nice man. He didn't always treat Mildred well."

"In what way?" Dixon asked.

"He was demanding and controlling. He would talk down to her like she was a second class citizen. Even in front of others he'd call her stupid and tell her to shut up, criticizing everything she did. I pulled him aside once and told him I didn't appreciate the way he belittled Mildred. He seemed shocked at my objection, almost as if treating women like that was something all men did. It was probably the way he was raised, I don't know, but he did stop with the emotional abuse, at least when I was around. Mildred often hinted to me that his behavior didn't change at home. She often called him a brute. Moving into that big house in the Garden District helped. She loved to garden and told me on more than one occasion that whenever Frank came home grouchy, which was often, she'd head straight for her garden and stay there until it was time to make supper. I was the one who found the house for them. I'm in residential real estate." He handed Dixon his business card.

"How did he die?" I asked.

"Heart attack. Fell over dead at the dinner table. Right here during Sunday night dinner."

"Here at your mother's house?"

"Yes, we had just sat down to eat. He started having chest pains. It wasn't his first heart attack. He died right there at the table. I hate to say this, but I was relieved he died. I know that sounds heartless. Mildred deserved much better. Frank was a good business man, there's no doubt about that, but he was not the right husband for my sister. Although she would never admit it, I know Mildred was relived to be free of him. Oh, she was clearly upset at the funeral, but I think her distress was the prospect of spending the rest of her life alone. Mildred was never a strong, confident person."

"So, who do you think would want to kill her?" Dixon asked.

"That's what's so weird. Mildred had no enemies."

"She obviously had one."

"You think she knew something about your missing friend?"

"Possibly. Rip Thigbee's a detective. Your sister hired him to find out who was disturbing her husband's tomb," I said. "She came to his office this morning and learned that Mr. Thigbee was missing. His secretary told your sister we were friends of his and that we were staying at the Pontchartrain Hotel. Evidently, she came to see us. We weren't there when she arrived." I glanced at Dixon and he nodded. "Unfortunately, we didn't get the chance to meet her."

"Why?" Elliott Ivy said.

"She was killed in our room while we were out," Dixon said.

"I spoke to Lily at the hotel," I said. "She told me Mildred went to see her."

"Lily," Elliott Ivy called again. Looking like a dog being reprimanded, Lily walked over.

"Lily, Mildred came to see you at the hotel this morning? Why didn't you tell me?"

"Don't use that tone with me, Elliott Ivy," Lily said. "Mildred was upset. She didn't say why, just that she needed to see these people. She wanted their room number. I couldn't give it to her." Lily hesitated. I took it that the pleading expression on her face meant she wanted us to continue the story, but I wanted to hear it again in her own words.

"Lily, why don't you tell Elliott the rest of it?" I said.

Elliott listened and when Lily was finished he said, "Mildred often overreacted, but this sounds like it was much more than that. No one was with her when she came to the hotel?"

"No, she was by herself," Lily said.

Elliott looked at us. "What do you think?"

"Your sister was obviously frightened by something," Dixon said. "When she couldn't find Mr. Thigbee, she came to us."

"You think something happened this morning that led to her murder?" he asked.

"Most certainly," I said. "We haven't a clue what it was. That's why we're here."

"Do you know anyone who would vandalize her husband's tomb?" Dixon asked.

"I didn't know his tomb had been vandalized."

"Your sister reported it to the police first. The damage wasn't serious enough for them to look into it further. She also complained to the cemetery caretaker, then went see Mr. Thigbee, hoping he could find out who was responsible."

"We were there earlier today, and the damage was significant," Dixon said. "It appeared as if someone had tried to open the vault last night. The lip was chipped away and red paint splashed over the tombstone."

"And you believed my sister was murdered because of Frank's tomb being disturbed?" Elliott asked.

"We don't know," I said. "We're trying to piece things together. But not knowing Frank or Mildred, we're working at a disadvantage."

"Damn. The police weren't reassuring. I apologize for the way I behaved earlier. I certainly hope you can help us sort things out."

"We'll do what we can while we're here, but we plan to return to Austin soon," Dixon said.

"You have my card. Please call if you hear of anything."

"You do the same, Mr. Ivy. We're still at the Pontchartrain Hotel. Before Sydney and I leave we'd like to talk to your mother, unless you think it's not a good idea. In a murder investigation, it's best to gather information quickly."

"I understand. I'll introduce you."

Mrs. Ivy was inconsolable over the murder of her daughter. It took a few minutes for her to catch her breath before we could talk. At first she seemed put out over us being there, but after she learned why we came, she warmed to us. She assured us that everyone loved Mildred. She was a loyal member of their church, and volunteered for a lot of community organizations. She was never in trouble, not even a parking ticket. Mrs. Ivy couldn't think of anyone who would harm her daughter. She went as far as saying that maybe the killer mistook Mildred for someone else, which seemed highly unlikely. We asked her about her son-in-law and her expression turned sour. "I thought Frank would make a good husband for Mildred, but I was wrong. I was too eager for my daughter to marry. Frank wasn't right for her. I was the one who introduced them. I feel everything is my fault."

"Mother," Elliott said. "Don't. You can't blame yourself."

"I do blame myself and I blame Frank Threadgill. The moment he walked into our lives, it's been one bad thing after another."

"Mother, please. You're exaggerating. Don't make things worse."

"Uncle Jonathon died soon after Mildred and Frank were married," Lily explained.

"My husband tried to dissuade Mildred from marrying him, but little good that did." Mrs. Ivy began to cry. "I tried not to judge Frank, but I never learned to like him. He immigrated here with very little money, and managed to start a business and do very well, very quickly. He was able to buy them a nice home in the Garden District. Despite that, I know Mildred wasn't happy. Frank's presence cast a shadow over our lives."

"Were you aware of any specific problem he and Mildred had?" I asked.

"Oh, every married couple has problems, you know. I shouldn't talk."

It was clear that Mrs. Ivy was uncomfortable with my question. Telling family secrets wasn't easy. I thought of my parents and their crazy relationship and my mother's insane behavior, but no one ever murdered her, at least not yet. I couldn't help but think of Lydia and I wondered how she was doing. I made a mental note to call her at the theater after we returned to the hotel.

"I just don't understand," Mrs. Ivy dabbed the tears from her face. "Mildred came to you for help and was killed in your room? And no one saw anything?"

Before we could answer, Lily said, "Someone obviously saw something, Aunt Alma." The ire in Lily's voice surprised me.

Mrs. Ivy snapped her head around and stared at Lily. For a brief instance, I thought Mrs. Ivy was going to give her niece the what-for, but her faced softened. "We can only hope," she said, "and trust the police to figure things out."

"That's not going to help Mildred, is it?" Lily said.

I had a feeling Lily was closer to Mildred Threadgill than she claimed. Lily turned to us. "After I spoke to Mildred, she must have gone up to the Dixons' room, Aunt Alma. Lavine Rose, the maid, works that floor."

"Maybe Lily's right," Mrs. Ivy said. "Will you speak to the maid, Mr. Dixon?"

Dixon and I failed to discuss how much we wanted to reveal while talking to the Ivys, so I let him answer Mrs. Ivy's question. "We have. Miss Rose found your daughter, Mrs. Ivy. We didn't learn much. The young lady was pretty upset."

"Perhaps you should speak to her again," Lily said.

Dixon and I glanced at one another. Mrs. Ivy also seemed confused by her niece's comment.

"Excuse me," Lily said. "I have to get back to work."

"Oh Lily, are you sure you should be working at that place?" Mrs. Ivy said. "I'm so worried about you."

"Don't bother, Aunt Alma. I can take care of myself," Lily called over her shoulder as she headed for the door.

Seems Aunt Alma was not Lily's favorite relative. I watched her go, certain she was holding something back.

Dixon nodded toward the door. "Please accept our condolences, Mrs. Ivy," he said. "We'll be on our way. Your son knows how to contact us if you need to."

"You will talk to the maid again, won't you?" she said.

"As soon as possible," I said. "I have to ask this, Mrs. Ivy. Did you know that Mildred was involved with voodoo?"

Mrs. Ivy coughed up the tea she was drinking. "Voodoo! That's ridiculous. Mildred would never involve herself in such heathenistic practices. What makes you ask that?"

Revealing to Mrs. Ivy that her deceased daughter was very much involved with heathenistic practices would only alienate the woman, so I downplayed it for now. "Oh, just something I heard. I'm sure you're right."

CHAPTER NINE

Dixon and I decided to walk back to the hotel. We held hands, both silent in our own thoughts. Finally, he said, "What was with the question about voodoo?"

"I'm not sure. It slipped out of my mouth. The Ivys annoyed me, especially Mrs. Ivy. Did you get the feeling Mildred Threadgill was an enigma to her entire family?"

"I didn't pick up on that, but your intuition runs on a different wavelength than mine, which is good. That's why we make a great team." He squeezed my hand, and we walked on.

The evening had cooled, the humidity lessened, and there was a calm stillness in the air. It was as if a quiet beauty had settled over the city. Winding through the historic neighborhood offered a nice change from all the activity surrounding the French Quarter. We found a local café with a few tables on the sidewalk and ordered drinks. "We're not getting anywhere," I said.

"Are you kidding? We've been all over the city, met the local voodoo queen, spent some time in the NOPD interrogation room, became acquainted with some locals, alive and dead, and managed to become involved with a new murder at a new hotel. All after being told we have to wait twenty-four hours before getting married."

"I was talking about this case. We have no suspects and no motives."

"I know, but those are the best kind of cases, the ones we can sink our teeth into. By the way, we just got started. Look at it this way, we have a track to follow. Money and murder, a lead in itself. Frank sold his business and made a bundle. I assume

Mildred inherited. Did she have a will? If so, who did she leave her money to?"

"The idea of family killing family for money is disgusting."

"It is, but it happens. A lot. We need to check if any of the Ivys were having financial problems."

"How do you propose we do that?"

He pulled out Elliott Ivy's business card. "He owns Tulane Real Estate. It shouldn't be too hard to find out what kind of shape his company's in."

"What if money isn't the motive? Mildred Threadgill was unhappy. She had a loveless marriage to a man few people liked. There's more to it, I'm sure."

"So am I. Frank Threadgill hasn't lived in New Orleans long. Where is he from? What's his story? There's also Rip's assistant, Betsy Radley's disappearance."

"You don't think she was kidnapped?"

"I think she bolted for some reason. I have to ask this. How much do you really know about Rip Thigbee?"

"In terms of a suspect?"

"In terms of anything."

"I trust him. I haven't known him very long, but when a guy saves your life and then works with you to solve a murder, you develop a strong feeling about his character."

"I'm sure you're right. I hope I get to meet him soon."

"Back to Elliot Ivy. What's your opinion of him?"

"No opinion yet. He bothers you, though."

"He gives me the willies. Once he loosened up, I felt he was overly friendly. But after listening to him, the stronger my suspicions became. He hardly knew us and he was gabbing about his family as if we were friends."

"Sometimes grief does that."

"You're usually not this maudlin. What's up?"

"I think it stems from running into my sister, Loretta, after all these years. After we went separate ways, I hardly gave her another thought. Then she shows up, wreaks havoc, and almost kills you when you were investigating the Johnny Pine case in San Antonio."

"You think her showing up was no accident?"

"Don't you? She's calculating and manipulative."

"I agree with you. I don't for one moment think she stumbled upon us by accident. But how did she know you were even in Austin? Could she have been in contact with your family?"

"She hates our mother. I believe my grandmother when she told me she hadn't heard from Loretta. Don't forget, Loretta was involved with a notorious bookie whose contacts spanned the entire Gulf of Mexico coast. Johnny Pine's connections brought him to Austin. And he and Loretta were seeing one another. It's not something we should worry about now. She's disappeared again, so as far as I'm concerned, she's not our problem now."

"But do you think she'll show up again?"

Dixon looked at me over the rim of his wine glass. "Without a doubt. We haven't heard the last of her." He was quiet for a moment. "Perhaps if I'd paid her more attention when she was growing up. I was so involved with my own life, I had no time for her."

"Feeling guilty for what should have or might have happened isn't going to help. This is not your fault. Your mother's the one who should shoulder the blame."

"Maybe."

By the time we finished our drinks, the long drive to New Orleans yesterday and the crazy day we had seemed to take its toll on both of us. It wasn't that late, but sleep called. Once we returned to our room, I was out minutes after fluffing my pillow.

CHAPTER TEN

I opened my eyes to another beautiful day in New Orleans, until I remembered how yesterday had unfolded and how with Loretta Dixon had invaded my dreams. Dixon was up and dressed, ready for work. I loved that brown suit and starched white shirt. He'd taken to wearing red suspenders lately, which I also loved. The man had style. My mother tried unsuccessfully during my parents' long marriage to dress my father. He would have none of it. Not that my mother didn't have decent taste, it was my father's way of getting under her skin. I watched them squabble about which shirt and tie he should wear to work before he retired, then took to wearing khakis and T-shirts. I knew long ago I wanted a man who could dress himself.

Dixon was slipping on his wingtips, giving them another quick polish with a wash cloth. I threw off the covers. "You tossed and turned all night. Stay in bed a while longer," he said. "I ordered you breakfast." We'd decided last night that he'd be at Threadgill's Appliances when they opened their doors at eight. I would go back to the kitchen and see what more I could find out since that's where Mildred Threadgill's trail started on her way to our room. "I'll meet you back here later. Good luck with the staff. If everything goes well, we'll be at the courthouse before noon." He bent over and planted a desirous kiss on my lips and then left.

CHEF PASCAL WAS WRANGLING with a fish monger when I showed up. "Yesterday, you bring me bad fish. I can get fresher fish off the cat-food production line."

"You do that. You should have been at the dock yesterday

afternoon like all the other chefs. You called me late in the day to deliver some fish so you get whatever's left." The guy grabbed his dripping crate and left.

"It's a good thing you made a big batch of stroganoff yesterday," I said.

Chef Pascal jerked around. "Ah, mademoiselle," he said. "You didn't show up last night."

"Something came up. Any leftovers?"

"Pigswill, never in my kitchen, and never for special friends." He winked. His French accent was barely detectable when insulting the fish monger, now he sounded like Maurice Chevalier."

"What's your special today?"

"Today is Lobster Thermidor. Was Mademoiselle Lily able to help you?"

"A bit. I still can't figure out how Mildred Threadgill got into our room. Lily gave her the number of our room by accident, but she did not give her the key."

"And you think I am able to help you. I do only two things, both with passion—cooking and loving. I don't concern myself with anything else, mademoiselle. And I would not worry. If the police thought you were involved, you'd be in jail now, oui?"

"*Non.* We . . . I'm still a suspect."

"Suspect? You might be the killer, *oui*?"

"*Non.* Why would I kill Mrs. Threadgill? I didn't know her."

"Ah, but maybe her husband. You and Mr. Threadgill were lovers, *oui*?"

I couldn't help but think of the little piggy who was denied roast beef and oui-ouied himself all the way home. I was getting nowhere with this guy and the flirting was no longer any fun. Without warning he threw his hands in the air. "Non!" he shouted at the sous chef. "You imbecile! The hollandaise has separated. Throw it out and start again." A waiter came in with a special order not on the menu, and Pascal flew into another tirade. For a few minutes he busied himself chewing out his staff. The interruption gave me a chance to figure out my strategy. He came back mopping his forehead. "See what they do to me, these imbeciles. They waste my time and food. Mademoiselle

Lockhart, please come back tonight when I get off work. We can talk then."

"I can't wait until tonight."

His eyebrows shot up. Cupid would have been proud.

"No, no. I mean, I need to find out how Mrs. Threadgill got into my room. Lily couldn't help me. Maybe someone else in the kitchen saw Mrs. Threadgill come in to talk to Lily."

"Ohhh. I think you are guilty and are trying to find a, how do you say, a scraped goat?"

"Scapegoat." If it wasn't for the voice and accent, I'd have thought I was talking to Ruth.

"Do not worry. The police will handle it. They are good at interrogation."

"I am better." I pulled a card from my pocket. "I can talk to your kitchen staff now before the breakfast rush, or I can park myself here and become a nuisance. You'll have more to worry about than separated hollandaise sauce."

My bossy attitude and the discovery that I was a detective, seemed to stoke Pascal's passionate flame. He allowed me a few minutes to talk to his staff. I hoped this would be my last time in the kitchen.

It was a waste. There were four waiters working. Not one of them saw Mildred Threadgill come in to talk to Lily Morton. The sous chef and two line cooks claimed the same. The dishwasher had talked to her briefly. She rushed in and asked where her cousin was, and he pointed her in the right direction. He didn't think anyone was with her, but he didn't know. He was busy placing dirty dishes on the conveyor belt.

MRS. IVY AND HER SON ELLIOTT were waiting in the lobby of the Pontchartrain Hotel when I returned. She popped up and ran over as soon as she saw me. Elliott was close behind. Oh, Mrs. Dixon, things are not good," she said.

"I hope you don't mind us coming here on the spur of the moment. I told Mother we should wait until Martin looks into things further, but she insisted we come to see Mr. Dixon, and . . . and you right away."

I realized that Dixon and I didn't make it clear yesterday that we weren't married. I had to bite my tongue to keep from saying, "My last name is Lockhart. It is not Dixon—yet. We aren't married—yet," but before I could get out a decent word, Mrs. Ivy said, "Is Mr. Dixon available, dear?"

"He's taking care of other business," I said. "Ralph Dixon and I are partners, Mrs. Ivy. If you don't think I'm capable, you and Mr. Ivy can come back later."

"I will not wait!" Mrs. Ivy said. "I want answers now."

"Please accept my apologies, Mrs. Dixon" Elliott Ivy said. "We didn't mean to suggest that you—"

"I could use some coffee," I said. "How about you? We can talk in the restaurant."

"Yes, thank you," Elliott Ivy agreed.

"Maybe something a little stronger for me," Mrs. Ivy said.

The bartender brought my coffee. Elliott ordered a bourbon for himself and his mother. The bartender didn't even raise an eyebrow at the early morning request for a drink. After all, this was New Orleans.

"The police knocked on my door yesterday with the news that my daughter had been murdered, and now this awful news from Martin." Mrs. Ivy gulped her drink. She made a sour face, but I had the feeling gulping liquor in the morning was not new to her.

"Martin?"

"Our friend, Martin Brant," Elliott said. "He's also our lawyer. Frank and Mildred's too. He came to offer his condolences yesterday. When most of the people left, he sat me down and asked if I knew about Frank and Mildred's wills. At first I wanted to tell him that now was not the time to discuss this matter, that we haven't even buried Mildred yet. Then I realized that he's too proper not to bring it up if it wasn't absolutely necessary. I didn't tell my mother until this morning."

"You shouldn't have kept it from me," Mrs. Ivy said.

"Mother, it would have been too much for one day."

"Do not coddle me, Elliott." She turned to me. "Someone stole my daughter's money—everything!" Mrs. Ivy said.

"Now, Mother, we don't know that yet."

"Then where is it?" Mrs. Ivy balled up her napkin. I thought she was going to throw it across the room, but she dabbed her face instead.

"Let me explain, Mrs. Dixon. My deceased brother-in-law sold his business shortly before he died. It was an appliance store."

"Yes, I know. Lily mentioned that he sold it recently."

"It happened all of a sudden. He didn't even discuss it with Mildred. She was shocked when she found out. He told her he was tired of the business and it was time to retire. Frank said he no longer enjoyed his work. Anyway, he said he got a fantastic offer."

"Lily told me that too," I said.

"Lily needs to learn to keep her mouth shut. That's family business," Mrs. Ivy said.

"Mother, calm yourself." He called for another bourbon.

"How much is fantastic?" I asked.

"Eighty-five thousand dollars. Mildred was to inherit everything."

"That didn't happen? He changed the will?"

"Oh no, everything went to Mildred, even the house in the Garden District and a small vacation cottage in North Carolina. But his bank account was empty. Frank withdrew everything the day before he died. The account was in Frank's name only. Martin is at the bank now to see if he can find out anything more, but I seriously doubt the bank knows anything."

"He drew out the cash?"

"Yes, all of it," said Mrs. Ivy.

"What's also odd is that Martin didn't even know Frank had sold the store until afterwards," Elliott said. "Martin was shocked. You would think Frank would let the family lawyer handle things. Martin had always handled the family's legal transactions. He drew up all the documents when Frank bought the store. But Frank closed the deal himself."

"You think this has something to do with your sister's murder?"

Mrs. Ivy let out another wail. "Of course it does. It has to. What other explanation is there? she said.

I could think of a bazillion reasons why Frank would withdraw all his money without telling his wife—gambling debts being the main one, supporting a secret wife and kids coming in second, planning to run away from a wife who he didn't give a hoot about. My thoughts were interrupted.

Mrs. Ivy must have read my mind. "I know why Frank took the money without telling anyone." This time the balled up napkin, now stained with makeup, sailed across the dining room. "He had another woman."

The secret life and kids scenario won out.

"He was planning to take his money and run away with a mistress," Mrs. Ivy said. "I never trusted him."

"Mother, you don't know if there was another woman involved, and you liked him when you first met him."

"I was a fool, and what else could it be if he didn't have another woman? He never cared about Mildred. I never thought I'd say this, but she's better off dead!"

"Mother!"

"This would break her heart."

"Mrs. Ivy, Dixon is at the appliance store now to see what he can find out. Please, don't upset yourself any further. There might be a reasonable explanation for all of this."

"She's right, Mother. I told you it was a good idea to come see the Dixons."

The Dixons. Jeez. Would we be lumped together as one entity from now on? No longer Sydney Lockhart and Ralph Dixon? If so, at least Dixon would benefit from keeping his own name.

"They are already looking into things, Mother. When I hear back from Martin, I'll let you know what he found out, Mrs. Dixon. Mother, why don't you go the lady's room and tidy up? You'll feel better."

"If it were only that easy." Mrs. Ivy shuffled off to the restroom.

Elliott Ivy grabbed my hand. The look in his eyes went from concern to desperation. "Mother will never rest if we can't figure this out. It's not about the money, with my mother, it's more about Mildred's reputation."

"I don't understand."

"It's just that Mother was always embarrassed by Mildred's

choices, her situations. She always felt she had to take up for her daughter, justify to all her friends Mildred's mistakes."

"It's not Mildred's fault she was murdered."

The word *murdered* made him shudder.

"No, but it's a scandal, isn't it? What if Frank did give his money to another woman? That would make it even worse."

I couldn't believe what I was hearing. Mrs. Ivy's main concern was how her friends would view her in light of the tragedy that befell her daughter?

"Please don't think we expect you and your husband to investigate this out of the kindness of your heart. I am happy to pay for your services."

I wanted to set him straight again on my name, but at this point it was probably a good idea for him to believe Dixon and I were married. I'd hate for Mrs. Ivy to be embarrassed by an unmarried couple staying together in a hotel room investigating her daughter's murder.

"Mr. Dixon and I are involved in this case regardless. Let's see what the rest of the day brings."

"You're right. Thanks for listening."

"How do I get in touch with you? Dixon has your business card, but why don't you give me one too. We often work different angles of the case."

"Yes, I understand." He pulled out his card and turned it over. "I'll write my home number on the back, that's the best place to call me. I'm usually out showing property and it's hard to catch me in the office. Truth be told, I think it was probably another woman."

"Do you know something, Mr. Ivy?"

"No, it is just a feeling."

"The big question is where's the money. If Frank was having an affair and planned to leave Mildred, would he have taken out $85,000 and just handed it to his girlfriend? That doesn't make sense."

"Or he could have hidden it somewhere, in which case we might never know."

Mrs. Ivy came back looking a bit more relaxed. "Elliott is right," she said. "I'm sure things will work out."

"I hate to bring this up, but I have to ask. Did Mildred have a will?"

"Yes." Elliott blushed. "She left everything to me."

CHAPTER ELEVEN

Dixon hadn't yet returned, and I had too much pent-up energy to sit and wait. The St. Louis Cemetery was a short walk away, so I headed in that direction to see if Frank Threadgill's tomb had had another nighttime visitor. A slight breeze blew in from the Gulf, but did little to quell the warm, stickiness of south Louisiana's subtropical climate. Pungent smell of seaweed mixed with the odor of car exhaust, cooking aromas from greasy-spoon restaurants—what I imagined as a soft, spongy subterranean muck settled over the city. Most of New Orleans is below sea level and is slowly sinking. In my wild imagination I could hear the sucking of tidal waters pulling the city into the Gulf.

I grew up in Houston, a city similar to the Big Easy, both located near the Gulf of Mexico with the same muggy climate, but the feeling was different. Houston was seriously urban, New Orleans delightfully sinister.

I thought over the conversation I'd had with Elliott and Alma Ivy. Could Elliott have killed Mildred to get to her money? If he did, I could imagine the shock at discovering that the money was gone, but then there were still the two Threadgill homes. Now Elliott Ivy's homes.

The cemetery could wait. Suddenly, I was in the market for a new home. I headed over to the chamber of commerce office to ask about real estate agencies in town and received an alphabetical list. Tulane Real Estate was on it. I asked the clerk if she could recommend one. Her response was that all members of the chamber were reputable. I told her that someone had recommended Tulane Real Estate. "We're not allowed to recommend one over another, you understand." She lowered her voice to a whisper. "But I can tell you that we purchased our home through Tulane, and were happy with how the company did business." I asked if she knew Elliott Ivy personally. Her eyes lit up and I learned that Elliott Ivy was such a nice young man. He had gone to high school with her son, and was a pleasant person to do business with. I thanked her and left without knowing any more than when I came in, feeling like a novice in the investigation business. Perhaps Dixon would have a better idea how to find out about Elliott Ivy's financial status.

I decided to walk toward the French Market and along the river before heading to the cemetery. My long thick hair had begun to feel like a hooded cape made of dense wool. I pulled it back into a ponytail. When that didn't help, I rolled it into a twist and held it in place with a clip I kept in my bag.

A weeks ago, the idea of spending time in New Orleans had not crossed my mind. This was my second time here in less than a month. I could understand Rip's desire to open his new business and make a life for himself here. I felt drawn to it too, not enough to put down roots though. Texas is my home, and for all its oddities—and there are a lot—it offers a magic found no place else. But New Orleans vibrates with mysticism and offers something different. I'm not sure what. Being here with Dixon was nice. Getting married here felt right.

As I approached the waterfront, I noticed a crowd had gathered and cops were trying their best to keep people back.

"What happened?" I asked a guy standing on his tip toes and craning his neck.

"Looks like another body is being pulled out of the river. Oh, this is a good one. Look." He moved aside so I could see.

"Another body?" Several cops had just lifted a body wrapped in a tarp onto a stretcher.

"It happens more often that you might think. Someone dumps a body into the Mississippi in hopes that the river will carry it out into the Gulf. If the current is right the tide takes the body out to sea. Gone forever. But not always. Two months ago during a low tide, an Oldsmobile was seen stuck on a sandbar. Turns out it belonged to a local gangster. The Olds was too heavy to be washed away. The car was pulled out of the water. Stuffed in the trunk was the gangster. I'm getting closer for a better look."

I was right behind him, shoving and edging my way through the crowd. That's when I noticed the guy pulled out a notebook. Hanging around his neck was a camera.

"You're a reporter," I said.

"*The Times-Picayune.* Oh, this is *really* good." He ducked under another mass of arms and elbowed and inched his way closer to the scene. I followed as best as I could, but I lost him in the melee. I didn't have to get closer. My height came in handy at times like these. Over the heads of gawkers, I had a clear view of the excitement. I spotted the reporter. He'd managed to edge closer and snapped a few photos.

Shoved up against a police car was a man dripping wet and covered in mud from head to toe. His suit coat was ripped. Despite his appearance, he was in much better shape than the poor sod on the stretcher. A cop kicked the man's legs apart, shouted at him to place his hands on top of the patrol car, and frisked him. Handcuffs were slapped on and the car door opened. The guy didn't resist. He acted as if he were sliding into the back of a limo and the cop was his chauffeur.

The reporter snapped away. "Turn around, buddy. This picture will be on the front page of the evening news."

At that moment, the guy being arrested turned his head. Our eyes locked. A surge of adrenaline had me shoving people out of my way as if my life depended on it. But I was too late. With lights flashing and sirens screaming, the patrol car turned the corner and Dixon disappeared from sight.

CHAPTER TWELVE

This is my third time in the New Orleans downtown police station. The first time, two weeks ago while on the Johnny Pine case, the second time was yesterday. It was becoming too familiar. The front desk was built high above the main floor with a long marble counter that divided the public from the police, a staunch reminder that once you walked through the door and up to the desk, you'd better have a damn good reason to be here. The police station in Austin looked like any city police station—overused, grimy, somber, sobering. It brought on feelings of desperation and despondency. This place spoke of all of the above along with a heavy dose of indifference. I squared my shoulders and stood staring up at the desk sergeant. He didn't bother to raise his nose from the newspaper he was reading. "You here to report a crime in our fair city? If someone picked your pocket, it was your fault. If someone stole your purse, it was your fault too. You should know better. If you're lost, go find a map. I don't give directions."

"None of the above," I said. "It's about someone who was just arrested."

"Let him sleep it off. Come get him tomorrow."

I folded my arms and stood there. He finally looked up. The look on my face said I wasn't going anywhere.

"Wait over there." He pointed to a bench.

I was certain Dixon was with Detective Bergeron whom we encountered yesterday. I'd been pacing for what seemed like hours, although only twenty minutes had transpired, when the reporter I stumbled upon in the crowd came in. He was on a first name basis with the sergeant.

"What have you got for me, Jim?"

"I don't have much to give you, Calvin."

"Come on. You know that answer won't do."

I sidled up next to the reporter. Sergeant Jim shot me a death look. "Beat it, lady. I'm busy."

I reached up and pulled the newspaper from his hands. "Reading the police blotter to find out what's going on in your fair city? As I was saying, I'm here to see someone who was just arrested and I'm tired of waiting."

This seemed to shake the sergeant's brain awake. "*You*," he said, finally recognizing me. "You were here yesterday."

The reporter turned to see who'd gotten the officer's attention. "*You*," he said.

Sergeant Jim lifted the phone receiver. "Tell Bergeron there's someone out here he needs to see."

"What's your interest in the case?" the reporter said.

"That's none of your business, Calvin," Sergeant Jim said.

Calvin ignored the sergeant. In my experience, sometimes it's better to stay silent and sometimes it's better to get as many words out in the little time you have. I chose the latter. "They've arrested my partner. We were hauled in yesterday over the murder at the Pontchartrain Hotel. The victim was found in our hotel room. I'm Sydney Lockhart, the Lockhart part of the Dixon, Lockhart, Ludlow Detective Agency, and you are?"

"Calvin Logan. This must be my lucky day. See, Jim, I can get more out of the general public than I can get out of you."

"I wouldn't call this woman the general public," the sergeant said. "And I'd keep my mouth shut, Miss, it I were you."

"Miss Lockhart, I've been looking for you. Follow me." Detective Bergeron turned down the hall, not waiting to see if I'd follow. I did, right on his heels.

"I'll be here when you get back, Miss Lockhart," Calvin Logan called after me.

The interrogation room felt as claustrophobic as a submarine.

"I was about to send my posse after you," Bergeron said. "Sit down."

"I'd rather not. Why did you arrest Dixon?"

"I'll ask the questions if you don't mind. Where were you about two hours ago?"

I checked my watch. "I was at the Pontchartrain Hotel talking to the kitchen staff." I didn't tell him about Elliott and Alma Ivy coming to the hotel. It's best not to complicate things.

"Not happy with the restaurant's food?"

"No, detective. I wanted to get a lead on who killed Mildred Threadgill in our room."

"And did you?"

"Nope. But Dixon and I were at Alma Ivy's house last night. She's Mildred's mother. Did you know Mildred was into voodoo?"

"Who in New Orleans isn't?"

"How about you? Are you into voodoo, detective?"

"I'm into arresting murderers."

"Oh, good, then you can let Dixon go. We've already told you we had an alibi for the time Mildred Threadgill was murdered. Didn't you check it out?"

"Or course I did, but you sort of lied. As far as I know, you had an alibi, not your boyfriend."

"But we were together at the cemetery. The attendant vouched for us."

"Nope."

"What do you mean, 'nope?'"

"He vouched for you, not Mr. Dixon."

"Dixon was standing at the door."

"The guy only saw you. Anyway it doesn't matter. We got your Mr. Dixon on a second murder."

"What murder?"

"A young woman. We caught Mr. Dixon with her body on the riverbank. He said he was trying to pull it out of the river, but we have information that tells us something different."

"And what might that be?"

"We have witnesses that said they saw him carrying the body and watched him throw it into the river."

"That's absurd. Dixon was a detective for the Hot Springs Police Department before he went private."

"Cops kill too." Bergeron walked out. Two minutes later he was back. "I'm having your alibi checked out."

"I thought you already did."

"This is for the second murder."

"Who were these witnesses?"

"Can't tell you that."

"Maybe these witnesses were wrong about what they saw."

"They weren't. The murdered woman was a maid who worked at the Pontchartrain. Her name was stitched on her uniform. Lavine Rose."

Lavine—she was our best bet. She had information. Had we not let her leave our room so quickly, would she still be alive? Guilt punched me in the stomach. Poor Lavine, what had she gotten herself into? "We spoke to Miss Rose at the hotel after the murder. She was scared and clearly hiding something. Dixon has no reason to kill either of these women."

"I was willing to give him the benefit of the doubt, but with a second murder victim linked to the hotel, things changed. What were you and Mr. Dixon doing at Threadgill Appliances this morning?

"I told you I was at the Pontchartrain. Dixon went to Threadgill Appliances."

"Need a new ice box, did he?"

At that point, I decided I'd said too much. I knew what he was doing, trying to trip me up. I'd played that game before. Bergeron and I were several minutes into a staring contest. A contest that was broken by a knock. Bergeron went to the door, had a short conversation with Sergeant Jim. My alibi checked out.

"I want to see Dixon," I said.

"You have fifteen minutes. Sergeant, accompany Miss Lockhart, but stay close by."

"Dixon did not kill anyone," I said, as I rose from the chair.

"We have witnesses, remember."

CHAPTER THIRTEEN

I never thought I'd live to see this," I said.

"Me neither." Dixon smiled. "I never go out in public looking like this. Maybe a slightly wrinkled dress shirt, but river mud on my suit, never."

"This is no time to joke. In fifteen minutes, tell me what happened?"

"Sure. Here goes. I went to Threadgill Appliances. It's still operating under the same name. I asked to see the new owner. By the way, his name is Walt Garrison. I was told he wasn't in. So I walked around to the back through the showroom, past the small appliances and found the offices. The door to Garrison's office was closed but I heard an argument going on inside. Sounded like two guys. I went to the loading dock and milled around. A few minutes later, the foreman came up and asked me if I was lost. He didn't sound happy. I told him I was tired of doing business with companies that delivered damaged goods, and that I was planning on switching to Threadgill's. I wanted to check out the loading dock. It was a weak story, and he didn't buy it. He told me to get lost. I turned to leave as he was paged over the intercom. As soon as he went inside the store, I checked out a few of the storage rooms. I found one that was locked but managed to get inside."

"Was it full of dead bodies?"

"No bodies, but I found a woman's shoe. I wasn't able to look around because I heard commotion coming from outside. The foreman was back, giving a guy an earful. I didn't like what I heard. I stepped out in time to see them toss something in the trunk of a car. I didn't like what I saw. They both sped off. I followed."

"Cab, bus, train?"

"I borrowed an old Ford pickup. The keys were left inside."

"You stole it?"

"I used it."

"So, besides Bergeron having you down for murder, he'll probably add car theft to the charges."

"Don't worry about that. You're getting me off track. The car pulled up to the river. The two guys got out, opened the trunk, and pulled out a lump covered in a burlap sack. I've seen enough dead bodies to know that's what was inside. I fired a couple of shots and told them to stop. They threw the body into the water. I jumped in. It was a stupid thing to do, I know, but there was a chance that the person was still alive. I underestimated the current and went down a couple of times, but I managed to grab the body. I held on the best I could. The two guys ran along firing shots at me. I lost my grip on the body, and it started drifting downriver. I swam after it and grabbed it again. I was finally able to crawl out of the water. I pulled the sack open just as the police drove up. It was Lavine Rose."

"I know. Bergeron told me."

"He seemed pleased to find me in the interrogation room again. First words from his mouth, 'Why did you kill that girl?' I told him what I'd seen and that I was trying to rescue her. He asked me if I made a habit of rescuing dead bodies."

"The guy's an idiot."

"Actually, I could see myself asking the same question. Evidently the two guys from the warehouse called the cops, gave them my description, and told them they saw me dump the body into the river."

"Both guys worked at the appliance store?"

"I'm not sure. The foreman wore a green jump suit with the Threadgill logo and the other one was dressed in regular clothes."

"What did they look like?"

"The foreman was middle-aged. About my height, on the heavy side. The other guy was bigger. Dopey walk. Didn't act too smart. I gave a description of the car they drove and the license number to Bergeron, but he didn't believe my story. I'd be surprised if he bothered to check on the car's registration."

"I'll go back to the appliance store, see what I can find out."

"I don't want you going back there."

"I understand, but what choice do we have? You're in jail. I need to find you a lawyer and try to get you bailed out. I'll call Marcella. She's not licensed to practice in Louisiana, but maybe she can recommend someone." Marcella Wheatly came into my life right after the first of the year. Dixon and I were just getting to know one another. I was in Palacios, Texas, staying at the Luther Hotel. Dixon was still a police detective in Hot Springs. I'd been wrongly arrested for the murder of Sam Buckner and was sitting in jail like Dixon is now. To make a long story short, Marcella and her law partner from Houston rescued me. It turned out that Marcella is Ruth's half-sister, a surprise Ruth is still having trouble accepting even though Marcella handles some of Ruth's philanthropic projects.

"Good idea. I trust Marcella's judgement and I have faith in your abilities, but don't go to the appliance store alone. I'm sure Lavine was not killed in the warehouse. There wasn't any blood in that room."

"Think she was killed at the hotel?"

"Maybe. We need to speed this game up. I knew you'd be here soon, so I used my one phone call to arrange for some help for you." His dimples were at their all-time deepest.

"But who . . . No! No! No!"

"Palmer is flying Ruth here as we speak. They should be at the hotel soon."

"I could slug you."

"You'll have to wait until later. In the meantime, get me some clean clothes and hurry back. I smell like the underbelly of the Big Easy. You have a lot to do." He had the nerve to blow me a kiss. A prickle of anger damped the back of my neck as I stormed out of the police station.

I had a good mind to let Dixon sit in his soiled clothes. I'm the one who usually pulls the crazy stunts in this partnership. I darted into the phone booth across the street. I called Marcella collect and gave her a quick summary of what had happened. She didn't know any lawyers in New Orleans, but she would talk to her ex-lawyer partner. She should have a name as soon as possible. I hung up and turned to leave only to find the reporter waiting outside the booth like a hungry coyote.

"You look flustered. Buy you a drink?"

"It's too early for me to imbibe, I need to keep a level head."

"Yeah, right." He chuckled. "Come on. I was talking about something more sustaining."

THE WAIT LINE AT CAFÉ Du Monde snaked out into the street, but Calvin Logan muscled his way in and found a table. "The coffee's the best in the world."

"I've been here before."

The waiter came over. "Full order, Lewis," Logan said.

"Yes, Mr. Logan, right away."

Logan pulled out his notebook. "Now, what did you learn from your boyfriend?"

If this guy thought that superb coffee and a full order of beignets was enough to provide him a news story, he had another thing coming.

"My boyfriend?"

"Boyfriend, husband, whatever. Sergeant Jim told me that you two were in yesterday for questioning over the Pontchartrain murder."

"I don't think he's authorized to give out that information."

Calvin Logan shrugged. "We're old buddies. So, what was your guy doing with the body?"

"Pulling it out of the river."

"He saw what he was sure was a body wrapped in a sack, decided to jump in the river, and pull it out?"

"That's right."

Our coffee and beignets arrived and Logan closed his notebook. He took a sip of his coffee and stuffed a beignet into his mouth.

"Mr. Logan—"

"Calvin."

"I am not going to jeopardize Dixon's situation by talking to a reporter."

"Or course not, but you need me on your side. I know the city. I know the cops. I know how things operate. Reporters can be a valuable resource for private detectives."

He was right. I knew from experience.

"This murder and arrest are linked to the murder at the Pontchartrain, right?"

"What makes you say that?"

"Oh, come on. I was standing right there when Sergeant Jim said Bergeron was looking for you. I saw you go back to his office."

"Off the record."

"Sure."

"Dixon and I are staying at the hotel. The murder was committed in our room. We were questioned. We were released. End of story." I finished my coffee and left.

I made my way down the street, passed a phone booth, and decided to look up Frank and Mildred Threadgill's address. I hailed a cab and was soon standing outside a mansion that took my breath away. It was a two-story stone structure with Gothic arched windows. Like many homes in New Orleans this one had a wrap-around porch on both floors, a necessity that allowed breezes to flow through the upstairs bedrooms. A multitude of narrow windows stood tall. Lacy curtains, drawn and parted in the middle, hung from each one. I told the driver to wait, and I walked up the steps onto the front porch and looked in the window to see an elegantly decorated dining room. Embroidered seat covers on the chairs. Matching pillows on the sofa. I doubted dust ever settled on the Cherrywood furniture. Mildred Threadgill would never enjoy this room again, if she ever did, from what I learned from her family. Up until this moment, all I felt for the woman was anger that she made it to our room, got herself murdered, and ruined our wedding plans. Looking into her home, I felt sadness for this poor woman who I'd never met. I vowed to find out who killed Mildred Threadgill and why.

CHAPTER FOURTEEN

Eager to get back to the hotel so I could bring Dixon some clean clothes and figure out my next move, I told the driver to step on it. On the way over I thought about what I needed to bring him—Did he bring an extra pair of shoes? Of course he did. Socks, underwear, tie—that too. I was two steps into the lobby when I heard, "There she is."

I looked up to see Palmer, Ruth, and Lydia coming toward me. *Was Dixon trying to help me or send me to an early tomb?* "The plane is a two-seater. How did you manage to get Lydia here?" I asked.

"They strapped me to the wing," Lydia said.

Palmer giggled. He was Ruth's new pilot boyfriend who owned his own plane and was teaching Ruth to fly. I have to remember to ask him if Ruth ever confessed to borrowing his plane without him knowing when we were on the San Antonio case. My crazy cousin actually flew us to New Orleans and back. It was her solo flight. The only reason I agreed to it was because I had amnesia and wasn't sure who she really was. Unfortunately, I regained some of my memory once we were in the air. I will keep the plane theft under my hat until it is absolutely necessary, although bribes didn't work on Ruth.

"I wish," Ruth said. "I can't believe she blackmailed me into taking her along."

"I had my concerns over getting us all in the cockpit," Palmer said. "But we worked it out. Ruth flew the plane and Lydia sat in my lap."

"Which was my idea," Lydia said. "It was either that or I sit in Ruth's lap, which would not happen in a million years. Easy decision. I'd rather crash than be that close to your weird cousin."

"Do I have to listen to this disrespectful brat?" Ruth said.

Ruth and Lydia did not get along—not ever.

The pounding in my head started at the base of my neck, rushed up the back of my skull, over the top, and slammed into my forehead. I was glad Palmer was here. He'd lend some peace and common sense to this insane situation.

"Call me when you're ready for me to come get you, Ruth" Palmer said.

"You mean you're not staying?" I asked.

"I have a client I have to fly to Abilene tonight." He kissed Ruth on the cheek. He was thwarted by a low rumble coming from Lydia when he tried to pat her on the head. He gave me a hug. I hung on and whispered in his ear. "Please, don't leave me here with these two." He giggled, pried my fingers from his lapels, and was gone.

"Where do we start?" Lydia said. "I didn't get the whole story. Something about a murder."

"How about we start by you telling me why you came? Don't you have a play to produce?"

"Flu epidemic in Austin. I cancelled rehearsals for a couple of days."

"Liar, liar," Ruth said.

"That's what I told your mother, thinking she would go back home," Lydia said. "Especially since you disappeared again. She wanted to stay with your brother, but Scott's boyfriend said no, so she checked herself into a hotel and insisted on staying. I had to call your dad to come get her. He's a really nice guy. I can see why you like him best."

"Sydney, you're brainwashing this child with all that bad talk about your mother. Aunt Mary Lou is not that bad." Ruth did a slow three-sixty, ogling the lobby. Wow! This place is swanky. That chandelier looks imported from Italy. And I love this black and white tile floor. And those deep red ceramic, or is that marble planters. I'm getting some fabulous decorating ideas just standing here. I guess if I am forced to stay in another hotel and help you solve another murder, the Pontchartrain is the place to be. Good choice, Sydney. But why did they name it the Pontchartrain? I've never heard that word before. Maybe Pontchartrain was the name of a blue-blood from the area."

"It's named after a place in France," Lydia said.

"How the hell would you know?" Ruth said.

I headed for the Bayou Bar and downed two shots of tequila, then took the elevator to my room. Unfortunately, the wealthy socialite and the autocratic adolescent followed. Ruth started her inspection as soon as I opened the door. She walked around our suite, inspecting every inch, the size of the closet, the inside of each dresser drawer, the firmness of mattress, the softness of the bathroom towels. She went into the second bedroom. I heard a few tsk, tsks. I held my breath and I called the front desk. I was told the hotel was full. The hotel down the street was full. The boarding house across the street had a no vacancy sign. If Dixon wasn't sitting in jail, I'd head back to the bar for seconds.

"I'm taking this second bedroom," Ruth said. "I cannot stay in the same room with Lydia the Liar."

"Everyone lies, Ruth. Right now I have a couple of murders to solve."

"Of course you do," Ruth said.

I hate it when Ruth uses her smarty-pants voice.

"Two murders?" Lydia said. "That's even better. Hey, did you have a chance to celebrate before you became involved with dead people?"

Oh, no, no, no, no. I can't deal with this now.

"Celebrate what?" Ruth asked.

Lydia, the smartest person among the three of us, realized her error. I had not told Ruth that Dixon and I were eloping. I was eager to hear Lydia's cover up.

"Celebrate . . . Mardi Gras," she said.

"You mean that parade where drunk people dress in gaudy costumes and toss plastic beads into the street?"

"That's the one," Lydia said.

"Sydney, why would you want to celebrate that?" Ruth said.

"It was a wild idea Dixon and I had. It's not important now. When Dixon called, did he tell you about the case?"

"Very little," Ruth said. "He told me you needed help and asked me to come because he was in jail. What did he do anyway? I can't conceive of him breaking the law."

"He didn't," I said. I told them about the case and the situation that led up to the murders.

"That's ridiculous. Dixon wouldn't murder anyone. We simply have to solve this case and get him released." Ruth continued scanning the room. Her perspective on life leaned toward topsy-turvy. She could take serious situations like murder and make them sound trivial, like breaking the heel off her shoe, or hotel towels not being soft and fluffy enough.

Lydia pulled a small notebook from her pocket and took notes. "I think the brother did it," she said. "What if he killed Frank, the husband, because of the trouble he caused Mildred, the wife? I don't buy that heart-attack story. But then, come to think of it, why would the brother kill Mildred? He loved his sister. What if the answer to this puzzle is hidden in Frank's coffin? Otherwise why was someone trying to open it? Or, what if Frank is not really dead?"

I answered Lydia's questions the best I could. I don't think she wanted answers. Her nose was back in her notebook and she was scribbling away. I would not be surprised if this story was soon woven into the plot of one of her plays.

"Hmmm," Ruth was having another go with the dresser.

"Ruth, have you been listening?"

"Every word. But there's a major problem here."

"Go on," I said.

"The problem is where am I going to put everything? True, I only brought two suitcases, but there's only one chest of drawers in this room and the wardrobe is tiny. And there's only one bed in each room. Where will you two sleep?" Ruth paused, tapped her front tooth with her ruby red fingernail.

This two-room suite was clearly not going to be big enough. Truth is, a twenty-room mansion would not be big enough. A knock on the door interrupted my silent Hail Mary.

"Room service."

I opened the door to see the large vase of yellow gladiolus. I read the attached card and my heart sank. Instead of sharing this lovely room with the man I loved, I was here with a small demanding woman and a child who was fascinated with solving murders and had no interest in playing with dolls.

Ruth took the flowers from my hands. "This saves me a phone call. Please bring up a fold-up cot." She handed the bellboy a tip. "That was so nice of the hotel to bring us flowers.

I grabbed the vase from her hands. "They're my flowers! Dixon ordered them for me."

"They let him order flowers from jail? How sweet. I'm moving this dresser into my room. I need it for my clothes." Ruth said.

"We were supposed to bring clothes?" Lydia asked.

"Clothes!" I needed to send my brain out for an overhaul. I started grabbing Dixon's things and sent Ruth downstairs to hail a cab.

"Sorry, I almost spilled the beans about you getting married," Lydia said. "Where's your wedding ring?"

I shook my head.

"Stupid question, I know," Lydia said. "Sorry."

CHAPTER FIFTEEN

Sergeant Jim was nice enough to grant me another five minutes with Dixon so I could give him the things he needed. I also gave him an update on Ruth's and Lydia's arrival. He had the nerve to chuckle.

"Lydia asked a good question," I said. "What if Frank isn't really dead? What if the coffin is empty? Or what if it contains another body?"

"Hon, slow down. First things first. We deal with who we know is absolutely dead before we start exhuming bodies. Will I be spending the night in jail?"

"Most likely. Marcella's looking for a lawyer. I doubt she can arrange anything this late in the day."

Sergeant Jim poked his head in. "Time's up. Detective Bergeron wants to talk to you again, Miss Lockhart."

"Be nice," Dixon said.

"SIT DOWN, MISS LOCKHART." Detective Bergeron looked too pleased with himself. It was almost as if he could tell that he made the hair on the back of my neck stand up. "I was serious about you not meddling in this case."

"I heard you."

"Good, 'cause if I find out you are meddling, you'll be sitting in a cell next to your boyfriend."

"Yeah, you mentioned that before."

"And I'll make sure your PI license is jerked."

I didn't bother to challenge him on that threat. This was Louisiana, not Texas.

"I don't have a high opinion of private detectives, especially women. My wife knows her place. She takes care of the house and kids. She does a great job 'cause that's what she's made for. I know all about what girls did for the war effort, working in factories and what not. Hell, my wife even volunteered at the local hospital. Volunteered! Women in Louisiana know their places. Do I make myself clear?"

As clear as any misogynist can make it, I thought. "I'll stay out of your way, Detective."

"Remember, I'm warning you, Miss Lockhart."

"You wouldn't be the first."

"Uh, Detective?" Sergeant Jim came in. "I hate to interrupt."

"Miss Lockhart and I are finished, Sergeant."

"Good. 'Cause I thought you'd like to know that a small, sassy blonde woman and a foul-mouth young girl, at least I think it's a girl, are squaring off out front. Personally, I'm putting my money on the girl."

Time to go. "They belong to me," I said, scrambling out of the office.

RUTH WANTED TO MAKE dinner reservations at Commander's Palace, but after the day I had, I insisted we stay in the room and order three Monte Cristos from room service. Ruth and Lydia argued over every little thing imaginable. Window open; window closed. Lamp on; lamp off. Leave the chair by the window; move the chair to the other side. Luckily, we ate our dinner in silence. I'd like to think Lydia and Ruth had nothing else to argue about, but it was the delicious French sandwiches that kept them quiet. I suggested we get to bed early since we'd have a long day and tomorrow would prove even longer. I was about to put on my PJs when room service knocked.

"Miss Lockhart, we have your champagne."

"I didn't order champagne."

"Compliments of the house. Oh, and I have a note for you."

I read the note. "Miss Lockhart, your Lobster Thermidor is ready."

Damn. I'd forgotten about Pascal. I slipped on my shoes.

"Where are you going," Ruth said. "Who's the champagne for?"

"You. I'll be back in a moment."

THINGS HAD QUIETED DOWN in the kitchen. When the sous chef saw me come in, he nodded to an open door in the back. Chef Pascal was putting the final touches on a candlelight dinner for two. He lifted the silver dome lids from the plates and the aroma of lobster lifted me off the floor. "I have a Bordeaux perfect for my creation." He placed his hand over his heart and raised his eyes as if offering up a prayer.

"A passionate chef," I said.

"That is me exactly, Mademoiselle, although Pascal is only a poor passionate boy who is lonely for his dear France."

His romantic mood disappeared and he hung his head. For a moment I thought it was for effect, but the guy was truly conflicted.

"Chef Pascal, are you okay?"

He handed me a glass of wine. "Yes, but the problems of a French chef should not trouble a beautiful lady."

We clinked glasses.

"Ummm. Nice, rich, smooth," he said. "You chase away my sadness." He lifted my hand and slathered my fingers with kisses. "Your Texas accent. When you say my name, I feel warm with beautiful butterflies inside. You feel it too."

Jeez Louise. I couldn't let this get out of hand. I came right to the point. "There's something you need to know, Pascal. I'm sure you've heard by now that there's been a second murder. Lavine Rose, a maid who worked here."

He dropped my hand. I thought he was going to cry. Unlike the fluctuating passion he exuded moments ago, these emotions were sincere. "Poor Lavine. She was a mixed up girl, but did not deserve that."

"Did you know her well?"

"No. But she was French like me."

"I detected a slight accent."

"Are you worried something will happen to you, Mademoiselle?

I'm sure you have nothing to worry about. Please, sit. We eat and talk, no?"

"Okay. But I do have something to worry about. The police have arrested a friend of mine for both murders."

"This friend, he is a boy?"

"Well, yes, a man actually."

"I see. This man is special to you. I noticed the ring." He buried his head in his hands and sighed, then quickly straightened up. "We will not tell him about our little dinner. Pascal can keep a secret."

"I appreciate that, but I need to find out who the killer is."

"I will help. Nose around, ask questions, but tomorrow. Tonight we do not worry."

We were halfway through the meal when I heard the sound of sharp heels tapping on the tile floor. "There you are. I got worried when you didn't come back."

"How did you know where to find me?" I asked.

"Please!" She turned to Pascal. "Hi, I'm Ruth." She stuck out her hand.

Pascal almost choked on his lobster. Ruth had that effect on men. He dribbled butter down his chin and knocked his wine glass over onto his lap. He turned pink. The guy was smitten. Once he found his voice, he muttered, "Two tempting Texas women. Pascal is a lucky man."

WE LEFT PASCAL TO CLEAN himself up. "Thanks for coming to my rescue."

"You know better than to run out of the room in a place where a murder has been committed," Ruth said.

"Are you serious?"

"Well, no. Curious."

"I figured I'd be right back. I couldn't very well leave after Chef Pascal prepared dinner. I might need his help."

"I like him."

"Seems he likes you, which is a relief. But you have Palmer."

"Yes, true. You think he will really try to help us?"

"Are you kidding? We are 'two tempting Texas women.' Where's Lydia?"

"She wanted to check out the hotel so she went downstairs to the lobby."

"And you let her?"

"I didn't try and stop her. Besides she wouldn't have listened."

There were still a few people in the lobby and a crowd in the bar. Lydia was not one of them.

"Where could she have gone?"

"Maybe she ran away."

"This is New Orleans, Sin City."

"It's the city I'd worry about, not the girl."

I wanted to strangle Ruth. What the hell was Dixon thinking when he called her? She's helped out on cases before, but I didn't want her in New Orleans. I went up to the concierge. "Have you seen a young girl around the lobby tonight? She's twelve, blonde hair, and dressed in overalls and lavender patent leather shoes."

"You mean that one?" He pointed to the front door.

Lydia walked in acting like she owned the place.

"Don't tell me you were wandering around the city after dark," I said.

"New York is not the only city that never sleeps. Besides it's not that late," Lydia said. "I wanted to get the lay of the land. There's a different kind of vibe at night. Did you know the Lafayette Cemetery was only a few blocks away?"

"From now on, I want you back at the hotel before dark. Here, take this." I handed Lydia a twenty. "But if you're going to be out at night, take taxis. I don't want you walking."

"Yes, mommy."

WE WENT BACK TO OUR room. All I could think about was crawling into bed and disappearing under the sheet.

"What the hell?" Ruth yelled from her doorway. "Did you do this, you little brat?"

It was evident that Lydia had rearranged the furniture and moved Ruth's clothes. Lydia went into *her* room and slammed the door. Sharing a hotel room with Ruth meant I'd sleep in a sofa, chair, or on the floor. I'd be lucky to have a flat, lumpy pillow. At least this time there was a cot.

"That child is a royal nuisance." Ruth stomped her foot. "Her father lets her run wild. She should be in school. She's certainly not being taught anything at home despite all those home-school textbooks strewn around that bawdy theater. She needs to be taught to behave."

"I don't think of Lydia as a child," I said. "As far as her behavior, I find it refreshing. I have to admit, though, she is smarter than the two of us put together."

"Oh please. Hey, look at this." Ruth held up the hotel's brochure, kicked off her heels and crawled into my bed. "It says Tennessee Williams wrote *A Streetcar Named Desire* while staying here."

"Yeah, I heard that."

"I wonder which room he stayed in."

"The concierge could probably tell you."

"Why would any playwright name a streetcar Desire as part of the title?"

"Go see the play."

"He could have named it, *Streetcar Named New Orleans* or *Streetcar Named Louisiana.*"

"Ruth! He named it *Desire* after the street in New Orleans named *Desire.*"

"Why would anyone name a street *Desire*? What's wrong with Oak Street or Elm Street, or Main Street?"

"I can't answer that, Ruth. But you have to admit that the title *A Streetcar Named Main,* doesn't have the same ring to it. It's flat. Something named *Desire* has a sultry, maybe passionate or erotic feel."

"Hmmm, now that I think about it, why would anyone name a child Tennessee?"

"I don't know. Maybe he was born in Tennessee."

"Thank goodness, he wasn't born in Massachusetts."

I threw a pillow at her. "I'm getting up early and going to the appliance store. I want you to stay at the hotel and poke around."

"By the way, I saw the movie a few months ago. It was hard to envision Vivien Leigh as Blanche DuBois. She will always be Scarlet O'Hara. But now that I think about it, I have to agree with you about passionate and sultry. The name Blanche DuBois is, I don't know, sexy and sultry. But what kind of name is Stanley Kowinski? It just doesn't fit Marlon Brando."

"Kowalski!"

"That doesn't fit either. Brando deserved a better name."

"It doesn't work that way, Ruth. The play was written first, and then the movie, and then the actors were cast."

I crawled onto my cot and stuffed a pillow over my head. I prayed a room would be available for Ruth tomorrow.

CHAPTER SIXTEEN

Ruth and Lydia were still asleep when I left the next morning. It was early, but I was eager to hear if Marcella had found a local lawyer for Dixon. I called from the lobby phone.

"Collect call from a Sydney Lockhart, will you accept the charges?"

"Yes, please, put her on," Marcella said.

"I hope I'm not calling too early."

"I'm on my second coffee. I was waiting to call you. Found a guy named Jake Noles. I spoke to him late last night. He works out of his home. He's a criminal lawyer and he's from New Orleans. Some of the cases he's won are bordering on legend. I gave him as much information as I knew. He's willing to go see Dixon today. Do you want me to come to New Orleans to help?"

"Not unless you want to babysit Ruth and a young girl named Lydia."

"I'm not my half-sister's favorite person and I've heard of little Lydia. She sounds like someone I'd like to know. If she and Ruth are together, God help you."

"Lydia is well on her way to making herself at home in New Orleans, and Ruth has pretty much behaved herself. But my cousin's been here less than twenty-four hours. Give her time."

Marcella laughed. "My offer still stands. I can be there in a few hours. How's Dixon holding up?"

"I'll see him later this morning. But you know him. He's tough."

"So are you, Syd. Hope you two had time to tie the knot before all this happened?"

"How did you know about our plans?"

"Uncle George called me."

"He was supposed to keep his mouth shut."

"Don't give him a hard time. Uncle George was giddy over you getting married. He really likes Dixon. He told me he was worried that you'd back out."

"I'm wearing my engagement ring and I bought Dixon a ring as soon as we got here, but we haven't tied the knot yet."

"The next time you call I want the operator to tell me that a Mrs. Sydney Dixon is on the line."

I didn't bother telling Marcella how I felt about changing my name. She, of all people, understands my need for independence, but she's still a romantic at heart. I thanked her for her help and hung up.

MUCH TO THEIR CREDIT, RUTH and Lydia were awake and ready to start the day when I returned. With all the other things I needed to do, I now had to find clothes for Lydia. We headed out on foot. There were no children's stores in the neighborhood, nor in the French Quarter. I didn't have time to wander all over the city. Lydia was content with what she was wearing, but with the heat and humidity, she'd certainly need a change of clothes soon. We walked past Burrow's costume shop. Costumes are what the twelve-year-old prefers to wear. The first time I met her, she was dressed in a First Communion dress and was wearing lavender patent leather shoes. Our agency was hired to find out who killed a Texas gubernatorial candidate. Lydia's father was one of the suspects. She insisted on helping with the investigation and for the rest of the time wore a Sherlock Holmes hounds-tooth cape and a deerstalker cap. Having the prop/costume room at the theater at her disposal provided her with everything she needed. If she wasn't in costume, she was dressed in overalls and a T-shirt, and her signature lavender leather shoes.

Lydia went inside the shop and dove in.

"Are we supposed to get a disguise?" Ruth asked. "You didn't tell me anything about disguises."

"Don't worry about it. I'll see if there's anything in there Lydia can wear."

Lydia held a Mexican sombrero in her left hand and what looked like a black dress made of cobwebs in her right. "I think they clash," I said.

"I know. I'll keep looking."

"You have five minutes to find an outfit. I don't have time to waste."

Lydia tossed the sombrero to Ruth. "Here. Put the strap under your chin. It might help keep your mouth shut." She took something off the rack and ducked into the dressing room.

"I'm going to strangle that child one day."

"Don't let her get to you. You might try being nice. She doesn't have a mother."

"That's because she was hatched from a pterodactyl egg. Ooh, look at this." She pointed to a swath of drab green fabric. On closer inspection, I saw it was an off-one-shoulder dress that barely covered the important parts. "I could wear this to a costume party."

"I never thought of you as the Jane type. Did you know that Tarzan was raised by apes in the African jungle?"

"No he wasn't. I happened to know he was an Olympic swimmer, and if I remember correctly, he was born in New York."

I didn't bother explaining to Ruth the difference between fact and fiction. I needed to get these two out of here.

Ruth walked up to the counter. "I need something for Mardi Gras," she said.

"Mardi Gras?"

"Yes, that crazy holiday you New Orleans people celebrate."

"Mardi Gras is celebrated all over the world," the sales girl said.

"Not in Dallas. Just get me a costume before my cousin has a conniption."

"Mardi Gras costumes are back there. Knock yourself out."

Lydia came out dressed as a pirate, complete with a stuffed parrot on her shoulder. "What do you think?" she said.

"If you like it, that's all that matters."

Something caught Lydia's attention on a nearby rack. "Look."

She held up a wedding dress.

"It's used," the sales girl said. "But I don't think it would fit you."

Lydia ignored her. "Sydney, do you have a dress?" She lowered her voice. "You know, for the wedding."

"Brides who elope can wear street clothes if they want. Put that back before Ruth sees it. You know I do not want her to know that Dixon and I came here to get married."

"Yes, you already told me, but the clothes you wear are important."

"You sound like Ruth."

"I'll ignore that. You ever wonder why I dress up in costumes?"

"Not really. Dressing in costumes just seems to fit your quirky personality."

"Costumes get you into the necessary frame of mind for whatever you need to do. Why do you think I dressed up like Sherlock Holmes when Serge was a murder suspect? I needed to help you prove he was innocent. I needed a sharp deductive mind because as a kid, I'd have ended up in an orphanage if Serge went to jail for life. I needed all the help I could get."

"What about the Communion dress you were wearing when we first met? It was after midnight. Explain that."

"It was a blue moon that night. Anything goes during a blue moon."

"I can't believe I'm hearing this."

"Okay, wear whatever you want. It's just a stupid wedding day. No big deal."

Ruth came out of the dressing room, wearing a peacock costume. "What do you think? It comes with a bird mask and a hat made of real peacock feathers."

"Would you like to wear it out or take it with you?" the sales girl said.

"Ruth, really, you don't need a costume. We don't have time to fool around."

"You're right. Someone has to set a mature example." Ruth stuck out her tongue at Lydia.

"I'm glad you understand," I said.

"I'll just take this pink boa. It matches my shoes."

"By the way, Miss," the sales girl said. "Mardi Gras is in February."

I threw some cash on the counter and we left.

"Is it really in February?" Ruth asked once we were outside.

"In New Orleans, it's always Mardi Gras."

Hurrying down Bourbon Street with a rich woman wearing Ferragamos and a cheap pink boa, and a child dressed as a pirate, didn't seem to faze the locals.

On the way to the jail, I told Ruth more of what went on at the hotel, the story Lavine told us, the story Lily Morton told us, and the story the Ivys told us. "We have three locations to focus on. Your task is to stay at the hotel to find out how Mildred Threadgill got into our room and how Lavine Rose put herself in a situation that got her killed." I assigned Lydia to Rip's office and the voodoo shop. It was the least dangerous location and I knew she wouldn't fall for any of the hocus pocus stuff. I was going to the appliance store.

CHAPTER SEVENTEEN

I stepped off the bus, arriving at Threadgill Appliances a few minutes before opening time. I'd hoped to case the building before the staff arrived. However, a few cars were already pulling into the employee parking lot in back. The warehouse door was open. The place looked just as Dixon had described. A few workers in green jump suits were smoking and drinking coffee outside. None of them fit Dixon's description of the two thugs who dumped Lavine's body in the river and shot at him. At that moment, a car drove up. The guy getting out could have been the heavy-set guy Dixon mentioned.

"Hey, Vinny," someone called. "I thought you weren't coming in today."

"Yeah, yeah. Things changed. I need to talk to Garrison."

I walked around to the front of the store. I was the first customer of the day. I'd prepared my outfit so I wouldn't stand out; white tailored blouse, brown pencil skirt, and black heels. I'd never given much thought to accessories, until I became a detective. In order to conceal my holster and gun, I added a lightweight, summer jacket, and added a small bag with a shoulder strap. With my hair wrapped in a tightly coiled French twist, I looked the part of an average housewife out to spend her husband's money. I barely had time to scan the place when a sales clerk appeared. "Good morning, ma'am, what can I help you with today?"

"Hello, I'm looking for a new washer and dryer. My housekeeper keeps showing me your newspaper ads. She claims if I purchased a modern set, my family's clothes wouldn't suffer the rigor of the outdated washer we have now. I'm not sure if I agree with her. But the way housekeepers jump from one place to another, according to who's paying what, well, I can't afford to be without her. I'm sure you know what I'm talking about."

"Your housekeeper is right, ma'am. Our newer washers have a gentle cycle that cleans more efficiently and have many labor-saving features. What is your housekeeper using now?"

"I'm not sure. It came with the house when we bought it five years ago. I don't think it's all that old." At times I amaze myself. Where in the hell do these lies come from? You wouldn't know I was raised Catholic. "And we don't own an electric dryer. The clothesline is fine if you ask me."

"Except when it rains, which it often does here. Let me show you our latest model. It comes in several colors. We carry Westinghouse, and Maytag—which is my personal favorite. We have automatic top and front loaders. No more hand-cranking. These washers have a state-of-the-art spin cycle that removes excess water fifty percent better than the roller types."

I followed him to the washer/dryer section. These machines sparkled. I smelled the newness. I ran my hand along the surface of a washer that was so smooth I wanted to rub my cheek against it.

"The most popular color this year is turquoise. This washer sells for $259."

"Pricy. I can hear my husband now."

"You can get the set for $375. They also come in pale green and white."

"The turquoise is beautiful."

"These are built to last and they come with a five-year warranty. Delivery is free. Think about how nice they'll look in your laundry room."

"I'm sure you're right. I rarely set foot in the laundry room, though. I'm sure Sadie would be pleased with the set, but I have to think about it."

"I can throw in a new electric iron that will glide across any fabric. No more scorching. It will save Sadie a lot of time to do other chores around the house."

"You've sold me, but I'll need to consult my husband first."

"Take this brochure. It should answer most of his questions. My name is Mr. Wells. I'm here Monday through Saturday. We can install the new set tomorrow afternoon, and we will dispose of your old model."

"How nice of you. Do you mind if I look around? Your store is gigantic."

"New Orleans's finest."

"That's what Sadie said. Her uncle works here. In the warehouse, I believe."

"What's the man's name?"

"I don't know, but Sadie said he's the foreman."

"That would be Vinny Zimmer."

"She told me if I saw him to tell him hi."

"You'll probably find him in his office down that hallway. Take your time looking around. I'll be on the floor if you have any more questions, Mrs.?"

"Dixon."

"Mrs. Dixon."

He went to help another customer and left me to wander around the store. A melancholy feeling set in. Is this what married life was all about? Housewives coercing their husbands to buy fancy, new appliances? I would never be that type of Mrs. Dixon. I would never be Mrs. Dixon at all. Being married to Dixon felt right, but living the traditional life didn't. I know he would never expect that of me. Married or not, I would always be Sydney Lockhart. But what's the harm in having a modern turquoise washer and dryer set? Would it fit in his cottage in Tarrytown if that's where we decided to live? Up to now, we each did our own laundry. When we're living under the same roof, it would make sense to throw our clothes in together. He could do the laundry one week, I could do it the next. I needed to slap myself out of this domestic daydreaming, or nightmare. I was not a housewife, nor would I ever be. Once I get Dixon out of jail and we solve this case we'll have a little chat about me never washing his socks.

I was now in the back of the store in the small appliance department. I found the offices Dixon told me about. I had a name and an excuse, and I'd wasted enough time. The hallway was empty. There were three doors. The first door's name plate read Walter Garrison, Owner. The office next door was open, but empty. A name plate read Vinny Zimmer, Foreman. The raised voice coming from Garrison's office told me that Zimmer was probably talking to his boss. I stepped into Zimmer's office. On his desk was a glass half filled with water. I emptied it into a potted plant. Now with my favorite listening device in hand I heard Garrison giving Vinny a dressing down.

"You idiot!" Garrison said. "That's not what I asked you to do! What about the guy who stole your truck and who was snooping around and chased you?"

"We pushed the truck into the canal. Piece of shit anyway. I wouldn't worry about the guy. He was just some nosy Good Samaritan."

"Nosy Good Samaritans don't carry guns. He chased you. He must have seen you put the body in the trunk. None of this would have happened if you'd done exactly what I told you. You've created more problems for me. He'll come back and so will the police."

"I had the room cleaned up. There wasn't much blood on the floor anyway. If the cops come, they won't see anything."

"I don't need them to come at all! I have a good mind to sack you. This guy who was helping you, he knows about this now."

"Relax, boss. You can trust Bugger."

"I doubt that. At this point I don't even trust you. Stay away for a couple of days. I don't want you anywhere around here until things cool down. Now, thanks to you, I've got a bigger mess on my hands. Get out!"

I set the glass down on Vinny's desk, dashed out of his office and collided with him. "What the hell?"

"Excuse me, I was looking for the restroom."

Garrison was standing at his door, fuming. "That way." He went inside his office and slammed the door.

I entered the restroom, locked the door behind me, and tried to catch my breath. Vinny and Bugger were the two thugs who dumped Lavine's body and tried to kill Dixon. It was clear Walt Garrison, the new owner of Threadgill Appliances, was behind this. That should be enough to sway Detective Bergeron and convince him it's time for Dixon to leave his jail cell. A knock on the door brought me up short.

"Just a minute," I said. I washed my hands and opened the door.

"Oh, glad you're still here," said Mr. Wells. "I was about to call you. I think I can offer you a better price on that washer-dryer set you were interested in."

At that moment, Garrison came out with his hat in his hands. "Mr. Garrison," Mr. Wells said. "This is Mrs. Dixon. She's here to buy some new appliances."

Garrison nodded and left. Zimmer walked by and stopped. I didn't like scowl he gave me. I followed Mr. Wells back to the showroom. I glanced down the hall and Zimmer was still watching. I thanked Mr. Wells and told him I'd talk to my husband, but I was sure the price would suit him. I left the store. The next bus was due in fifteen minutes. I decided to walk around the block for another look at the store. I turned the corner and almost bumped into Vinny Zimmer. "Mrs. Dixon, I thought you'd like to know that I don't have a niece named Sadie." The last thing I remembered was someone rushing up behind me and pressing a cloth over my nose and mouth.

CHAPTER EIGHTEEN

I woke to complete darkness, the kind that tells you you're in big trouble. Darkness where nothing else exists. Darkness that smells of doom. Darkness that told me I'd screwed up again. My mind cleared a bit. Two unpleasant realizations hit—I was soaking wet and gasping for air. Drowning—not again. I'd almost drowned on the last case and here I am again, except this time, I was bound and wrapped in a sack, probably the same kind Lavine Rose was wrapped in. Panic began to set in. Then a glimmer of hope. I was not in the river. I was lying on the ground and I heard thunder. Rain pelted down.

"She's coming to," someone said. "I told you to bash her in the head. You couldn't kill a fly with a brick." I recognized Zimmer's voice.

"I'll take care of it, she'll be dead in no time. I didn't want to do it before we put her in the trunk. This way we won't have to clean up any blood. Why don't you go sit in the car? I'm almost finished."

"That hole has to be deeper. What if someone comes along and sees this? Or what if a coyote or something digs it up?"

"Who's going to come along here? The big bad wolf? Besides, if I dig much deeper water will seep in. The ground in this cypress swamp is a sponge. That's why you should have dumped her into the river like the other one. Let the alligators take care of her quickly."

"The other one was pulled from the river, Bugger. I want to make sure this one never surfaces. Stop talking and do as I say. I want to see this hole covered up when you're done. Understand?"

I had to do something quick. There was no way I'd stand for being buried alive. The only problem was I couldn't move.

I heard Vinny slosh away, and I figured I had two minutes at the most. Although I was tied up, I wasn't gagged. "Bugger," I whispered. "Can you hear me?"

"What the hell?" I heard the shovel drop. "Momma, is that you. This isn't my fault. You know I'd never kill anyone."

Momma? Who was Bugger talking to? Was there a woman with them?

"Please, Momma, help me. I know I was a big disappointment to you. I know you're in a good place. Give me another chance. Give me a sign from the other side. Momma?"

The guy no longer sounded sure of himself over what he was about to do. His voice began to quaver. Was this guy speaking to his dead mother?

"Momma, please, talk to me," Bugger sobbed.

With a slight Louisiana twang to my voice, I whispered, "Bugger, this is your mother." A silence followed. Had Bugger passed out, or was he frozen in fear from hearing his dead mother speak?

"Bugger," I said again.

"Momma, Momma! You're here."

"You don't have a lot of time, so listen closely."

"Yes, ma'am."

"Hide the woman behind some cypress trees. Then fill in the hole. Hurry!"

Bugger took hold of the sack and tossed me over his shoulder. He started moving through the brush, evident by several tree branches slapping me, but at least he was following my, or his mother's directions. Then he dropped me on the ground and threw some twigs on top. I heard him walking away. "Bugger go back and untie the sack." Again Bugger did what he was told. I heard him scurry back and start shoveling.

"Thank you, Momma," I heard Bugger say.

"Bugger," Vinny yelled, "who in the hell are you talking to?"

"No one, Vinny. I was just saying a prayer over the body. I'm almost done here."

"Stupid cuss. Did you bash her head in?"

"Several times, with the shovel. She's good and dead."

I waited until I was sure they were gone. I managed to sit up. Dizziness from the chloroform wafted over me. I took a few deep breaths and wriggled out of the sack. Rain splatted on my face—a welcome feeling after being stuffed in suffocating burlap. Luckily, my captors hadn't bothered to search me. I felt my gun nestled under my left arm. My hands and feet were tied, but I was alive and as safe as I could be for the moment. My head cleared. I looked around. The swamp seemed alive and dead at the same time. From my last experience in the swamp, I learned that when you hear nothing, when nothing moved, you could be sure that those moments were followed by a loud animal sound. One caught by another. An alligator snatching a blue heron. A cougar pouncing a raccoon. A water moccasin swallowing an entire nest of baby birds. Then just as quickly, silence returned. I didn't want to be a predator's next meal.

I looked around for something I could use to slice through the ropes around my wrists. All the trees were covered in spongy moss. Their bark soft and crumbly. There were no sharp rocks in a swamp. A soft breeze moved the canopy above and a lone sun ray reflected off an object a few feet away. I scooched over. In a clearing I saw what I thought was a trash heap. It turned out to be an old camp site. Lying near the remainder of a camp fire was a rusty tin can. The lid sticking up, still attached. I kicked it over and black water spilled out. When was the last time I'd had a tetanus shot? Not important now. I maneuvered the can into my hands. Within minutes, my palms were scratched and bloody but free of ropes. The footprints the men left led me to a muddy road, little more than a wooded trail covered in tree roots. Thick mats of water hyacinth grew over a creek and reminded me that one false step would have me hip deep in water. I understood why they decided to bury my body out here. No sane person would be caught dead in this creepy environment. Truthfully, I don't know why they even planned to bury me. My body would be devoured in days and the rest decomposed soon after.

The main road came into view. Tire tracks led me in the right direction. Ten minutes into my track, I spotted a curious object lying in a shallow puddle—a shovel—a fairly new, rust-free shovel. I fished it out. It must have been the one Bugger used to dig my grave. If there were any fingerprints left on it, the water probably took care of that. I brought it with me anyway. Having another weapon never hurt.

Soon I found my way to a shack. The sign out front said Gully's Bait Shop.

My clothes, stained with mud and blood, and me looking like a deranged nutria, I walked in. The guy behind the counter seemed unfazed by my appearance and the shovel in my hand. He was sitting at a counter peeling a pile of boiled shrimp.

"Hey, lady, been out skinnin' a hog?"

"Are you Gully?"

"Yep. That be me."

"Well, Gully, that's exactly what I've been doing, skinnin' a hog. Can I use your phone?"

"Got night crawlers, crawdads, and minnows, but no phone."

"How far is it to the city?"

"Ain't no city here."

"New Orleans."

"About seven miles." He popped a shrimp into his mouth."

"I'm happy to pay you if you'd give me a ride."

"Ain't got no car. Riley out back got one."

I heard jaunty zydeco music coming from behind a back screen door. I stepped out. A guy who looked to be older than Moses was seated on a wooden bench with his feet propped up on the porch railing. He was playing an accordion. Another guy was thumbing the washboard, and the third was burning up a fiddle. These guys were good. It was hard to keep my hips from swaying. The necks of beer bottles poked out from an iced-filled wash tub. If I wasn't involved in a murder investigation and time wasn't of the essence, I'd grab a cold one and stay awhile. "Which one of you is Riley?" The accordion player nodded. I didn't bother explaining my presence, it didn't seem to matter. "I need to get back to New Orleans fast. Can you drive me there? I'll pay you."

"Nope."

"Nope?"

They started up another tune. I had to sit down to keep from dancing. "Please, it's important."

Riley smiled. "Can't."

"Why? Gully said you had a car."

"I do. Ain't got no gas."

I considered my options. I could walk back, even in bare feet, I could probably make it in under three hours. I thought about hitchhiking, but I hadn't seen a car come by on this road. And I wouldn't dare get into a car with anyone who stopped to pick up someone looking like me.

"I could take you in my pirogue," Riley said.

That's when I noticed a creek running behind the bait shop. "How long would that take?"

"Be there before the sun go down."

I didn't have the entire day to waste on a pirogue floating down a swamp creek with a Cajun at the helm. "That won't do."

"It's pleasant out on the Honey Creek. We'd have real good time, right, Beau?"

"Right pleasant, it be," Beau, the washboard guy said.

I no longer wanted to dance. I wanted to take my shovel and swat all three of them upside the head. "Wait. Did you say Honey Creek?"

"Yep, that be it behind me."

"You don't happen to know this guy named Lucien Thibaut? Looks a lot like a bear."

"Old crazy Lucien? Yeah, we know'd him," said Riley.

"I think he be dead," the fiddle player said.

"He was alive a couple of weeks ago," I said.

Lucien Thibaut was a guy Rip and I ran into when we were here chasing a crazy woman who'd knocked off a couple of people in San Antonio. Lucien lived on a shanty and ate rotten squirrel stew, but otherwise, he was harmless. The best thing was he had a pickup truck. "I'll take the chance he's still alive. How far away is his shanty?"

"Five minute float," Ridley replied.

"Let's go," I said. "Now."

Gully was standing at the door listening. The four of us climbed into Riley's pirogue, instruments, beer tub and all. In fact, the music never stopped. Gully climbed in too. With him using an oar and me using my shovel as a paddle, we took off.

Shortly after, I detected a pungent odor—squirrel stew—and knew we were close. We rounded a bend. There was Lucien sitting on his porch. It looked as if he hadn't moved since the last time I saw him.

Lucien squinted when he saw us and then his face lit up. "Sydney!" He jumped up. Riley threw him a rope and Lucien tied us up to his houseboat. "Good to see, ya, gal."

"Good to see you, Lucien. I didn't think you'd remember me."

"'Course I do. Anyone who'd give me an entire beer truck full of beer be hard to forget. I know'd ya come back to see old Lucien."

"You did?"

"Yep. Been waitin'. Le me give ya a hand." He plucked me out of the pirogue and sat me down on the porch. Lucien's hug came close to crushing my rib cage.

The shanty started vibrating and swaying. I looked up to see a big guy come out from inside. He was wearing overalls like Lucien. His beard was heavy and he smiled like a monkey. "Rip!"

"Sydney! I can't believe it. Lucien kept telling me you were coming."

"How did you know, Lucien?"

"I read it in them bones I throw. They tol' me ya was coming," Lucien said.

"I didn't believe him," Rip said.

"I can guess you're here hiding out, but why?"

"Long story, Syd." I needed to hear Rip's story, but I had to get a move on. "My story's long too, Rip. You've got to come back to New Orleans with me right away. You left a nasty trail behind. Since Dixon and I arrived two days ago, two people have been murdered. If it wasn't for Bugger's dead mother, I would have been the third. Mildred Threadgill and a maid named Lavine Rose who worked at the Pontchartrain Hotel being the first two."

A woman screamed and came running out. Rip took her in his arms. I wasn't surprised to see Betsy Radley. I figured that wherever Rip was, Betsy would be there too. "Lavine and Betsy were friends," Rip said.

CHAPTER NINETEEN

On the way back to the city, I rode with Rip in his car and Betsy followed in hers.

"I really screwed up this time," Rip said. "Things were heating up in New Orleans and phone threats were being made against me and Betsy, warning me to leave and to stop asking questions about Frank Threadgill. Someone even broke into my office. I thought it best if I left for a few days to figure things out. Then Betsy showed up and told me about Mildred's murder. I think Frank Threadgill was murdered too. I told Betsy where I was going and to make up a story about me disappearing. I thought it might keep her safe. I wasn't sure how old Lucien would feel about me showing up, or if he'd even remember me. But it seems like once you shared a beer and squirrel stew with a Cajun, you're friends for life. I took a chance and told Betsy to come to Lucien's if things got bad for her. And when she showed up, Lucien was so excited, he took a bath and washed his overalls. I don't know about all this, Syd. I just wanted to investigate lingering ghosts of people who died mysteriously, not murder victims."

I failed to see the logic in that statement, but I let it go. "Any clue why someone would want to murder Frank?"

"I hadn't found out yet. Mildred told me that her husband had secrets. She didn't know what, but before he died, he started going off without telling her where he was going. He'd come home in the wee hours of the morning. The phone would often ring, and whenever she answered whoever was on the line, would hang up. If Frank answered, he'd tell her to go into the bedroom and shut the door while he talked. Every time she questioned him, he'd fly into a rage. Then once, when Frank was gone, someone called and told her to give him a message. She was to tell Frank that he 'wasn't going to take them to his grave.' She wasn't able to give him the message because he died suddenly."

We pulled up and parked behind Rip's office. Although I felt as if I'd been away for two days, it was only approaching mid-afternoon. Betsy got out of her car. She looked as if she hadn't stopped crying the entire drive back to New Orleans. Frida Mae must have heard us drive up. She came running out of her voodoo shop. "Betsy, are you okay? I was so worried. Come back into the kitchen. I'll make you some tea."

We walked into the House of Voodoo where I found Lydia working the register. She was dressed in a voodoo queen costume complete with a turban. I didn't bother to ask.

"Lydia, can you mind the shop while I take care of Betsy?" Frida Mae said.

"Don't be too long," Lydia said. "I have to deliver this mojo bag to my friend Jacko." She turned her glare at me. "Well, Sydney, where have you been? I thought you were going to the appliance store." She picked up a bandana and covered her nose. "You smell like rotten eggs. There's moss in your hair. Who's the guy with you? Let me guess, Rip."

"Yes, this is Rip. I did go to the appliance store, but made a slight detour on the way back. Rip, this is Lydia. She's here from Austin. Helping out, I guess."

"Frida Mae got busy and since Betsy wasn't here, I pitched in. I'm glad you found the ghost investigator. He might be able to explain this." She handed him an envelope. "It was slipped under the door, probably last night. The note inside says 'Stop meddling or you will be sorry. You will pay with your life.' It was written by a woman. Notice the floral embossed stationary and the feminine handwriting."

"Do you always read other people's mail?" Rip asked.

"I do when we're investigating a murder, and since you disappeared, which I never really believed you had, I felt justified. I also thoroughly searched your office in case there was something Sydney and Dixon missed."

Rip turned to me.

"I know, but trust me, she's real."

"All this because some wacky woman wanted me to investigate her husband's ransacked tombsite?" Rip said. "Damn. This gets crazier all the time."

"Who's Jacko?" I asked Lydia.

"The bartender at Pat O'Brien's," Lydia said.

I found a stool and sat down. "You know a bartender who works at Pat O'Brien's?" I didn't bother questioning Lydia about how she got into the infamous bar. She could easily find her way into the Vatican and talk the Pope into letting her assist in saying Mass.

"I do now," she said. "After I found the note, I walked up and down Bourbon Street asking people if they noticed anyone shifty snooping around the shop last night. Someone told me about Jacko. He knows everything that goes on around here, but he wasn't working last night, so he couldn't tell me a lot."

"Any idea who the note could be from?" I said.

Rip rubbed the back of his neck. "No. This case has me stymied."

"It might involve money," I said. "Mildred Threadgill's brother and mother told me that Frank made a hefty profit from the store's sale, but that his bank account was empty."

"I'm not surprised."

"Why?"

"From talking to Mildred, I understood that even though she was married to the man, she knew almost nothing about what he did."

"What does Betsy know about Lavine?"

"We talked about that. Betsy met Lavine when she came into the voodoo shop while Betsy was visiting Frida Mae. Lavine said she was having trouble with a boyfriend. Some guy who worked at the Pontchartrain. Betsy took Lavine out for coffee and they became friends. Lavine would call Betsy often."

Betsy came in from the backroom. "That's true," she said. "Lavine was so troubled, but she never would say much. I just sat with her while she cried. I have a feeling that whatever was bothering her was more than boyfriend troubles."

"Lavine was scared," I said. "Who was the boyfriend?"

"She wouldn't say. Just that he'd worked at the hotel and was a good person, but she didn't like some of the things he did. She wouldn't say what."

"I'll see if I can find out who this guy is. Mildred's cousin, Lily Morton, works in room service. She might know. The message about not taking something to his tomb, could that mean someone wanted Frank's secrets revealed? Somehow Lavine was involved. Two separate murders is too much of a coincidence."

"Was Lavine murdered at the hotel too?" Betsy asked.

"I'm not sure. I plan to find out."

"By the way," Rip said. "How's your cousin? Has she done away with any boyfriends lately?"

Rip had become smitten with Ruth during the San Antonio case. I made up a bunch of stories about Ruth knocking off boyfriends. I needed Rip to focus on the case, not Ruth.

"I sort of lied about that."

"I figured."

"She's here in New Orleans."

"She joined you and your boyfriend on your vacation?" He chuckled.

I hadn't known Rip Thigbee long. I met him at the Keynote Club in San Antonio where he was a bouncer. When the owner of the club told him to kill me and throw me into the river, Rip switched sides and became my protector. I always thought of him as body strong and mind mediocre, but I'm beginning to realize I underestimated him.

"After Dixon got arrested he called Ruth in to help with the case."

"I figured I'd better come along," Lydia said. "To help with Ruth."

"Are you going to tell the police what happened to you?" Rip said.

"After I talk to Dixon. You and Betsy lay low for a while. Do you mind if I take your car?"

"I'm not going anywhere. I'll be here if you need me."

Lydia walked with me to Rip's car. "I'm staying here at the

voodoo shop," she said.

"Are you an official hire?"

"Just helping out. I plan to look for more clues."

"Lydia—"

"About Frank's murder."

"We don't know if he was murdered."

"Frida Mae said you can cause someone to have a heart attack. There are all sorts of ways to do that, voodoo dolls, potions, incantations, and gris gris." She pulled out a match-box side pouch, which dangled on a string hanging around her neck. "Before you ask, gris gris is a bag that contains weird little objects and verses written on small pieces of paper used to cause evil to someone. Frida Mae said that in Haiti, gris gris is considered a good luck charm, but African slaves living in New Orleans used it to bring evil upon their abusive owners. Frida Mae said you could even learn chants that will make someone keel over and die. I had her make up one especially for me. It causes the hair on all blonde rich women from Dallas to fall out."

"You know, Lydia, Ruth is wealthy, but she does a lot of philanthropic work."

Lydia shrugged. "I'll see you at the hotel later. I'm going to stick around here for a while to see if I can learn anything more from Betsy. She seems like a wimp. After I deliver Jacko's mojo bag, I'm going to make my way up and down Bourbon Street, get to know the neighborhood folks. They notice things. Jacko said they can tell the difference between tourists and trouble makers. Jacko can even feel when someone who's up to no good walks into the bar, or even passes in front of the bar. I showed him Frank and Mildred Threadgill's wedding picture to see if he could sense anything. Before you ask, I got the picture from Frida Mae. Mildred brought it in to the voodoo shop because she was so unhappy with her marriage and wanted a potion to help in that department. At least that's what Frida Mae said. I think Mildred's real reason was to figure out a way to get rid of her lousy husband."

"You don't really believe any of that voodoo stuff?"

"No, but it couldn't hurt. If Frida Mae has time, she's going to show me how to make voodoo dolls. I have a list of people I plan to use them on."

"Lydia, you did good getting on Frida Mae's good side. The last time we were there, she refused to talk to us."

"I can turn on the charm when necessary. See you later."

"No, wait. I'm not finished. I'm not sure you should be hanging around this neighborhood asking questions. And, you don't know this Jacko guy."

"I know enough."

"Tell me about him."

"He's been working at Pat O'Brien's for most of his adult life. He's pretty active for an old guy. He grew up in New Orleans, has four kids, six grandkids, and a wife who smiles only when he's getting ready to leave the house and go to work. He's of Creole origin, that's not the same as Cajun. His father is from Great Britain and his grandmother was born and raised on some island in the Caribbean. His skin is the color of coffee with a dash of cream. He plays the accordion. He sings in the River Baptist Church choir."

"You found all this out today?"

"He likes to talk."

I SUSPECTED I'D HAVE TROUBLE getting into the hotel and back into my room. I looked like Medusa and smelled like the swamp. The doorman's mouth fell open. I thought he was going to stop me from going in. "I'm staying here." I fished my key out of my pocket, held it up, and walked in. Although some stared, everyone gave me wide berth. The elevator operator had the courtesy to keep his eyes on the floor numbers as they rolled by. Just as the door slid open something stabbed me under my left arm. "Damn!" I threw off my jacket and slipped my gun out of its holster. The elevator operator fell to his knees and covered his head with his arms. I looked down to see a crayfish crawling out of the holster. It scurried manically along the floor. Little claws clicking like castanets. "It's yours if you want it," I said to the operator.

I didn't take time to clean up. I grabbed a pair of shoes and drove to the police station. I was past due for a visit with my jailbird.

One look at Dixon told me he wasn't enjoying his time in the slammer. He'd cleaned up, but the bags under his eyes looked heavy and dark. The creases around his mouth were deep. "Where the hell have you been?" he barked. "What have you been doing?"

"Where have I been? What have I been doing? I just finished having étouffée with Huey Long's ghost. It's great dining with a ghost. They never look at my plate and ask, "Are you going to eat that?" Then I strolled down to the French Market where I ran into a homeless woman begging on the street. Since I didn't have my purse with me, I gave her my black pumps. Then barefoot and suffering from indigestion from eating too much spicy food, I decided to take a nice swim in the Mississippi River. On the way back to the hotel, I stepped on a nail the size of Louisiana. I'm feeling tetanus creeping up my back causing muscle spasms. It's now on its way to my jaw."

"Did we just have our first fight?"

"We did. That's good. I was beginning to think you were perfect."

"Come here. Ever kiss a guy behind bars?"

"Let's give it a try."

"It's harder than I imagined, but better than nothing." He licked his lips. "Good lord, did you really swim in the Mississippi?"

"Close."

"Sorry, I snapped at you, hon. I was worried. Fill me in."

I told him everything that had transpired since I last saw him. When I got to the part about me almost being buried alive, Dixon hit the ceiling again and spewed off a long stream of cuss words.

"Prison life doesn't suit you. You're usually not this jumpy."

"It's frustrating because I can't do anything to help."

"You can digest the information I bring you like Nero Wolfe waiting for Archie Goodwin to bring news."

Dixon laughed. "Except Wolfe wouldn't leave his home because he chose not to. That phone message Mildred Threadgill got is a curious one. What had Frank taken to his tomb that someone wants revealed? Someone really was trying to exhume his body."

"I'll make sure Bergeron knows about the message. We have enough evidence to get the charges dropped, but Detective Bergeron, the misogynist, warned me about meddling in his business."

"I know, so I don't think it's a good idea for you to talk to him," he said. "Maybe Rip should go to Bergeron instead of you."

"But, I was almost murdered. Surely, Bergeron can't accuse me of meddling now, since I was a victim. With Rip backing up my story, Bergeron will believe me."

"I wouldn't count on it."

"I need to get you out of jail."

"Maybe you should clean up first."

"I was, I will. I wanted to give you the latest. You'll be out in no time."

"Let's hope."

CHAPTER TWENTY

I bathed, donned fresh clothes, and fixed my hair in record time. Lydia was right, I did have swamp moss in my wavy red locks. I was afraid I'd clogged up the bathtub. My first stop was Pat O'Brien's. I had to meet this Jacko fellow. I trusted Lydia's judgement, but who's the adult here? I found a space on Bourbon Street and parked. I got out of Rip's car and saw Lydia walking toward me. "Casing the neighborhood again?"

"I had to get out of the voodoo shop. Betsy was driving me crazy."

"I'm glad I found you. You can introduce me to Jacko."

"You don't trust me, mommy?"

"Stop calling me that."

I spotted Jacko right away. Lydia's description was dead on.

"Hey, Lydia," someone called from one of the tables. "Nice to see you back."

"Hey, Luke." Lydia waved.

"Look, Jacko, Lydia's brought in a friend," said a waitress whose name I learned was Claudia.

A bus boy walked by and asked Lydia if she remembered to bring him a vile of black salt from the House of Voodoo to help ward off negative energy. Lydia reached in her pocket and tossed him the vile. "Frida Mae put it on your bill, Jerry."

We walked up to the bar. An elderly man hopped off his stool. "Sorry, about sitting on your stool, Miss Lydia. I didn't think you were coming back in today."

"No problem, Jesse. Hey, Jacko, I'll have the usual. This is my friend Sydney. She's here to make sure you're not an axe murderer." Jacko held out his hand. "Nice to meet you, Miss

Sydney. Lydia has told me a lot about you. Did you really have amnesia a few weeks ago and forget who you were?" He set a Dr. Pepper in front of Lydia.

"I'm the one. I'm much better now."

"I'm sorry about your boyfriend's arrest," Jacko continued. "I sure hope that's cleared up soon so you can go ahead with your wedding plans. Here," he handed me what I assumed was a Hurricane. "It's on the house."

"Satisfied?" Lydia asked.

"Very."

I left Lydia with her new family and swung by the Finder of Lost Souls office, picked up Rip, and was back at the station in half an hour. Detective Bergeron listened to both of us without saying a word. He took notes while we talked, which was encouraging. When we finished, he read over the notes, underlined a few things, and scratched his head. Tiny dandruff flakes rained down on his notebook. He didn't seem to notice. I scooted my chair back a few inches.

"So, sitting in front of me is a voodoo detective and a woman who claims to have been kidnapped and almost buried alive. "You're saying a bunch of swamp trash residing on the Honey Creek Swamp can substantiate part of your story?" He tossed his fountain pen on the desk. "Any sane witnesses I can rely on?"

Rip and I looked at each other. "Betsy Radley," Rip said.

"The woman who helps you locate dead people? You gotta be kidding me. You have one minute to get out of my office before I lock you both up."

Rip and I stood in front of the police station and shared a cigarette. "That went well," he said.

"I think Detective Bergeron's bigotry includes Cajuns."

"But I can see his point. I'm not sure I'd believe the story we just told him."

"Whether he believed it or not, looks like Dixon will spend another night on a jail cot. And I'll spend another night without Dixon."

"You have Ruth and that Lydia girl to keep you company. Don't forget about them."

"It's hard not to. Drop me off at the Pontchartrain. Pick up Betsy and hurry back to the hotel. We'll put our heads together.

LYDIA MET ME AT OUR room with the door opened. She had changed back into her pirate costume, most of it. "Tired of the voodoo outfit?"

"That's just for work."

"Where's the parrot?"

She pointed to the bed where a mass of colorful feathers lay propped up on the pillows. "I had to remove him from my shoulder. The thing must weigh five pounds. I was beginning to walk crooked. Did you take a bath?"

"I did. I still smell of swamp water, right?"

"You and this room. That's why I had the door open."

"I thought it was my imagination."

"It's not."

"God help me. Call room service and order me a pitcher of martinis. Rip's on his way. While I try to remove the swamp from skin pores, you and Rip can get to know one another." I went into the bathroom and slammed the door. I had just slid under the bubbles when room service delivered my martini pitcher.

"Are you decent?" Lydia said.

"Decent is the last thing I am. Come in. I was joking about the martini pitcher."

Lydia poured me a drink and sat down on the bathroom floor. "They forgot the olives."

"Of course they did. Any news from the world of voodoo?"

She pulled out her notebook.

"Lydia, what's with the notebook? You've never used one before."

"I was just getting my feet wet with the dead gubernatorial candidate case. I'm more experienced now. I might be late on the uptake, but it's not above me to improve on my tactics. There wasn't anything that's happened at the voodoo shop that has any relevance to the case. A lot of crazies coming in for spells and potions. One woman came in wanting a potion to feed to her neighbor's cat to keep the animal from stalking and killing birds in her backyard. Frida Mae threw some smelly nodules in a sack along with a sprinkle of red dust. The lady left happy, and Frida Mae stuck a five-dollar bill in her register. An old man wanted to know how much longer he had to live because he wanted to make sure he didn't die before his money ran out. Frida Mae told him she wasn't a fortune teller and recommended one down the street. But she then sold him an immortality oil made from a recipe from one of the seven Jinn Kings. By the way, if you need a Jinn King's help, you must never ask them to do something for you. You may request that they send one of their subordinates to help you out. The Kings themselves are too powerful. Another five dollars in the till. There's money in this business, not like live theater. Speaking of that, your father called and left a message at the front desk." She held up an envelope.

"Open it and read it to me.

"I already read it. It's good news."

"He called to tell me my mother moved to Saturn?"

"The good news is for me. He said he'd talked your mother into coming back to Galveston. That means I have to go back to Austin and resume rehearsals. I can stay tomorrow and help with the case, but I have to leave the next day. Palmer's flying in and taking me back. Oh, and I managed to get Ruth a room in another wing. I requested a special room for her. It's right over the bar."

I looked at Lydia over the rim of my martini glass. She was a cherub. Wavy blonde hair, violet eyes, heart-shaped face. Who was this twelve-year-old girl who called her own shots? Who made her own way in the world? Who could book rooms in a hotel simply by asking? Who, in a matter of hours, could befriend a bunch of locals in a notorious bar in New Orleans? Who had a 200 IQ and an imagination that would make Disney's creators seem like morons?

"What?" she said.

"You arranged this all yourself?"

"Is that a question?" She refilled my martini glass.

"Thank you, Lydia. You're always there for me and you don't ask me for anything in return. I'm glad we're friends."

I expected a curt reply. What I got instead were tears, not adult hysterical tears, but soft, child tears. "Lydia?"

"You're my only friend, Sydney. I knew we'd be friends the night you walked into the prop room at the theater. It was the night of a blue moon, remember? I'd been reading a book of spells trying to contact my dead mother, instead you showed up. Don't tell anybody. Especially Ruth."

Even a gulp of martini wouldn't wash down the lump in my throat. "I won't. I promise."

"Okay, enough of that. Here's what else I discovered today." She took my washcloth and rubbed her face. "Since I didn't find out anything significant at the voodoo shop, I went back on the street and then to Pat O'Brien's. Jacko was still working. He wanted to see that picture of Frank again. Because the picture was several years old, he didn't recognize Frank at first. But after another look, Jacko was pretty sure Frank Threadgill had come in once and made a nuisance of himself. The guy was a light weight. After one drink, he started ranting and raving about how he hated Americans."

"That sounds like Frank Threadgill. His brother-in-law and mother-in-law described a loud, judgmental, domineering, unfriendly man. Good work, Lydia. Anything else we need to know? Go on."

"Frank talked about his time before he came to the U.S."

"When he lived in Belgium?"

"Jacko said he didn't think Frank really lived there. Or if he did, he wasn't from there. Frank had an accent and it wasn't Belgian. Polish maybe. Anyway, he'd talk about how people from the U.S. were spoiled and greedy. Evidently, he'd had a difficult life, wherever he was from, but he wouldn't shut up about spoiled Americans. Jacko finally had to throw him out."

"Elliott Ivy said Frank immigrated to the U.S. after the war. I need to find out if that's true. New Orleans is a port of entry for immigration. I'll check there."

"I already have. I went to the immigration office and told the clerk I was doing a research project for school. I had to write about my grandfather who died before I was born. I told her I couldn't ask my father because he's dead too. Died in the war when I was two. I managed a couple of tears and continued. I said that my mother didn't talk to me much because she works all day to support me and my four brothers and sisters."

"You didn't wear the voodoo costume, did you?"

"No, I changed back into my rag-a-muffin clothes. Anyway, she couldn't get off her stool fast enough to help me. A few minutes later she said she couldn't find any record of a Frank Anthony Threadgill coming in through New Orleans."

"Anthony?"

"Before I went to the immigration office, I dropped by the newspaper office and read Frank's obit. It didn't say much about his life before he came to New Orleans. The immigration clerk said he may have come through New York. She's checking for me and will call me when she finds out."

"Call you where? Being from a poor family, she wouldn't believe you live at the Pontchartrain, but I'm sure you've thought of that."

"I told her to call my Uncle Jacko who works at Pat O'Brien's and leave the message with him. He called right before you walked in. No Frank A. Threadgill immigrated through New York either. It must be an alias. I agree with Jacko. I don't think Frank was from or ever lived in Belgium. Poland or Germany, some Eastern European country, is my guess. You need to get out of that tub before you turn into a prune."

"True. I don't have time to luxuriate. Hand me my robe."

A loud knock on the bathroom door brought us up short. "What's going on in there?" Ruth said.

Lydia opened the door. "We're going over the case."

"In the bathroom?" She didn't wait for the answer. "Sydney, you've been gone all day. Where's Dixon? I thought he'd be released by now."

"So did I, but Bergeron was having none of our story."

"So, you've been luxuriating in the tub, drinking martinis while Dixon's in jail. Am I the only one working this case? Oh, I found out from the front desk that I have my own room now."

"That's good news," I said.

"It's not good news." She stomped her foot. "I'm down on the second floor. It's so noisy, I'm afraid my earplugs will not help tonight when I try to sleep. This was all your doing, Lydia?"

"Don't be ridiculous. A twelve-year-old can't reserve rooms in a hotel."

"I don't need to listen to you two bicker. Get out so I can get dressed before Rip and Betsy arrive. Lydia, fill Ruth in on what happened today. Try to do it without sarcasm."

CHAPTER TWENTY-ONE

I walked out of the bathroom to find Ruth sniffing the air and turning over all the pillows. "What's that godawful smell?"

"It's either my clothes or Lydia's gris gris. Don't ask about either." I opened the window to air out the room. "Lydia, did you tell Ruth what you found out?"

"I'd rather you do it. She never listens to me."

"Ruth, sit down. Lydia, grab your notebook and write. This is what's happened since Dixon and I arrived. Mildred Threadgill came to see Rip a week ago about the disturbances of her husband's tomb. He wasn't interested in the case, but she insisted. She told him that someone called the house and left a message about Frank not taking something to his tomb. All it took was a few quick visits to the tomb to earn Rip menacing phone calls. When the caller threatened to harm Betsy, Rip took off for a couple of days, leaving Betsy behind to tend to the office.

"That was rather rude if you ask me," Ruth said. "Leaving Betsy to take care of herself."

"Just listen. When Dixon and I showed up on the scene, Betsy pleaded for our help. We went to the cemetery where Frank Threadgill was buried and found his tomb vandalized. In the short time after leaving Finder of Lost Souls, Mildred Threadgill came in and Betsy told her about us and where we were staying. Mildred rushed to the hotel, entered our room, and got herself murdered—knife in the chest."

"Mildred sounds like a flake," Ruth said.

"Nevertheless, she's dead," Lydia said. "Stop interrupting. Continue, Sydney."

"Dixon and I were hauled down to the police station for questioning. Our alibi got us released, at least mine did. Dixon went to the appliance store, found a body, and saw two guys dump it into the river. He was arrested when he pulled the body from the water. We discovered the body was Lavine Rose— the maid who attended to our floor; the maid who saw Mildred Threadgill go into our room; the maid who, scared and crying, swore to us she knew nothing about the Threadgill murder. Lydia, tell us what you found out about Frank Threadgill."

"Besides having a weird wife, Frank Threadgill, previous owner of Threadgill Appliances, had a mysterious past. I don't know much more than that, yet, but I'm working on it. Back to you, Sydney. Tell us about the swamp part. That's my favorite."

"Speaking of weird," Ruth said.

"Stop it, you two. Okay, I went to the appliance store where I was chloroformed and almost buried alive in the swamp. Luckily, I escaped by convincing some guy named Bugger that I was his dead mother. I found Rip and Betsy hiding out in the Honey Creek Swamp because Rip received a note in the mail telling him to stop meddling or he would pay with his life. And to think, Dixon and I came here two days ago to . . . to have a vacation. Damn, I couldn't make this shit up if I tried."

Rip and Betsy arrived. Rip rolled his eyes and nodded toward Betsy as they walked in. By the looks of her puffy, red face, she hadn't stopped crying.

"Time to fill in some blanks," I said. "Rip, tell me more about your visits to Frank's tomb."

"The first time, I noticed the smashed vase and the chipping on the lid. I figure someone was trying to open it and got interrupted. I went to talk to the guy who oversees the cemetery. He took a look and said it was probably kids out after dark getting their kicks. It happened a lot, he said. Then he cleared away some of the larger pieces of the broken vase. I went back two days later. Again more damage. Someone wanted that casket opened. I went back to the cemetery guy. He said he'd keep an eye out, but he didn't sound too bothered by it."

"Footprints?" I said.

"Afraid not. It rained hard the night before."

"What about the threats you received?"

"At first I thought it was all a bunch of hogwash, especially since Mrs. Threadgill was certain the disturbances were caused by evil spirits. I told her what the cemetery guy said and she flew into a rage. She was willing to pay, though, and I didn't have any other clients, so I said I'd stake out the cemetery after dark. Nothing happened. The next morning I got the first threatening call, telling me to mind my own business. No big deal. You know me, Syd. I don't scare easy. I went back that night, got another call the next morning. Much nastier, this time. The caller threatened to cut my throat."

"Man or woman?"

"Hard to tell. Out of meanness, I went back again the next night. Have you ever been in a cemetery at night? I like it. Peaceful and quiet. Not like what you'd think. Anyway, I left right before sunrise. I got back to the office to find blood splashed over the office window. Someone had drawn a face in the blood and under the face was written 'Betsy.'"

"Why me?" Betsy wailed.

Frankly, the girl's hysterics were weighing on my nerves. I tossed her a box of tissue, which made matters worse.

"Rip, what I don't understand is why you hid out and left Betsy to mind the store alone?'

"Well, I didn't really take off. I was upstairs camping out in Frida Mae's storage room. I wanted to find out what was going on. I told Betsy not to tell anyone I was nearby. When you and Dixon came upstairs to search my apartment, I was taking a cat nap. Staying up all night for several nights takes a toll. I left town when I found out Mildred Threadgill was murdered. Betsy and I left at the same time."

"Betsy, Lavine was your friend. She told you she was having trouble with a boyfriend who worked here at the hotel."

Betsy nodded and blew her nose.

"You told Lavine that Rip was hired by Mildred Threadgill to investigate the situation surrounding Frank's tomb, didn't you?"

"Betsy!" Rip said. "Did you?"

"Please don't be mad," Betsy said. "I thought it was funny. Investigating evil spirits. I was just trying to cheer her up."

"You know you're not supposed to talk about my cases." His face turned crimson and the veins in his temple pulsated. I'd never seen the big guy riled before.

My mind attuned to three women: Mildred, Lavine, Betsy. The first two were murdered. I didn't want Betsy to follow in their footsteps so I ramped up the heat.

"It was you who told Lavine we were staying here and that Mildred Threadgill was coming to see us," I said.

"No. That's not true," Betsy said. "Please believe me."

Blue flame time. "Do you realize you're responsible for two murders, Betsy, and you might be the next?"

Betsy tumbled over in a dead faint.

"Well, that was fun, but I'm starving" Ruth said. She picked up the phone and called room service. "I'm calling from room 702. Send up five bowls of your famous duck andouille gumbo."

Up until now, Ruth had remained quiet during our discussion. Quiet, but impatient. Tapping her fingernails on the arm of her chair. Getting up, pacing, sitting down. I didn't like the look on her face. W.C. Fields with a secret.

"While you're at it, bring a bottle of brandy," she said.

"I don't like gumbo," Lydia said.

"Make that four bowls, two large orders of hushpuppies."

"I don't eat anything named after a dog," Lydia added.

In the middle of the food feud, Rip picked up Betsy and laid her on the bed. He ran to the bathroom for a washcloth.

"Add five Caesar's salads."

"I don't like anchovies." Lydia folded her arms across her chest.

"Excuse me," Ruth said. She cupped her hand over the receiver. "Listen, young lady, you'll eat whatever I order. Sorry, and bring five orders of bread pudding and a pot of the wonderful Louisiana coffee. Thank you."

Lydia picked up the phone. "About that order for room 702, please add a cheeseburger, medium, order of French fries, a chocolate malt, and a slice of your *famous* chocolate cake."

"If you continue to eat like that, young lady," Ruth said, "one of these days you're going to turn into a beach ball."

"Ruth, Lydia, we don't have time for this bickering," I said. "Dixon's sitting in jail charged with two murders."

The washcloth idea hadn't worked. Rip brought Betsy around with a few slaps on her face.

"Well, everything I've heard from all of you was sadly interesting," Ruth said, "but none of it will help the situation because it's your words against the police."

"We know that, Ruth," I said. "That's why we're hashing things out."

"As I was about to say, we need something that will convince the police that Dixon is innocent. And I know what that is." Her head wobbled in that smarty pants way she was famous for.

"Well?!" I said.

"I nosed around the hotel kitchen," Ruth said. "Chef Pascal is a charming fellow. Every time I tried to get information out of him, he changed the subject to passion and romance. He loved my pink boa."

"I thought you discovered something important," Lydia said. "I should check things out myself. I'll add the French chef to my investigation list."

"You most certainly will not," Ruth said. "The hotel is my domain."

"Yeah, well good luck with that," Lydia said. "By the time you find out anything useful, like Rip said, Betsy could be dead."

Betsy went down a second time.

"I hope that brandy arrives before Betsy goes into a coma," Lydia said.

"Stop it, you two," I cut in.

"I was about to say, before this rude child interrupted me, Lavine was fooling around with Chef Pascal."

"That's it? We already suspected that," I said. "How in the hell is that going to get Dixon released?"

"Well, it's obvious that Pascal's the one who killed her."

"It's not obvious, Ruth," I said.

"Well, there was a blood smear on his locker."

"He's a chef," Lydia said. "Maybe the blood came from a slab of meat."

"Well, then, why was there a bloody steak knife inside?"

"How did you manage to search the employees' lockers?" I asked.

"Easy. It was obvious that Chef Pascal was attracted to me."

"My dear cousin, he's attracted to any woman who comes near."

"Whatever. While you were trying to get yourself buried alive, and Sherlock Holmes here was hanging out in bars and telling lies all over New Orleans, I stuck to my assignment, which was to stay at the hotel, which is where the first murder, and probably the second murder, took place, if I recall. I waited until things got really busy in the kitchen and went into the employees' room. I started opening the lockers. I saw the blood smear on one and found the bloody knife. The name on the locker was Pascal La Duc."

"What did the blood on the knife look like?" Lydia said.

"What do you mean what did it look like? It was red, red, red—red, blood."

Ruth punctuated each "red" with a foot stomp. I'm surprised the people staying in the room below didn't call the front desk and complain about heavy objects hitting the floor above.

"Did you smell it? Taste it? Was it fresh blood or dried? Was the blood a splatter, a smear? Was it on the handle or just the blade? It could it have been the result of Pascal cutting oneself while slicing onions?"

The food order arrived. Ruth flung the door open and scared the waiter. "Where's the wine?"

"You didn't order wine, ma'am. You ordered brandy."

"Well bring up a bottle of wine anyway, dammit," she said stomping again. "And tell the bartender to send up a double immediately."

"A double of what?"

"Everything!" Stomp. Stomp. Stomp.

I needed to step in before we had two distraught women in the room. "Everyone grab a plate," I said. "Ruth, you did good, but Lydia's questions are valid."

"I didn't have time to study the bloody knife," Ruth said. "Who do I look like, Dracula Gross. There was dried blood in the serrated edges of the knife."

"Dried blood looks brownish, not red," Lydia said.

"It was freshly dried!"

"Did you wear gloves?"

"To hell with gloves."

"You should have worn them. It could have been the murder weapon," Lydia said. "But if Pascal's the killer, he wouldn't leave the evidence where it could easily be found."

"Unless he was in a hurry to hide it," Ruth said.

"But he's had plenty of time to come back and remove it," Lydia reminded her.

"Someone else might have found it and tried to implicate Pascal," Rip said.

"True. Okay, the police need to know this," I said. "But Rip and I are the last people who should call it to their attention. And not Lydia or Ruth, since they were seen with me at the police station."

"Who then?" Rip asked.

"Lily Morton. Enjoy the food. I'm going to see if she's still here."

Without going into detail, I told Lily what I needed. She was hesitant, but agreed to call the police. Reluctantly, I rejoined the melee in my room. Luckily, the booze had arrived. There was enough food to feed everyone on our floor. Despite the heavenly aroma, I didn't have an appetite. I found a water glass and poured myself a full glass of red wine.

"You have to eat something, Sydney," Ruth said. She handed me a bowl of gumbo and a few hushpuppies. "I must ask Pascal for the recipe."

Lydia looked into the bowl. "That shrimp still has its head on. Look at the little black eyes and feelers. Yum, shrimp eyes, my favorite."

"You're so childish," Ruth said.

Lydia grinned and shook her head. "That's because I am a *child*."

The phone rang. "Miss Lockhart," Lily said. "There was no bloody knife in that locker."

I broke the news to everyone, which instantly stifled the festive mood.

"What if Lily was the killer?" Lydia said. "She could have taken the evidence."

"At this point it could be anybody," I said. "Whoever killed Mildred came into the hotel through the kitchen. Went up to our room. Killed Mildred with a knife and on the way out, put it in Pascal's locker."

"Who took it then?" Ruth asked.

"Pascal," I said. "If you found evidence of a murder that pointed to you, you'd get rid of it. And, remember, Mildred was killed on Wednesday morning. Two days ago. Pascal would have had plenty of time to get rid of the damaging evidence."

CHAPTER TWENTY-TWO

The phone rang again. "Mrs. Dixon, this is the front desk. There's a man here wanting to come up to your room. He's very insistent, but he wouldn't give his name."

"I don't want to go up to her room. I want her to come down here."

I recognized the squeaky Alfalfa voice, shouting through the phone line. My blood froze. I hung up and pulled on my boots. "I need to check on something. I'll be right back."

Bugger was on his way out the front door by the time I made it down to the lobby. "Bugger, wait." He started to run. He was no match for a long-legged woman who was on her college track team. I caught up with him two blocks away and strong armed him into an alley. Dixon described him as a big guy, but most of his bulk was soft and doughy. With my gun under his chin, Bugger didn't struggle.

"How did you find me?"

"The newspapers. The story about the murder. The guy who was arrested was named Dixon. The story said he'd been staying at the Pontchartrain with a woman. When Vinny and I took you to the swamp, he said, 'We need to get rid of Mrs. Dixon.' I'm glad you made it out of the swamp. I didn't want to kill you. I put it all together and called the hotel and found out you were still staying here. I was sitting in the lobby when you came in earlier today."

"Why did you call my room and then run?"

"I came to tell you I was sorry, but I chickened out. Please put the gun away."

"No. First you talk."

"It's my momma. She was a good Catholic. She's been talking to me ever since she talked me out of burying you. I'd spent a lot of money on spirit stuff trying to get momma to talk to me after she died. I even went to one of them ghost meetings."

"A séance?"

"Yeah, with a woman who knows how to talk to the dead."

"A medium."

"If you say so. But nothing worked until you came along. I figured you must be one of them spirit women, and my momma was talking through you 'cause she couldn't get to me herself. It's like you opened the door. She hasn't shut up since. She told me I needed to come see you or I was gonna be sitting on the devil's pitchfork forever after I died. I couldn't let that happen. It was just me and my momma, and I wanted to meet her in heaven. Know what I mean?"

"I know exactly what you mean, Bugger."

He let out a heavy sigh. A wave of bad breath hit me in the face. I stepped back. I could empathize with Bugger. Catholic guilt was often responsible for people hearing voices. If Bugger wanted to believe I was a channel to the other world, fine. Standing in an alley in the dark, holding a gun on someone was not a good idea. I was tempted to take him up to the room #702 insane asylum, which a couple of days ago was to become a honeymoon suite. We stepped across the street to a park bench.

"Your momma didn't tell you to turn yourself into the police, did she?"

"Oh, no, she didn't."

Of course, she didn't.

"Listen, Bugger, there's an innocent man sitting in jail right now because of what happened. If you don't go to the police, not only will you get the pitchfork after you die, I'll see to it that you meet the devil much faster than you anticipated."

Bugger sat there chewing over my threat. Then his eyes widened. "What? No, momma, no." He clamped his hands over his ears. A low wail escalated into a yawl. A couple strolling by stopped and stared. Two elderly woman quickened their pace and fled.

"Bugger! Bugger!" I pulled his hands away from his head. "Calm down. You're causing a scene."

"She won't shut up. I'm gonna lose my mind."

"I'll help you, but you have to tell me everything that happened at the appliance warehouse. Maybe we can figure this out and make your momma happy. Who killed Lavine Rose?"

"Who?"

"The woman you and Vinny dumped into the Mississippi."

"I don't know. All I know is Vinny—I do odd jobs for him sometimes— told me that if I wanted to make a little extra money, I could help him with something, but I never did anything like bury people in the swamp. When I walked into the warehouse and saw the body, I told him I wanted no part in it. He told me it was too late. I saw too much. If I didn't help him, he'd make it look like I was the one who did it. I didn't know who that was on the floor. I didn't want to know."

"Did Vinny kill her?"

"I said I don't know. I didn't ask. I just did what Vinny told me to do."

"Where's Vinny now?"

"I don't know. Oh God." He bent over and put his head between his knees and rocked back and forth. I thought he was going to throw up. The wailing started up once more, low from the bottom of his stomach, then it rose into his chest and spilled from this mouth—hot lava roiling up from a volcano. Evidently, his momma was talking to him again. If momma and I succeeded in talking Bugger into turning himself in, the cops would toss him out onto the street. Another lunatic hearing voices in his head. I'm sure there were a lot of those colorful people around here. But I couldn't let this guy go. If I did, I'd never see him again. I needed more information, and momma was going to help me.

"Bugger, momma and I know you are lying. We know you're not telling me everything. Your momma is not going to stop talking to you. You have to come clean, understand?"

"Vinny said he'd kill me."

"Tell me where he is. I can't help you if you don't tell me the truth."

"He'll find me. I know he'll find me."

"Where is he, Bugger?"

"Promise you'll let me go if I tell you."

Jeez. "I can't promise that. You're not in a position to bargain. If you don't tell me, I'll take you to the police myself."

Bugger gave his head a vigorous rub as if his scalp was on fire. "In a house in the Lower Ninth Ward. Vinny told me we'd stay there until things blew over. I left while Vinny was asleep this morning. If I go back, he'll kill me. I know he will. I'm a dead man."

"Where's the house?"

"It's as you cross over the canal where Sister Street turns in to Dauphine down by the river."

"Take me there."

"No! No way am I going back."

"Give me a house number?"

"Four-hundred something. It's an old house, a dump like most others on the street. The windows are boarded up."

"What are you doing out here, Sydney?"

In that one brief moment a thousand things assaulted my mind. That brief disruptive moment that caused hope to vanish and fear to set in. That brief annoying moment when I visualize my hands around my cousin's throat as she walked up with Rip in tow. Bugger's eyes bugged out and he leapt off the bench and ran. Rip and I gave chase. Bugger darted into traffic, and I followed. I narrowly missed getting hit by a car. A taxi sped by as Bugger turned to look behind him. The car clipped Bugger's coat, spinning him around—a perfect pirouette, then a stumble before he caught his balance and ducked down a side street. I followed. Rip was close behind before he overtook me. Bugger, only a half a block away and almost in reach until a bus turned the corner in front of us. That's all Bugger needed. The bus passed. Bugger was gone.

I motioned for Rip to keep going. I took the side street, ran to the end of the block, turned left, another left back to the main street. Bugger could have ducked into any of the doorways along the way. I saw Rip up ahead, looking around until he took off again. Two blocks down Bugger was bent over gasping for air. He saw us and took off again, turned the corner, darted into a Chinese restaurant. Rip rushed in behind Bugger. I ran around the block to the back of the building, hopefully we'd be able to corner the guy. The back door of the restaurant flew open and Rip and I smacked into one another, turned and ran back inside. A waiter pointed to a side door. Another lucky break. The door led to a hallway and a door at the end, which led to a dark alley. We didn't see Bugger standing in the shadows. We didn't see the gun in his hand. Didn't even suspect he had a one.

He fired. The shot ricocheted off the side of a building inches from my head. Rip and I hit the ground. Bugger was off and running again.

Bugger, crazy, spooked Bugger just upped the ante. Driven by a surge of anger, I scrambled to my feet and plunged after him. I knew I could keep up the chase longer than he could.

Back on the main street, people were glancing around having heard the shots, looking back and forth between Bugger and his pursuers. A woman, seeing my gun, screamed and passed out. I leapt over her and kept going. Nabbing Bugger meant getting Dixon out of jail, and nothing was going to stop me from making that happen. Wherever Bugger's momma was now, she must have given up talking sense to her son.

Bugger dashed across a grocery store parking lot crammed with cars, ducking and bobbing as he went. He reached the street, turned to look back, and tripped over a curb, tumbling into traffic. Tires squealed, but the driver of the truck couldn't stop fast enough. Bugger flew into the next lane, landed in the middle of the street, bounced and rolled several yards down the road. He tried to stand, but collapsed. I slipped my gun back into my holster and shouted for someone to call an ambulance. When I reached him, he was bleeding from a gash in his head and his left leg was bent at an ungodly angle. He tried to raise up, but fell back. "Bugger, take it easy," I said. I took off my jacket and placed it under his head. His lips moved. "Don't talk," I said. He coughed up blood, then whispered something. I leaned down.

"Grey house. Cockeyed mailbox." He passed out. I felt his pulse, but he was bleeding so heavily, I was afraid he wouldn't last long.

Rip came up behind me. "Go, Sydney. I'll take care of this."

I didn't know how Rip knew. It must have been the look of desperation on my face. I didn't hesitate. I was gone. Three blocks away I heard the sirens and said a prayer for Bugger. I grabbed a cab. "Lower Ninth Ward. Sister Street."

"You sure, lady? Not a good part of town, especially at night."

"Just go."

We crossed over the canal and Sister Street came into view. I told the driver to turn right. The street numbers, those that existed began with 1307 and continued increasing. No four hundreds.

"Sure you got the address right?" the driver asked.

"No, but keep going." Hope and excitement began to vanish. "Maybe it's on Dauphine." If Bugger lied . . . I pushed that thought away. There was no four-hundred block on Dauphine. "Keep circling the blocks." We covered every street in a half-mile radius.

"Sorry, lady. Want me to take you back?"

"Go ahead. Wait. Drive down Sister one more time."

"It's your money."

We'd almost reached Dauphine when I spotted it. A gray house with a mail box hanging cockeyed from a nail, windows boarded up. The numbers on the house were a four and a three and the other numbers missing. What now? I hadn't thought that far ahead. On the wrong side of town with a cabbie anxious to leave. "Drive to the end of the street, turn around, and park."

The face looking back at me in the review mirror was not a happy one. "I don't know what you got going, but I don't want any part of it."

"I'm looking for someone. It's important." I thought of Taco, the cab driver in San Antonio, who became my friend, my savior when I'd lost my memory after Rip threw me into the San Antonio river, thought better of it, and rescued me. Taco let me stay at his house. He cooked for me, let me drive his deceased sister's car, and eventually accompanied me all the way to New Orleans and helped me nab a killer. This guy was no Taco. "Keep your meter running and I'll throw in an extra twenty."

He turned around, leaned his elbow over the seat. He

followed my gaze to the house across the street. "Don't look like nobody's home."

"Sure doesn't, but I have to check."

"Wait." He rummaged around in the glovebox. "Take this. You might need it." He handed me a flashlight.

I pulled my gun from my holster and popped out of the car. "I'll be right back," I said, confident the driver wouldn't take off since I owed him money.

I tried the front door. It opened. The odor of mildew and spoiled milk wafted out. I flipped on the flashlight. Vinny wouldn't be doing any more jobs for Mr. Garrison, or talking to the police. He was sprawled on the floor, face up. The blood that had spilled from the hole in his chest was fresh. I turned off the light, closed the door, and got back into the taxi.

"You were right. No one's home. Take me to . . ." I didn't want the driver to connect me with the Pontchartrain. "Take me back to where you picked me up."

With Vinny dead and possibly Bugger, I wasn't sure about my next move. Three murders in three days. At least the cops couldn't pin this one on Dixon.

CHAPTER TWENTY-THREE

Back at the hotel bar, I found Ruth in a rare state, staring down at her empty brandy glass, shaking her head repeatedly.

"I'm responsible for killing that man," she blubbered. "I had no idea he'd take off running like that."

"It's not your fault. We don't know if he's dead."

"But what if he is. What if I go to hell? I couldn't handle it. I just wouldn't fit in there. You know how I feel about sweating. Who was he anyway?"

"His name is Bugger. One of the men who chloroformed me and took me to the swamp. He tracked me to the hotel and called my room from the lobby. If it wasn't for him, I'd be dead. He was supposed to bury me, but instead he dumped me behind some bushes and left me there. Seems his dead mother was pestering him to confess, but he was afraid the other guy, Vinny, would kill him. He'd gotten in over his head."

"Why did he run away?"

"He came to me for help, but chickened out and took off. I caught up to him."

"His dead mother talks to him?"

"To my advantage, and I helped a little. Anyway, I recognized his voice when he called the room. Before Bugger passed out on the street, he told me where he and the other guy, Vinny, were staying. I found the house. Vinny had been shot dead moments before I got there. As soon as Rip returns, we're going back to the appliance store. Where's Lydia?"

"She's upstairs with Betsy."

"Did you know that Palmer's flying in tomorrow to take Lydia back to Austin?"

"She told me. I don't like how she gets away with bossing everyone around and meddling into everything. I'm glad she's leaving."

"I like having her around, but this time, I agree with you. Things have become too dangerous. Please don't tell her you're happy she's leaving because she'll find every excuse to stay."

Rip walked in and I waved him over. "What's the latest?"

"I stayed around until the ambulance arrived and learned Bugger was to be taken to Charity Hospital. I followed. He was in the emergency room when I got there. I told the nurse on duty that I was a friend of his and I had seen him get hit by the car. I asked how he was. I had to wait, but an hour later the doctor came out to see me. Good news. Bugger's in bad shape, but he'll recover. He has a broken leg, a few broken ribs, and a cracked skull, which wasn't as bad as it looked when he was bleeding all over the street. He was awake. I got in to see him for a few minutes before he went into surgery to set his leg. He was on a lot of drugs and was talking out of his head."

"He was doing that before the accident. He hears his mother's voice."

"Yeah, I know."

"I'm relieved he's okay," Ruth said.

"He was mumbling about a guy named Vinny coming to get him. He got upset. I almost called a nurse, but he calmed down. I don't think he even knows where he is. I'll go back after his surgery."

"There's not much more he can help us with," I said. "He swore he didn't know what was going on. He was only following orders. I believed him."

"He also said the name Carl Wilner a couple of times."

"Carl Wilner?"

"Maybe it's some other dead person talking to him," Ruth said.

I asked the bartender for a phonebook, but there was no listing for a Carl Wilner. Lydia walked in, followed by Betsy. "This woman needs a drink," Lydia said. "Either that or a slap on the face."

"I think she's had enough," Rip said. "Betsy, you need to get ahold of yourself. Come on. We need to have a talk." Betsy fell into his arms and they went over to a table by themselves.

"Lydia, think you can get your friend at the immigration office to check another name?"

"Sure."

"Carl Wilner. It might not lead to anything, but I have a hunch."

"I'll do it first thing in the morning," Lydia said.

"Wait. I do not want you leaving this hotel by yourself. Three people have been murdered. You can do this over the phone."

"Don't worry," Lydia said. "I can handle it. Who's the other victim?"

"One of the guys who dragged me out to the swamp. The foreman at the appliance store."

"I'll have some information tomorrow."

"Wait, tomorrow is Saturday."

"I know. But don't worry. I'll manage."

"I don't want you to leave—"

"I won't leave the hotel. Just as long as I don't have to babysit hysterical women." Her eyes lowered to half mast. "And annoying women." I was ready for an argument, but she turned on her heel and headed for the elevator.

"Was she talking about me?" Ruth asked.

"Betsy. She was talking about Betsy."

"And me!"

"Shut up, Ruth."

Rip walked up. "I'm taking Betsy to stay with Frida Mae. I'll be back as soon as I can."

"Hurry, we're going back to the appliance store."

After they left, Ruth said, "She's such a mousy, whining thing. I don't know what Rip sees in her."

"I don't care what he sees in her, Ruth."

RIP RETURNED FROM DROPPING off Betsy and we made a quick trip to the hospital. I waited in the car while Rip went inside to see if it was safe for me to talk to Bugger. I wanted to inform him about Vinny's murder and see if he could tell me anything about Carl Wilner.

Rip waved me in and when no one was looking, Rip and I ducked into Bugger's room. He'd just come back from surgery and was still groggy, but he recognized me. The bandage covering his head gave him an angelic look. A plaster cast reached from his hip past his knee. "Bugger, how are you feeling?"

"Not good."

"Doctor said you'd be fine."

"No, I won't. I'm gonna die."

"None of us are getting out alive, Bugger."

He gasped, his eyes almost popped out of his head. While I had his attention I said, "Vinny is dead. Did you kill him, maybe in self-defense?"

He closed his eyes. "I never killed anyone."

"Who could have killed Vinny?"

"Mr. Garrison was mad and threatened him. Maybe it was him. I don't know."

"Have the police been to see you?"

"No!"

"I'd be prepared. If they can tie Vinny's murder to you, they'll be here, you know that. So, if I were you, I'd tell me everything you know. You might need someone in your corner. Have you done a lot of odd jobs with Vinny?"

"A few. Do you really think the cops will come here?"

"Bugger, think about it. Vinny has been murdered. Someone shot him in the chest in the house where you two were staying. Someone probably saw you there."

"When I left the house, Vinny was alive, I swear."

"Vinny didn't tell you anything about the body, why it was in the warehouse?"

"No, nothing. I already told you."

"Who's Carl Wilner? You mentioned him to my friend here. Remember talking to him? You said the name Carl Wilner before you went into surgery."

"You remember me, Bugger," Rip said. "I was the one who stayed with you until the ambulance came."

"I don't know anyone named Carl."

"Why did you run, Bugger?" I said.

He opened his eyes and looked around the room, then to the door.

"It's okay. We were in the park talking, remember? All of a sudden you jumped up and ran. What frightened you?"

"That little man."

"What little man?"

"I saw him at the appliance store when Vinny and I were putting the body . . . putting the body in the car. He saw us. I should have told Vinny, but I didn't. I saw him again across the street from the park when I was talking to you. He was looking right at me. He knew, he knew what we did."

"What did he look like?"

"Moustache. Black hair. Dressed funny."

"How?"

"A doctor."

"Where was he when he saw you moving the body?"

"In the back parking lot. Standing by a car. He was watching us."

"What would a doctor be doing in the back parking lot of the appliance store?" Rip asked.

"What are you doing in here?" A nurse had walked in with a tray. "He needs to rest. It is not visiting time. You were here earlier," she said to Rip.

"Yes, we just wanted to know how the surgery went," Rip said.

"Well, now you know, you need to leave."

Rip and I gladly took her advice. "That was not good. I was hoping we could get in and out without me being seen."

"I don't think we can get much more out of him."

"I think we can. He was lying about not knowing Carl Wilner."

CHAPTER TWENTY-FOUR

Rip and I made a slow lap around Threadgill's Appliances. A few security lights were on outside. The parking lot was empty except for one car. We parked on the street out front.

"What do you think?" Rip said.

"I doubt someone is still there this late, but we want to be sure. Let's wait." A thin sliver of moon peeked out from a cloudy sky. The smell of impending rain hung heavy. Even in the darkness you could see swollen clouds roil in from the east.

"I hope you don't mind me asking, but I've often thought about what happened to the racehorse girl, Nora Jasper, who brought us to New Orleans a few weeks ago," Rip said.

"I don't have a clue, except her name is not Nora Jasper, it's Loretta Dixon."

"Dixon? Any relation to your Dixon."

"Afraid so. Remind me to tell you about it when we have nothing better to do."

"Man. It's a crazy world. Look, someone's coming out."

I looked up to see Walt Garrison locking the door and getting into his car.

"Now we can go in," Rip said.

"I don't like what I just saw. Did you notice how he kept looking around when he came out?"

"I would too this late at night in this neighborhood."

"Instead of going inside, I have a better idea. Let's follow him."

"Are you sure?"

"If he goes home, we can come back and search the place."

Walt Garrison drove west out of the city on Gentilly Road.

There was little traffic, so we stayed as far behind as possible. A few minutes later we were still following.

"I don't think he's going home," Rip said. "Looks like he's turning. There's nothing here but swamp. Why is it whenever I'm with you, I end up in a swamp?"

"I was thinking the same thing about you."

Garrison slowed, made a turn onto a dirt road and was swallowed in the vegetation. Rip pulled over to make a U-turn. He parked on the side of the road and turned off the headlights.

Another car came along and followed Garrison's route, followed by a second car, and a third.

"I'm not sure if I want to go in there," Rip said.

"Me neither. Good thing we're armed."

Rip let out a grunt. "You know, Sydney, I have a confession to make. The reason I got the idea to investigate the dead is because I've seen enough violence. Ghosts are harmless. Don't look at me like that. I know it's just a way to cash in on the fallout of Marie Laveau's House of Voodoo. But here I am with you. We're following a murderer again. We have guns. Can't we just go back to the appliance store, break in, and see what we can find?"

"Great idea, after we find out what's going on in the swamp."

"I figured you'd say that."

We waited until we were sure no one else was coming to join the party, and made our way on foot. A light rain was falling and thunder echoed not far off. A few yards into the overgrowth I turned around. The highway from which we came was no longer visible. We were consumed in cypress, moss, and strangler vines, rising up from the ground in search of another victim. I thought of Houston where I grew up. We had bayous, lowlands, and rivers, all leading to the Gulf. Yes, there was mass vegetation, but for the most part civilization poked out every now and then. In Austin where I live now, we have rolling hills to the west and vast farmlands to the east. Getting lost in a dark forest was not something I ever worried about. Louisiana is a quagmire with a few cities and towns floating on spongy terrain ruled by man-eating reptiles and strangling plants. And yet, here I am—again. A line of parked cars led us in the right, or maybe, wrong direction. I'd like to say I felt comforted by the rain not reaching us through the canopy overhead, but that would be a lie.

Rip and I stopped in our tracks. At first I thought we were hearing the call of great-horned owls, but as we approached, the sound became a haunting chant that escalated the closer we got. Lights twinkled through the growth. We stepped off the path and wove our way closer. The ground submerged under two inches of muddy water. My heart stopped when I saw the bonfire beginning to blaze. Then terror swept in like whirling Dervishes as white-robes and cone-shaped hoods became visible in the flame's glow. I wanted to get the hell out of there, but my curiosity won over any good sense I had left. Careful not to get tangled in kudzu vine, or create a splat as we pulled our feet from the mire, we risked getting as close as we dared.

The Ku Klux Klan had experienced another resurgence since Senator Joseph McCarthy jumped on the bandwagon of the House of Un-American Activities Committee. The purpose was to hunt for communists residing in the U.S. to prevent them from overthrowing the government. Now the Klan had another group of people to terrorize, but this time with the blessing of the government, or so they believed. Fortunately, we didn't notice any victims prepared for punishment at this gathering.

I looked over at Rip. Even in the darkness, I saw that his face had turned white and his eyes bugged out. He leaned over to say something, but I held my finger to my lips. The leader stepped onto the bed of a pickup truck and began what sounded like a rally speech, to which the members shouted agreement and encouragement. During the speech a latecomer joined the crowd. As he put on his robe, he turned. My heart stopped a second time. It was Detective Bergeron.

We couldn't hear what was being said, but the speaker created a frenzy of excitement. Less than an hour later it was over. Some of the members left, those who stayed removed their hoods and gathered around. The ambiance changed from an angry mob looking for trouble to a group of guys enjoying a backyard barbeque. Finally, they filed down toward their cars. Walt Garrison, looking as ominous as when he caught me coming out of Vinny's office, shook Bergeron's hand. They spoke a few words, then parted. Then I saw another man I recognized, causing acid to burn in my stomach—Elliott Ivy.

Rip and I waited until we were sure we were alone. "Maybe I should move back to Texas," Rip said.

"The Klan's in Texas too."

"So Garrison is a member of the Klan."

"So are Elliott Ivy and Detective Bergeron." Seeing Bergeron here tells me that having the charges dropped and getting Dixon released was turning out to be one of the hardest things I've ever had to do.

"What next?"

"As soon as possible, I'm going to contact Elliott Ivy."

"Is that wise?"

"Probably not, but I need to check up on what's happening with Frank Threadgill's missing money, and I'll go from there."

On the way back to Rip's car, my mind spun a web that ran in different directions. My thoughts were interrupted when Rip let spew a few expletives and took off running. I looked around expecting to see one of the Klansmen. Then I saw Rip with his hands on the hood of his car and his head slumped to his chest. "All goddamn four of them," he said. He slipped his flashlight from his pocket and I saw the car's running boards and fenders nestled in the tall grass. All four tires had been slashed. "What the hell do we do now? We're at least three miles from the edge of the city."

"We walk. Stay close to the roadside in case we see headlights in either direction. After what we just saw, I don't want to meet anyone traveling this road."

"I can barely see my hand in from of my face and the storm is coming in."

"That's good for us. No sane person would be out driving in this weather. Turn off the flashlight. Let's go. If we hurry we should be off this road and in the city in about an hour." I turned up the collar of my jacket and pulled my hat down over my ears. The deluge started. Streak lightening lit the way.

Twice we dove off the road upon seeing headlights in the distance. Both times the cars turned off before reaching us. The third time, however, landed us thigh-deep in water. The ditch along the road had become a swift-moving river. The wind turned to gale force and Rip's hat disappeared into the brush. He looked like a drenched Frankenstein making his way slowly, careful not to trip. Every few yards, I had to stop and empty my boots of water. Even with Dixon's future looking bleak and the prospect of me becoming a widow before I married, I thought of Dixon and me walking into Pete's Western Footwear in Austin when we returned home. The image of him in those black cowboy boots, made me giggle. Rip turned and looked at me. I'm sure the sight of me is what made him giggle. Before I knew it, we were doubled over with laughter.

"I don't see what's so funny," I said.

"Neither do I," Rip said.

It was five minutes before we could catch our breaths and compose ourselves. "Look," I pointed. Up ahead was the glow of New Orleans.

"Maybe we can grab a cab to your hotel," Rip said.

"Well, good luck with that."

IT WAS ALMOST TWO WHEN we reached the Pontchartrain. The same doorman was on duty from yesterday when I came in wearing swamp. This time he just opened the door and looked the other way. I could almost hear his thoughts, *swamp woman found her a fella."*

"What do we do now, Sydney?"

"I have a plan."

"I was afraid of that."

CHAPTER TWENTY-FIVE

Lydia's door was closed and there was no light coming from under it. "Lydia's asleep," I whispered.

"That was one of the spookiest nights I've ever had," Rip said.

I brought two towels from the bathroom and draped them over the chair's seat cushion.

"I don't ever want to mess with those people. They are the worst of the worst. Violent vigilantes. I'm sure they are the ones who slashed my tires. Think they'll try and find out who owns the car?"

"Possibly. It might have been Bergeron. He was the last one to show up. You need to have it towed right away."

"I know a guy who can do it for me."

"Call him."

"Now?"

"You don't want your car sitting there. See if your friend will tow the car tonight. Call him while I clean up."

By the time I got out of the shower, Rip had taken care of his car. "He's going to replace the tires and keep the car at his automotive shop until I pick it up. Guess what? When I told him where the car was, he knew the area. He said, 'Is that near where the Klan meets?'"

"Is he a member?"

"No, but his uncle is. You said you had a plan."

"Fortunately for you, I've scrapped it. I've come up with a better one, I hope. Walt Garrison, Elliott Ivy, and Detective Bergeron, who are associated with this case are all members of the Klan. That's not a coincidence. I was going to suggest you infiltrate their organization and see what you can find out. Two reasons that won't work."

"You can say that again. I can think of several. Reason one: I'd refuse. Reason two: I've had my fill of swamps. Reason three: I don't look good in white."

"There's that, but also, Garrison might know who you are. You've never encountered him, but he might have had tabs on you since Mildred hired you. And, who knows when the Klan will have another nighttime outing. From what I understand, the Klan meets when they have an issue. We don't have time for another meeting to happen."

"You think last night's meeting has to do with this case? That it was an issue, like you said?"

"I am not sure of anything right now. What's your take on it?"

"There's nothing racial about the case."

"The Klan also targets Jews, homosexuals, and immigrants. Walt Garrison is an immigrant, yet he's a member. Want to bet Frank Threadgill was a member too?"

"You and me, Sydney, we can't go up against the Klan. That's plain crazy."

"No, we can't. But out of those three, Elliott Ivy is my best bet to finding out what's going on."

"I don't see how. You can't tell him you saw him at a Klan meeting last night."

"I'll think of something. Check on Bugger's condition again in the morning. I'll call you. I'm going to try and get a few hours of sleep."

I WAS DEAD TIRED, BUT despite everything that had happened, I was wide awake. I missed Dixon terribly, but I was glad I had this room to myself. I needed time to think. I got out of bed. I'd left my slacks to soak in the bathtub. In the short time they were submerged, the water had turned black, bits of moss and algae had risen to the surface, and the tub smelled of swamp—again. I soaped and rinsed a half a dozen times before most of the smell was gone. I'd send them out in the morning for a more thorough cleaning. I scrubbed my boots and set them on the balcony to dry. The way things were going, this outfit would become my uniform while in New Orleans. I should know better. I always pack light when I'm on the road, but when I'm on a case, I ruin most of the clothes I bring. I'd have to stop criticizing Ruth for packing half her wardrobe when she traveled. I crawled back into bed. Sleep refused to join me.

I pulled out my notebook and wrote down a list of what I knew as fact and a list of speculations, possibilities, and assumptions. Then I made a list of everyone involved in the case. I listed "local Klan," and under that I wrote Elliott Ivy's name and instantly remembered him mentioning that soon after he'd met Frank, he invited his brother-in-law to join a community organization. That had to be the Klan. It made sense if Walt Garrison was a member, then Frank was too. I'd put these questions to Elliott tomorrow. I wondered if he and his mother had discovered what had happened to Frank's small fortune. I'd use that as a reason to call.

Next I wrote down as much as I could recall from the two conversations I had with him; one at Mrs. Ivy's after the funeral, and the other was when he and his mother came to the hotel lobby. Was the bizarre story about wanting us to solve the case so that his mother could save face among her friends really true? I wondered how she'd feel if she knew her son was a member of the KKK. Maybe she wouldn't care. Maybe they were a bunch of racists. Jeez. Lack of sleep was doing a number on my level head.

CHAPTER TWENTY-SIX

I woke with a start. A clap of thunder had me up looking out of the window. Pre-dawn cast a soft, foggy glow over the city—another round of thunderstorms brewing on the horizon.

Memories of last night's dreams came into focus. Alligators in white hoods lined up on a riverbank, me standing on the other side of the river, paralyzed, watching them slide into the water one by one. I'd fallen asleep with my notebook open. Ink from my fountain pen had leaked, smudging some of what I wrote. No matter, most of it was little more than nonsense.

I listened for Lydia stirring in the adjoining room, all was quiet. A sadness, an aching covered me like a heavy blanket of doom. I wanted Dixon here beside me, not in a jail cell. He was the most emotionally strong person I knew, but I'm no stranger to being locked up and the toll it takes. I'd been in jail for two maddening days when I was in Palacios trying to find out who killed Sam Bucker while dancing with him last New Year's Eve. *Yeah, I know, it sounds weird, but the man was stabbed while he twirled me around the dance floor.* I threw off the bed covers, got dressed, and went downstairs in search of coffee.

A newspaper boy was filling the rack with the early morning edition. I walked over. "Read the latest, Miss." He handed me a newspaper. I was sure the latest news dealt with the case. I was sure the headlines announced Vinny's murder. If the cops connected me to that murder, I'd have to make myself scarce. The headline was not what I expected.

BODY IN CEMETERY REMOVED
FROM COFFIN AND MUTILATED.

Early this morning a maintenance worker at St. Louis Cemetery discovered the body of Frank Threadgill. The coffin had been opened and the body left on the ground and mutilated. Threadgill's tomb had been vandalized several times since his death a month ago. The body has been taken to the morgue for further examination. The police are investigating. In the meantime, the cemetery will be under a twenty-four hour watch.

The wait staff was setting up for breakfast. I managed a cup of coffee from a waiter in the dining room. Soon the caffeine pulsating through my veins woke me up, but also heightened my anxiety. I couldn't wait any longer. Every minute meant time to scheme, time to conspire, time to lie. I dialed Elliott Ivy's phone from the lobby.

"Hello, who is this?"

"Mrs. Ivy, this is Sydney Loc . . . Sydney Dixon. I know it's early, but may I speak to your husband?"

"Who?"

"Sydney Dixon, my . . . my husband and I were at your mother-in-law's house the day your sister-in-law died. Your husband asked me to look into some of her affairs."

"Oh, yes. Hold on."

I must have woken up the entire household. I heard a child fussing. Elliott grumbling in the background. No surprise, since he was out late last night too. Up until this point I wasn't sure how to approach him.

"Mrs. Dixon?"

"Mr. Ivy, I need to speak to you right away. It's important. Can you come to the hotel?"

"Do you know what time it is?"

"It's important."

"Is this about Mildred, about the money?"

Money? It's about her murder, you idiot. "Maybe. I'll buy you breakfast."

"I hope so." He laughed. "I'll be there soon."

The disappearance of Frank's money seemed an insignificant detail when you considered three murders in two days. When you considered my future husband was accused of two of those murders, the situation grew desperate. I was about to take a big gamble, a gamble I couldn't afford to lose. I went upstairs to get my notebook. When I returned Elliott Ivy was standing in the lobby, looking disheveled.

"That was fast," I said.

"I live down the street. Pardon my appearance. I don't often get summoned this early. What's happened?"

The restaurant wasn't open yet so I headed toward the hotel's Silver Whistle Coffee Shop. Ivy followed me to a table and I didn't hesitate spewing my opinions. "You mentioned that you had invited Frank to join a community organization, which one?"

"What?"

"Eagles, Masons, Elks, Salvation Army?" I couldn't keep the ire out of my voice.

"You think Frank left his money to a community organization?"

"Mr. Ivy, your sister was murdered three days ago. Another woman was murdered in connection with Mildred's."

"I read in the paper that someone was arrested for both murders. I just assumed—"

"You assumed—problem solved—let's move on to the money? Did you even wonder about the motive for the murders? Frankly, I find it curious, not to mention annoying, that your sister's inheritance is your and your mother's main concern. Mr. Ivy, did you kill your sister? Because if you thought that she was about to come into money, that would be a strong motive since you would inherit. I also discovered information that can tie you to Lavine Rose's murder. You knew she worked at this hotel." *I wasn't sure about this, but the bluff was worth a try.* "Even after Frank died, your sister continued to work at the appliance store, so she knew Walt Garrison, the new owner. You know him as well. Did you know that Miss Rose's body was found at the appliance store two days ago? There was a third murder. The foreman who worked at Threadgill Appliances. Know what

I think? I think you and Walt Garrison killed Mildred, or had her killed. I think Miss Rose was a witness and you killed her too. You didn't want the foreman to talk, so you added him to the list. So, yes, I guess you can say that this meeting is about the money and a bit more." I held my breath. If Elliott Ivy was pals with Detective Bergeron, things were about to get ugly. If I'd gone too far, I couldn't pull back now.

"You've been busy, Mrs. Dixon." His face hardened.

"Actually, it's Miss Lockhart. Dixon and I aren't married." Yet.

"If I were you, I'd pack it up and head back to Texas." He threw some change on the table. "I prefer to pay for my own coffee. Don't bother me again."

"Before you leave, maybe you can answer this question for me. What would Detective Bergeron say about all this?" I heard my heart pounding in my ears. My throat dried.

His back turned to me. He paused.

That's all I needed.

He sat back down. "You said something about breakfast?" He picked up a menu.

"I take it you haven't seen the morning paper. Before you order, take a look at this." I handed him the newspaper.

Ivy laid the menu down. "Damn."

The waiter came over. "How does the breakfast special sound, Mr. Ivy?" I said.

"Fine." Elliott waited until the waiter left. "I didn't kill my sister. I didn't kill anyone. I didn't open Frank's tomb or mutilate his body, and neither did Walt Garrison. Frank was not who he said he was."

"Tell me about him."

"I told you yesterday, I never trusted him. I had someone look into his background. After weeks, the guy I hired came up empty. It seemed like Frank just appeared out of nowhere. He claims he immigrated, but there's no record of it."

"We checked too," I said. "That's a good reason not to trust him."

"He hardly spoke of his past, only a few facts when pushed, but after a while I noticed that he contradicted himself. He claimed to have come from Belgium, but his Eastern European accent said otherwise. He said when he was five, his father was killed in the first war. Another time he said his father died right before he was born. This probably wouldn't have bothered me too much, except for him mistreating Mildred and for that gut feeling I had about him that wouldn't go away. Then recently, I stumbled on something. I can't tell you any more than that."

"But you wanted our help in figuring out what happened to your sister's money."

"I was appeasing my mother. I don't care about the money, but I do care about finding Mildred's killer."

"And you don't think the cops can do that?"

I saw movement out of the corner of my eye. Lydia had stepped off the elevator. She saw me and motioned for me to come over. "Excuse me, Mr. Ivy."

"I'm sort of busy right now," I said. "I thought you were still asleep."

"How could I sleep with you and Rip yammering in your room last night? I wish I could have been there with you."

"Why didn't you just walk in and join the conversation?"

"No, I'm talking about the Klan meeting. I always wanted to see a real Klansmen. Those guys are creepy."

"You were eavesdropping?"

"I was honing my investigatory skills. I wanted you to know that while you were hanging out with the Klan, Uncle Jacko called again last night. My immigration contact called him with more information. She found a Karl, with a K, Franklin Wilner who immigrated into the US by way of New York in 1945. She's doing some more digging. I'm on my way to see her. "

"It's barely seven o'clock."

"She likes me, so she's making time to see me."

"You're not leaving this hotel alone. Have you forgotten? We'll go together."

"I'm not leaving alone. Uncle Jacko's picking me up. What's going on? Who's that guy you're with?"

"Mildred Threadgill's brother."

"The guy who was at the Klan meeting last night? He looks shifty."

152 | KATHLEEN KASKA

The concierge walked up. "Miss Lydia, your ride is here."

"I'll meet up with you later." Lydia gave Elliott Ivy the evil eye on her way out the door.

"Try to stay out of trouble," I called and returned to interrogate Ivy.

"Sorry about the interruption," I said.

"Was that child dressed in a pirate's outfit or am I hallucinating?"

Explaining Lydia's behavior would take all day. "What do you really want from us, Mr. Ivy, because I'm about ready to tell this all to the police?"

"We don't want you to go to the police with any of this."

"We, as in you and Walt Garrison."

"That's right. Things are complicated."

"Tell me about Karl Franklin Wilner."

Ivy did his best to feign ignorance, but the flush that colored his face told me I'd struck a chord.

"I don't know anyone by that name."

"Let me help you with that. I think Karl Franklin Wilner and Frank Anthony Threadgill are the same person. There's no record of a Frank Threadgill immigrating into the US, but Karl Franklin Wilner immigrated in 1945."

"A lot of people immigrated in 1945. That means nothing."

"Except that one of the men who is connected to Lavine Rose's murder is familiar with the name Karl Wilner. Mr. Ivy, my fiancé is sitting in jail right now. He's been arrested for Rose's murder and your sister's. We both know he did not kill those women. If I can't prove his innocence, he will be charged."

"I'm sorry, but I've told you everything I know."

"You leave me no choice but to have another talk with Walt Garrison."

"If I were you, I'd leave Walt Garrison alone. He's a loose cannon, and going to the police at this point will make things worse. I need time. You'll have to trust me. And if I were you, I'd watch out for Detective Bergeron. I can't say more."

"Let me remind you that you are the one who opened this can of worms."

Our breakfast arrived and we both pushed our plates away, although I wanted to fling my eggs benedict in his face. My gut told me to trust the guy. My heart screamed no.

Tap, tap, tap. *Noooo! Not again*. I turned to see Ruth marching toward the table. With the most determined look I could muster, I motioned for her to sit at the next table. I couldn't believe she was up this early. Miracles never cease. But there she was— hair coiffed, make-up perfect, dressed in an outfit that looked as if it came fresh out of a Neiman's box. She opened her mouth. I bared my teeth. Nodded at Ivy. Pointed to my ear. The sun was barely up and I received another miracle. She got the message and took the table behind Ivy.

"I shouldn't have asked you for help," Ivy said. "That was a mistake."

"Too late to turn back now. I'll give you two days to figure this out. If I don't hear from you, I'm going to the police. I might not have a lot of proof, but soon, very soon, I will." *Lie*. "And I can deal with Bergeron." *Another lie*.

"I seriously doubt that." Ivy gave me a long hard look and left.

"Follow him," I said to my cousin.

Ruth was out the door in a flash, the high heels announcing to the entire world she was on a mission. Jeez!

CHAPTER TWENTY-SEVEN

I had to wait until the prisoners finished breakfast before I could get in to see Dixon. In that time, I rehearsed what I'd say so I could get it all said in our allotted time. I needed to catch him up and listen to his suggestions. It was hotter in here than yesterday. The door to the police station was open to the outside. Little good did that do. The storms that blew through sent the humidity sky high.

Dixon was stripped down to his undershirt. Sweat ran down his face. His five-o'clock shadow had turned to stubble, but otherwise he looked good. Despite his situation, he greeted me with his cool, sexy smile.

"How was breakfast?"

"Cold coffee, cold oatmeal, cold toast, but who's complaining?"

I filled him in on what had happened since I last saw him. It was hard to believe it was less than twenty-four hours. I related everything in as few words as possible—chasing Bugger, finding Vinny lying dead in a house near the canal, and stumbling upon a Klan meeting.

"That checks out with what Lydia told me," he said.

"She was here?"

"She just left."

"They let her in here to see you this early?"

"We're talking about Lydia. Who's ever stopped her from anything?"

"Her independence is going to get her in trouble."

"She's never been disciplined. You can't expect her to learn now."

"No, but I am responsible for her. I can't wrangle her in while trying to get you out of jail."

"She's leaving soon."

"Not soon enough. This situation is bad. Another murder and I can't go to the police."

"It's worse." He sat down on his cot. Ran his fingers through his hair. The front he displayed moments ago had disappeared. "The lawyer, Jake Noles, came to see me. Nice guy. But the judge denied bail. Noles said he wasn't surprised since I'd been arrested for a double murder charge. Seems the judge hates PIs more than Bergeron. Noles is working on getting me out though. He's going to put pressure on the prosecutor to charge me or let me go. He agreed the evidence against me is flimsy. Keep your fingers crossed that he knows what he's doing."

"Marcella recommended him, so that's a big plus."

"You're right. Okay, let's think. We need to tell the cops about the body you found."

"How do I do that without implicating myself? Once the cops find the body and it hits the paper, which will probably happen this afternoon, tomorrow morning at the latest, the cabbie who drove me will contact the police and report that he drove a tall red-headed woman to the house and watched her go inside."

"So keep quiet about it for now. In the meantime, try to find out more about this Bugger guy. Pray his dead mother is still talking to him. Once he stews over Vinny's murder, he might be willing to talk to the cops. Don't worry about hiding your involvement in all of it. It can't be helped. How long do you think Vinny had been dead by the time you found him?"

"I'd say no more than a couple of hours."

"Bugger could have done it before he came to see you."

"I seriously doubt it. Bugger was terrified of Vinny coming after him."

"Now, listen, I need you to be at your best and stop worrying about me and pray that Ruth does not get herself kidnapped again." He managed a laugh, then his brow knitted. "So, do you think Elliott Ivy is behind this?"

"I'm not sure, but he's certainly involved. I want to trust him, but I can't."

"See what happens. He's given us a lot to go on and that's what we need. Get what you can out of Bugger."

"Rip was going to the hospital this morning to see him. I'm going there too as soon as I leave here."

"Okay, don't waste any more time here. Remember my friend from the Houston Police Department who put me in touch with Billy when you were in trouble in Palacios?"

"I remember you calling him."

"The cop's name is Greg Stower. He's now a US marshal. He still owes me favors. Give him a call and ask him to see if Karl Wilner has a record. It might be a dead end, but it's worth a try. Call Stower right away."

"Dixon, I'm worrying about Detective Bergeron. We can't trust him. He's a Klan member and he might be involved in all of this."

"There's nothing we can do about it now."

"Maybe I should call Billy to come and help."

"I thought of that, but who knows what could happen by the time he gets here. We don't have time to wait. Besides, I'm sure he has his hands full with getting the office up and running after the fire."

"I'll call and see how things are going with the Nash case."

"Hon, don't worry about what's going on in Austin. If things weren't going well, he'd contact us. We have a pretty reliable team. Besides, the Nash case is small potatoes. I'm glad you found Rip and that he's willing to help. You have Ruth too. And Palmer's coming to get Lydia. That's good. She's been a big help, but we can't put her at risk. And with her gone, you can stop worrying about what she does. Also, find out what's going on with Walt Garrison. He's our common denominator."

"All three murders are linked to him."

"Right. You and I were almost numbers four and five. Whatever you do, do not do it alone. Hear me? Take Rip with you. Leave Ruth at the hotel and tell her to keep looking there. You did good, Sydney."

"Not good enough. You're still in jail."

"That can't be helped. Call Stower first. What's your next move?"

"Pascal and the bloody knife."

"Be careful, hon." He stood, leaned against the bars, and reached for my hand. "You have a wedding to attend."

CHAPTER TWENTY-EIGHT

Much to my surprise and also my relief, I found Lydia up in the room.

"How's Dixon?"

"Don't give me that, 'how's Dixon?' You and your Uncle Jacko were supposed to meet your contact at the immigration office, but instead you sneaked off to the jail to see Dixon."

"Not true. I did see Dixon, but only for a minute, and I didn't sneak. I never sneak, because I'm not a sneaker. I had some time to kill before I went to the immigration office. And the reason I went to see Dixon was because I wanted to see if your assessment of him matched mine. He tried his best to look upbeat, but I could tell he was worried."

"Of course he's worried. But I don't want you running around haram-scarum, or ambling around New Orleans, taking in the sights along with way."

Lydia looked me straight in the eye. A cold hard stare. I might have pushed the girl too far.

"In case you're interested, Karl Wilner seemed to have disappeared after he arrived in this country. Now for all my hard earned information, I think I'll just amble down to Pat O'Brien's and knock down a few Hurricanes."

"Are you serious? It's way too early for that." There it was—a smile—an itsy-bitsy Lydia smile.

"Prepare yourself. I'm about to hug you."

Lydia pulled out her gris gris and waved it.

Little Miss Voodoo and I went downstairs to the kitchen where Lily was helping herself to a plate of macaroni and cheese. I took it out of her hands and set it on the counter. "I wasn't finished," she said.

"It can wait. Where's Chef Pascal?"

"I saw him walk out into the garden. Is this about the bloody knife?"

"What do you think?"

"I'm not missing this," Lily said, and followed us outside.

We found Pascal sitting on the garden wall smoking a cigarette. Lydia pulled out her notebook.

"Go away. Pascal is very sad. Lavine, my little friend, is dead. The police were here again. She would not listen to Pascal. She would go to clean rooms while guests were out and she would take things. I warned her, but she would not listen." Pascal wiped away a tear. "I try, but I cannot help everybody."

"So, she must have let Mildred Threadgill into our room."

"I don't know, but if Madam Threadgill paid her, then maybe yes."

"Can you explain why the murder weapon, a knife, was found in your locker?"

He stubbed out his cigarette. "You play games with Pascal," he said.

"Someone found it in your locker yesterday, Pascal," I repeated.

"Are you the one who killed my cousin Mildred?" Lily said.

"I say phooey to all this murder and spying. Why would I kill that Mrs. Threadgill? I didn't know her. You think I stabbed her with one of my special knives and put it in my own locker. I do not even use my locker. And if I did, I would not put the murder weapon there. No one is that stupid."

"Whoever stabbed Mildred didn't use a chef's knife. They used a steak knife," I said.

"Look around. There are steak knives everywhere."

"Maybe you are the killer, Lily, and you tried to pin a donkey tail on Pascal."

"I had no reason to kill my cousin."

"But you gave Lavine the key and she let the killer in Mademoiselle Sydney's room."

"I did no such thing." Lily stormed out of the garden and went back inside.

"You are climbing up a wrong tree, Mademoiselle Sydney. I have work to do."

Lydia, good up to this point, snickered.

Pascal turned and paused and stared down at her. "And who is this *peu reine vaudou?* You are all a lot of crazy people from the Texas. I'm glad I do not live there." He stormed off too.

"That's French for little voodoo queen," Lydia said.

"I figured that much."

"You'd think after being in this country for a few years, one would have gotten a few simple aphorisms right," Lydia said. "Besides, I don't trust him. Serge says never to trust a Frenchman."

"But your father is first-generation French," I said.

"Right, now living in *the Texas,* so he should know. Since I'm stuck at the hotel, I'll continue to investigate the French chef."

"Ruth's domain, remember? Besides, the only investigation I want you to do is stay in the room in case anyone calls."

"I'll get claustrophobic."

"You'll survive. If I find out you left the room, I'll tell my mother you need help at the theater. She'll be waiting when you arrive back in Austin."

I straightened Lydia's turban. "My *peu reine vaudou.*"

Lydia made gagging noises on the way back inside.

BACK IN OUR ROOM, I CALLED Greg Stower's house in Houston.

"Stower residence."

"Mrs. Stower?"

"Yes, who's calling?

"This is Sydney Lockhart. I'm calling for Ralph Dixon. He's a friend of your husband's."

"I remember Mr. Dixon. Is everything okay?"

I wasn't sure how much to tell her, but I plowed ahead. "Actually, no."

"Oh, my. Greg is away on a fishing trip."

"This is important. Can you locate him?"

"Not by phone. I'd have to drive out to the fish camp, about eighty miles away."

"Mrs. Stower, Dixon, Ralph is in trouble. We're in New Orleans. He's been arrested and needs your husband's help as soon as possible."

"Oh my. There's a phone at the general store nearby where Greg is staying. I was going to drive out to the camp in the morning, but I'll call and leave a message for him that I'll be there today. He'd be more than happy to help Ralph if he can. What should I tell him?"

"Tell him we need to find out if a man named Karl Franklin Wilner has a criminal record. I suspect he's come into this country illegally about eight years ago under the name of Frank Threadgill. He's been living in New Orleans for a year. Oh, and ask him if he can check on a Walt Garrison too. He's also living here in New Orleans.

"Okay, how is Greg to get in touch with you?"

"Tell him to call the Pontchartrain Hotel. Dixon and I are staying there, or at least I am."

"Are you that redhead Greg told me about?"

"What?"

"Ralph told Greg he was seeing a tall, gorgeous, redhead who had turned his life upside down. In a good way, of course."

I was speechless. I couldn't picture Dixon having that kind of casual chat with a buddy. There was so much about this man I didn't know. I was flattered, and speechless. "I don't know about gorgeous, but that's me, Mrs. Stower."

"Call me Abigail. I'll go see Greg later today. I'm sure he'll come right back and start looking into it."

"Thank you so much. The conditions in jail are not good. Dixon's been denied bail."

"What is he charged with?"

"Two murders.

"That is bad. I'm on my way, but there's one condition."

"That is?

"We get an invitation to the wedding."

Abigail Stower hung up before she could hear me gasp.

CHAPTER TWENTY-NINE

Rip was slumped in a chair in the hospital's waiting room when I walked in. He looked as if he hadn't slept at all last night. "You haven't seen Bugger yet, I take it?"

"I caught a bus and got here early. Visiting time isn't until eleven. Fifteen more minutes. I don't know if we can see him though. The nurse kept telling me Bugger needs rest and not to disturb him."

"What's the word on your car?"

"It should be ready by the end of the day. The automotive shop had to search the city for the right tires."

"I saw Dixon this morning. A cop friend of his from Houston is going to see if he can find anything on Frank, like a criminal record. Lydia discovered that his real name is Karl Wilner."

A nurse came up and told us Bugger was awake. The doctor was happy with his progress, but we only had five minutes. The left side of Bugger's bruised, scratched, and swollen face looked as if it had been used for a punching bag. His head was bandaged to twice its size. His leg was in a cast and raised in traction.

"Bugger?"

He grappled for the buzzer to call the nurse. I beat him to it. "I want to help you, Bugger."

"Nurse," he cried.

I placed my hand over his mouth. "It's okay, I'm not going to hurt you. Listen to me, Bugger, Vinny was killed soon after you left the house on Sister Street. I'm asking you again. Did you kill Vinny?"

His eyes widened. He shook his head.

"I'm going to remove my hand and you're going to answer questions.

"He'll find me," Bugger said.

"I told you Vinny is dead."

"Not him."

"Who?"

"The little man I saw, the one that was dressed like a doctor. The one who saw us put the body in the car at the appliance store." He dropped his head back and closed his eyes.

"Here, drink some water." I held a cup to his lips.

Bugger took a sip.

"Do you remember anything more about this guy?"

"No. Go away."

"Just a couple of more questions."

"Momma, Momma."

The nurse came in. "Ma'am, you're going to have to leave now. He needs his rest."

I doubted at this point I could get much more out of Bugger. I was almost out the door when I heard him say, "He was one of them fancy cooks."

"A chef? Bugger, was the guy you saw a chef?"

"You'll have to leave now. He needs rest," the nurse said.

RIP AND I TOOK A CAB BACK TO THE HOTEL. I was getting out of the car when Ruth walked up. "Any luck following Elliott Ivy?" I asked."

"I followed him to his house. He was in a big hurry. A few minutes later he came out and left. I grabbed a cab and followed him to his office. He works in the Philips Building on Royal. After an hour, I figured he was in for the day. I was about to tell the driver to bring me back here, when Ivy left. I followed him to the appliance store, where he stayed a few minutes and left again. This time someone was with him.

"Stocky guy, in his late fifties?"

"Yeah, that's him."

"Walt Garrison. Where did they go?"

"I lost them. My cab driver was a moron."

"I gave Ivy two days to tell me what he had on Frank before I go to the police. If he doesn't come through, we're stuck. Bergeron won't believe a word I tell him. Rip, stake out the appliance store. I'm going to stick around here for now."

Ruth reached down and massaged her foot. "I never believed I'd say this, but if I'm expected to follow someone, I need more comfortable shoes."

"That's a great idea, since everyone can hear your heels tapping from a mile way. I recommend saddle shoes."

"I'd rather go barefooted than look like a Mouseketeer. Oh, how's that guy I scared yesterday? The one who was hit by the car. Tell me he's not dead. I don't want to carry that guilt the rest of my life."

The only guilt I've ever heard Ruth confess to was not being the first shopper on Neiman Marcus' doorstep for a sale. A duty she took seriously. The faster she got into the store, the more money she could spend, guaranteeing the retailer more sales. Ruth alone can keep Neiman's in business.

"His name is Bugger. You can rest easy. Sweating in hell is not on your agenda. He's not dead, and it wasn't you who caused him to bolt."

"Who then?"

"Come up to my room and I'll tell you."

"I'm going to the restaurant. I skipped breakfast."

"Me too," Rip said.

"I'll go get Lydia and we'll be down right away. I hate leaving her by herself for too long."

"She's such a pain."

"Well, she is leaving to go home to Austin this afternoon. She's been a big help, but I'll feel better if she's gone."

"Amen to that."

"Oh, Miss Ruth Echland, you have a telegram," I heard the front desk clerk call out as I stepped into the elevator.

WHEN I GOT UPSTAIRS, I found the door to my room unlocked. I pushed it opened. Everything looked the same, but I'm sure I locked it behind me when I left. I knocked on Lydia's door. "Lydia?"

I knocked again, then ran inside. I prayed she was annoying the hotel staff, but I had a sinking feeling that wasn't the case. Lydia is too smart not to keep the doors locked. I ran downstairs and asked the front desk, kitchen staff, housekeeping staff, valet, doorman, bellman, the concierge, and office staff. No one had seen her. I ran back into the kitchen. The staff was busy finishing lunch orders. Pascal was nowhere to be found. I went into the small alcove where Lily handles room service orders. She was gone too. I shouted above the clattering of dishes and clanking of cookware. "Where's Chef Pascal?"

"He came in for a few minutes. Said he was feeling bad and left," one guy said.

"How about Lily Morton?"

All that got me was a few shrugs.

Back in the dining room, Ruth was digging into her Belgian waffles and Rip was smothering his eggs with catsup. "Oh, Sydney, something terrible has happened. Look at this!" She held up a telegram. "Because of bad weather, Palmer is unable to fly in to get Lydia this afternoon."

"I'd hate for him to make a wasted trip. Lydia's missing."

"She's probably at the voodoo shop selling dead toads to tourists," Ruth said. "Or she's in the mayor's office telling him how to run the city."

"I told her, under no circumstance, was she to leave the hotel."

"You might as well have sneezed in the wind."

"Spit in the wind."

"I . . . don't . . . spit!"

Rip began laughing so hard he almost choked on his eggs.

I took both of their plates and dumped them into a bus tub. I grabbed Ruth by the arm and dragged her outside. Rip followed.

"Ruth, I want you to go to Marie Laveau's House of Voodoo and see if Lydia is there. Rip and I are going to the appliance store. Wait. I have a better idea. Ruth, call the police. Tell them that your daughter is missing. Rip and I will go to the voodoo shop and take it from there. If something has happened to that girl, I'll never forgive myself."

"The police won't believe I have a twelve-year-old daughter. I'm too young."

"Then, tell them she's your niece, your sister, your cousin. I don't give a crap what you tell them, just get them to start looking for her."

CHAPTER THIRTY

Frida Mae had not seen Lydia. We stopped at Pat O'Brien's. No one there had seen her. Rip and I stood outside, looking up and down Bourbon Street. "You really think someone took her?" Rip said.

"I hope to God that didn't happen."

"Maybe she's visiting Dixon again, or maybe she went back to the immigration office, or the appliance store.

"Okay, panicking is the last thing I need to do. Let's check those places."

"Another murder in the city," shouted a newspaper boy. "I tossed him a nickel and grabbed a paper. "Change of plans. Vinny's body has been found. I'm now on the run. Let's check out the immigration office before I have to go into hiding."

"DON'T WORRY, SYDNEY," RIP said. "We'll find her."

The clerk at the immigration office who helped Lydia was there, but Lydia hadn't been in today. I kept seeing her bounded and stuffed into a tow sack in some back room in Threadgill Appliances or worse, floating in the river. What will I tell Serge? How could he let his young daughter do as she pleased her entire life? I ran back to the car. Next stop, the appliance store. I didn't care what happened to me the last time I was there. Lydia was now my top priority.

WALT GARRISON, BUG-EYED AND pale, backed up against the wall behind his desk. "Who are you? Put the gun down."

"You don't remember me, Mr. Garrison? I was here shopping for appliances. Your salesman Mr. Wells was helping me pick them out."

"Mrs. Dixon."

"Surprised to see me? If you're going to hire thugs to do your dirty work, make sure they have IQs higher than fifty."

"If you're not happy with your appliances, I'm sure we can work things out without the situation turning violent."

"Cut the crap, Garrison. I swear I'll blow a hole in your head if I don't find that girl."

"I don't know what you're talking about, Mrs. Dixon," he said.

"Oh, but you do! And my name is not, Mrs. Dixon," I screamed. "I don't know what you've got going on here, but I'll get to the bottom of it if it's the last thing I do." I moved closer and held the gun higher. "Where's Lydia?"

"I don't know anyone named Lydia."

"You took her from the Pontchartrain Hotel, or had someone take her. My friend is searching your warehouse now."

"Your friend will find nothing."

"I know you killed Lavine Rose and your foreman. You tried to have me buried alive. You're responsible for killing Mildred Threadgill, and you're the reason an innocent man is in jail. And it's not beyond you to abduct a young girl."

"You've lost your mind, lady. None of that is true."

"Tell it to the cops."

"Sydney." Rip walked in. "She's nowhere around."

"Did your foreman take her to the swamp and bury her like he tried to bury me?" I aimed the gun between his eyes. I knew at that moment the last vestiges of sanity had slipped away. Killing him was all that mattered. If Lydia was dead, I didn't care what happened to me. I squeezed the trigger. The bullet whizzed past Garrison's head and hit the picture hanging on the wall. The next thing I knew, I was on the floor. Rip had torn my gun from my hand and had it pointed at me. Garrison made a move toward his desk. Rip turned and fired a shot, blowing the intercom on the desk to pieces. He backed up, reached behind him, and locked the office door.

"Keep your hands up, Mr. Garrison," he said. "Sydney, are you alright? Killing him is not going to help us find Lydia."

"You fools," Garrison said. "The police will be here any minute."

Someone started banging on the door. "Mr. Garrison? Is everything okay?" a woman called. Rip grabbed my arm and pulled me behind the door.

Garrison glared at me, then Rip. A look of resignation on his face. "Yes, Mrs. Seger." He walked over and unlocked the door. "My gun went off by accident."

"I didn't know you had a gun here, Mr. Garrison," Mrs. Seger said.

"I brought it from home this morning. There was an attempted break-in last week and I wanted the gun here just in case."

"I heard two shots," she said.

Garrison held out his hands in surrender and managed a sheepish smile. "I'm not too good with a gun, eh?"

"I'll send in the janitor to clean up," she said.

"Not necessary. He will think I'm an oaf. I will take care of it." He shut the door. We listened as her footsteps sounded down the hall. "My bookkeeper did not believe me," he said. "The police will come."

"We'd better leave then," I said, and nodded toward the door.

"I'm going nowhere with you."

"You don't have much choice."

Rip drove. Garrison rode shotgun, and I was in the back with a gun to the back of his head.

"Where are we going?" he said.

"To see Elliott Ivy," I said.

"He will tell you nothing."

CHAPTER THIRTY-ONE

Ivy was in his office, arguing with someone on the phone when we walked in. He turned and slammed down the receiver. "You were going to give me two days, Miss Lockhart. Walt, what are you doing here?"

"Things have changed," I said. "Walt is here against his will." I nodded to Rip who was now holding the gun on Garrison. "A young friend of mine, the pirate girl you saw this morning, has disappeared. Regardless of what Mr. Garrison says, you and he are responsible. If you've harmed her in anyway, your bodies will be the next ones buried in the swamp."

"For God's sake, what is she talking about, Walt?"

"Do not tell her anything," Garrison said. "I am warning you, Elliot. Do not let this woman and her big man with the gun frighten you."

"Things have gotten out of hand. I don't know where to turn, Walt." Elliott said. "They might be able to help."

"Yeah, I'll help. I'll help by going straight to the police," I said. Walt Garrison made as if to strike me, but Rip stepped between us.

"For God's sake, Walt, get a hold of yourself."

"You are not calling the shots here, Elliott," Garrison said.

"When you came to me for help, my sister was still alive and so were the others. They've been murdered, and the situation is rapidly growing worse. We have to do something. This has gone too far. The police—"

"I've gone over this with you before. Going to the police at this time will make things worse," Garrison said. "You will stand a good chance of being arrested on federal charges. And you,

Miss Lockhart, will look like a fool. I can easily arrange that."

"Idle threats don't scare me, Mr. Garrison," I said.

"Stop it!" Elliott said. "She knows way too much. She knows Frank was not from Belgium, that his real name is not Frank Threadgill, but Karl Wilner."

"Shut up," Garrison shouted.

"Karl Wilner was from Austria," Ivy said to me. "How he got into this country, we're not sure, but it doesn't matter at this point. Right after my brother-in-law died, Walt came to see me with this wild story."

Walt Garrison slammed his fist on Ivy's desk.

"There's no other way," Ivy said.

"You do not have the authority to do this, Elliott. I should have never brought you in."

"It's too late now. My sister's been murdered."

Garrison looked at Rip. "I will let this man shoot me before I talk." His face, now scarlet, his body tremoring in anger, his eyes glued on Ivy, as if daring him to say another word.

"Walt is working for the government, tracking illegals who have come into this country after the war. Frank, or Karl Wilner was one of them."

"You will regret this!" Beads of sweat broke out on Garrison's forehead.

"I already do," Ivy said.

"Are you part of McCarthy's hunt for communists?" I asked.

Garrison threw his arms up in the air and let out a string of expletives. "It's not radical American citizens we are concerned about. I can't tell you more."

"Garrison's people tracked Wilner to New Orleans. He came here because there are others of his kind, illegals. Garrison's agency is afraid these people will start trouble."

"IVY, THIS IS TREASONOUS!"

"Wilner was helping fund a group that was bringing others like himself into the country. They are up to no good. You see, Frank was a war criminal."

"Since he changed his name and came here illegally, I didn't think Karl Wilner was here seeking the American Dream," I said.

"Garrison?" Ivy said. "Tell her."

"This man with the gun must leave the room," Garrison said.

"Aint't gonna happen," I said. "I will go the police, I swear. So sit down and start talking."

Garrison deflated. "If I find out you spoke to anyone about this, I promise you will be staring at the dank walls of a prison cell for the rest of your life, if you are lucky. That goes for you too, Elliott, and you, big gun man. And that's not an idle threat." He got up, locked the office door, and began his story.

"I've been investigating Wilner for some time now, from New York to New Orleans. He is a threat to the government, but he is slick. I could not pin anything on him. My job was to bait him. He had just put his appliance store up for sale. As an excuse to find out more about him, I offered to buy it. While we negotiated, I worked on gaining his trust. Knowing his background, I made up a story about immigrating here to make a better life for myself, how I'd lost everything in Germany due to the war. But after a while, I realized that life in this country was in many ways worse. I told him I'd been a successful business man in Bonn, but here in America I could not find work. I took menial jobs, scraping by until I saved a little to start my own business, but every bank I went to turned me down for a loan. I continued to work and save. I invested most of what I had, and the money grew. I told him I had enough for a down payment and that I'd found a bank willing to loan me the rest. This was all a lie, of course, but Wilner began to trust me."

"You bought his appliance store to gain his trust?"

"You don't understand the gravity of this. At first I had no intention of buying the store. While we were still negotiating, he began to confide in me. One evening he invited me out for beer. As we talked, he became more comfortable, telling me how much we had in common. After a few more visits he told me about the group, Foreign Americans for Justice, and that he used the store for a meeting location.

"You've got to be kidding," I said.

"If you want to hear this, keep your snide comments to yourself, Miss Lockhart. The FAJ is a covert organization. I will say no more about them. I went back to my agency with the idea to buy the store and join his group so we could continue to keep tabs on Wilner and the others. Soon after I signed the papers and took ownership, I suggested to Frank that his group continue to meet there. He liked the idea. This would allow us to monitor their activities from the inside."

"Why was he selling the business to begin with?"

"He needed the money for whatever he'd planned to do. That was the reason he bought the store in the first place. He was a smart businessman and knew he could turn the business around and make money."

I looked at Ivy. "You knew all about this?"

Ivy nodded. "Not until recently."

"Did Mildred know?"

"I'm not sure. I have a feeling she was in the dark about all this, until the day she was killed."

"Why was she still working there after her husband sold the business?"

"That was Frank's suggestion," Garrison said. "He said he wanted Mildred there to maintain normalcy around the shop. Upon hearing that, I was sure Mildred knew what was going on. A few of Frank's employees were members of FAJ. I think Frank planned to use her to keep watch on me. But two could play at this game. Having her close by would give me another outlet into who Frank was and what he was up to."

"And how do you fit in, Ivy?" I said. "Why did Garrison need your help?"

Garrison and Ivy looked at one another.

"Walt approached me at Frank's funeral," Ivy said. "He asked for my help."

"With Frank dead, the members became suspicious of me," Garrison said. "I knew there were some bigger players in this group. Frank had not told me enough. I needed to find out more. Mildred was leaving work one day and I asked her how she was holding up. She smiled and said, 'I've never been happier.' And I knew she wanted to talk. We went out for drinks. She told me how unhappy she'd been married to Frank and that she was looking forward to starting over."

"She must have known that her husband's bank account was empty," I said.

"She didn't know," Ivy said. "Frank's will was still in probate and she couldn't get access yet to his bank account."

"Mildred told me she knew her husband had secrets," Garrison continued. "She said he went out a lot at night. She thought he had another woman, and I realized that she was in the dark about who Frank was and what he had going on. So I was back to where I started. I called Elliott and told him that his sister was acting strange. We met and I confided in him. It was risky, but I needed to find out more."

"Okay, let's say all this is true, but you can't expect me to believe you didn't kill anyone. Lavine Rose's body was found in one of your storerooms and later dumped into the river."

"Frankly, I don't care what you believe, Miss Lockhart. I had no idea who that woman was or why someone put her body there," Garrison said.

"Then why did you have your foreman dump her into the river?"

"When I discovered her body in the storeroom, I had to get rid of it. You understand that I could not have police involved. I told Vinny to take the body to a nearby alley and leave it there. The place is not located in the best neighborhood. I told him to make an anonymous call to the cops and report the body, but then your partner showed up. Vinny panicked and, well, you know the rest."

"And what about me?" I said.

"What about you?"

"You told Vinny to get rid of me yesterday."

"I did no such thing. Mr. Wells, my salesman, mentioned to Vinny that his niece recommended the store to you. I knew Vinny did not have a niece, so I told him to find out more about you. I didn't tell him to get rid of you."

"Well, your foreman chloroformed me and took me out to a swamp. He told the thug who was with him to bash my head in and bury me. Luckily, I managed to escape."

Garrison blanched.

"I told you this entire thing has gotten out of hand." Ivy pulled at his hair and began pacing in circles.

"That's putting it mildly, Mr. Ivy."

"Vinny acted on his own," Garrison said. "I do not kill people or have them killed."

"Was Vinny a member of Frank's notorious group?"

"He was not. The arrogant bastard. The man was barely smart enough to tie his shoes."

"When was the last time you saw Vinny?"

"Yesterday."

"Do you know where he is now?"

"No, he did not come into work today. I hope he is long gone."

"You got your wish. Late yesterday afternoon I found him lying dead in a house in the Lower Ninth Ward. The guy who helped him get rid of Lavine Rose's body, the same one who tried to bash my head in in the swamp, is in the hospital recovering from being hit by a car, and he's talking." Not exactly true, but my words struck another chord. Garrison buried his head in his hands and groaned.

"Walt, are you responsible for all of this?"

"You know I'm not!"

"Miss Lockhart, I've known Mr. Garrison for only a short while, but this doesn't sound like something he'd do."

"Well, somebody did it! This is not getting me any closer to finding my young friend and getting my partner out of jail. Mr. Ivy, if Mr. Garrison is innocent you say, then how does the Klan fit in? You are both Klan members, right? That group is not beyond brutality and murder."

"I am not a member," Ivy said. "After we talked, Walt told me about Frank's involvement with the Klan."

"Frank asked me to join," Garrison said.

"Why?" I asked.

"Frank wanted me to help recruit. He joined to recruit Klan members for FAJ."

"From what I understand, the Klan hates the communists."

"They also hate immigrants, but they didn't know who Frank really was."

"Did Police Detective Bergeron know who Frank, or Karl really was?"

"Yes," said Garrison. "I will not tell you more."

I looked at Elliott Ivy. He shook his head.

"Explain to me why Mildred Threadgill was murdered."

"I do not know that either," Garrison said.

"Could the FAJ be involved?"

Garrison thought before answering. "I suppose it's possible. They were a radical bunch. Many were war criminals."

"Why was Frank's body removed from the casket and mutilated?"

"I have no idea," Garrison said.

I looked over at Elliott Ivy again. He was twisting his wedding ring around and around. I waited. A quiet tapping on his office window drew my attention. A persistent bee flung itself against the glass, unable to move forward. I could empathize.

"Tell me about the night Frank died."

"The night he died?" Elliott said.

"Yes, Sunday night dinner at your mother's house."

"We sat down to eat and he began having chest pain and died. It was horrible."

"How was he up to that point?"

"Frank hadn't been well. He'd had a few minor heart attacks and he began to go downhill after the last one. He didn't look good that night when he and Mildred arrived. Mildred went in the kitchen to help Mother with the dinner. I tried to engage Frank in a conversation, but he was in one of his ornery moods. I think he and Mildred had an argument before they came over, which is not that surprising. Mother had made her usual beef stew. Frank started eating and then set his spoon down. He took a few breaths and Mildred asked him if he was okay. She suggested he take one of his pills. He rudely told her not to fuss. He started eating again and almost finished when the chest pains began. Then he gasped for air. Mother jumped from the table to call an ambulance, but before she could reach the phone, Frank fell over. I loosened his tie and unbuttoned his collar, but within a few seconds, he stopped breathing. He had no pulse. It happened so fast. So, there you have it, Miss Lockhart, for whatever good that does."

"Everything that's happened has to be connected."

"You thought Frank was murdered? Well, now you know. He died of a heart attack. There is no connection."

"There is. Even if Frank did die of a heart attack. I'm trying to make sense of what happened in the cemetery. Still, why was his body pulled out and mutilated? Why were Mildred and Lavine Rose murdered? And most important to me, where is my friend?"

"I don't know what the connection is," Garrison said. "My advice to you is to stop nosing around and let me handle this."

"Frankly, Mr. Garrison, I think you know a lot more than you're telling me. And with Lydia missing, and Dixon in jail for murder, there's no way in hell I'm going to sit back and let you handle anything."

CHAPTER THIRTY-TWO

Rip and I left Garrison and Ivy to their clandestine operation. Their story was too bizarre not to be true. We couldn't hold them at gunpoint forever, and unless they left town, which was unlikely, I knew where to find them. When we returned to the hotel, I went to the front desk just as the desk clerk was hanging up the phone. "Oh, Miss Lockhart. That message was for you. I just finished writing it down."

I studied the note.

"It's in French," he said. "I had to ask several times before I could get it written correctly."

"I don't speak French," I said.

"I understand a little. This first sentence . . . Oh, I'm afraid my French is too lacking to get this right. It says, 'I'm wearing a . . . *toque blanche* and a *chef blouse*. A chef's jacket and hat?"

"Excuse me?"

"It also says, 'Jacques is with me. Don't worry. Your *peu reine vaudou*.' That means little voodoo queen."

I snatched the paper from his hand and stormed out the door. "Sydney, where to now?" Rip said.

"To Pat O'Brien's."

Once we arrived at the infamous bar, Claudia, the waitress, confirmed that Lydia had called Jacko to come pick her up at the hotel. She claimed it was an emergency.

"What's all this about?" Rip asked.

"Lydia, she's fine." I flopped down on a bar stool and dropped my head on the bar. "I don't know how much more of this I can take. I adore that girl, but I'm so happy she's returning to Austin."

"That's great news that she's okay, but what did the message mean? Are you sure that guy translated it right?"

"It meant that she's now dressed as a chef and that her friend, Jacko, is with her. But she didn't give a clue as to where she was going."

I ordered both of us a Hurricane, sucked mine dry in record time, and ordered another.

"How did you and Lydia become acquainted anyway?"

"I met her in a dark prop room in a theater one night. She was standing next to a guillotine and listening to a Billy Holiday record—'Blue Moon'."

"Oh, that makes perfect sense. Only you would attract someone like that, wouldn't you, Sydney?"

"Yep, as well as an ex-bouncer, who didn't know how to spell his first name."

"That hurt."

"I could strangle that child for scaring the crap out of me, but then again if she hadn't done that we wouldn't have had that nice chat with Walt Garrison and Elliott Ivy."

"You think Walt Garrison is the killer?"

"If the story he told us is true, I don't think he's guilty of murder or kidnapping." Without warning, a loud buzzing sound echoed. "What was that?"

"What?"

"That whining sound."

"I don't hear it."

My head spun and the sound grew louder. "Oh shit."

"You okay, Sydney?"

"Now I know why these drinks are called Hurricanes. I feel as if a swarm of wasps have taken up residence in my skull. Let's go. I need to find Lydia."

"You need to get something in your stomach first."

I laid my head down again to stop it from orbiting the room.

Rip ordered coffee and a plate of oysters. "Hopefully, the coffee will wake you up and the oysters will soak up the alcohol."

"I don't think it works that way."

"I heard oysters have medicinal benefits."

"They have benefits, but I don't think they are considered medicinal."

"When we're finished here, let's go back to the hotel. Maybe Lydia will be there."

"It's a good thing you're driving.

Two dozen medicinal oysters later, I paid the bill and we left.

RUTH WAS IN THE HOTEL LOUNGE, a bottle of champagne sitting in a bucket on her table. "You were supposed to be looking for Lydia!"

"I did. I didn't find her, so I'm celebrating."

"Ruth!"

"Joking, it was a joke. I told the police about my maid's missing daughter."

"Your what?"

"You heard me. I didn't want to claim her as my relative. They said to come back in twenty-four hours. That she'd probably gotten mad at her mother and she'd run way. I explained to them that we were visitors to New Orleans, so they said they would look around. You'd think children disappeared all the time in this city. You've been drinking—a lot—and you dare accuse me of not working the case when you and Rip seem . . . ripped?"

"I'm sober, Miss Echland. But Sydney needed a little something to calm her nerves. Lydia's trail led us to Pat O'Brien's. Don't worry, we're working the case."

"Oh, how convenient. Was Lydia tending bar or playing the jazz piano?"

"We didn't exactly find her," I said, "but she's with an adult."

"Who?"

"Jacko, the bartender."

Ruth motioned for the waiter to bring two more glasses. "See, Syd. I told you not to worry."

"Is that all you did today, was report Lydia missing and drink champagne?"

"No, smarty pants. I was in the kitchen slaving over a hot stove. With all my experience in hotel kitchens, I was able to fill in for Chef Pascal."

"Your experience consists of less than a week at the Driskill Hotel."

"That was enough to know all I had to do was boss everyone

around. It was fun. I helped out a little too. You know me, I like to be useful."

"You are amazing, Miss Echland," Rip said.

"Yes, Ruth, you are a marvel. Now, what did you find out?"

"Never put dry rice in the water until the water is boiling. A quarter cup of Tabasco sauce is too much to add to a large bowl of jambalaya, and never, never chop onions with a table knife. Oh, and wearing a boa while trying to cook doesn't work. I accidently chopped off the end and it flew into the sauce that was simmering on the stove."

"I didn't know that about the rice and water," Rip said. "I'll be sure to remember."

Uh, oh. Rip had that enchanted look in his eye whenever Ruth got going.

"The case, Ruth, the case."

"I'm getting to that."

"There was something odd about the maid who was murdered, Lavern Ross."

"Lavine Rose."

"Whatever. She kept to herself. The only person she spoke to was Pascal. Everyone said she was smitten with him, but Pascal ignored her. She always seemed on the verge of hysteria, like ghosts were following her. The dish-washer guy said she would come to the back where he washed the dishes and break down in tears every time she worked. No one seemed to know where she came from, just that Pascal got her the job. She was also a terrible maid."

"Interesting," I said. "Betsy said that Lavine had a boyfriend who was causing her a lot of grief. I'm not surprised if it was Pascal. It makes sense."

"So, you think Pascal is the killer?" Ruth said.

"Chef Pascal had the best opportunity to kill Mildred Threadgill and Lavine Rose. And he was seen at the Threadgill Appliance Store warehouse watching Vinny and Bugger move Lavine's body. If he and Lavine were involved romantically, he might have had a motive to kill her, but why kill Mildred Threadgill? But right now, I need to find Lydia before she gets into real trouble."

"How do we do that?"

"Easy, find out where Pascal lives. She's obviously on his trail. We'll ask the neighbors if they've seen a young blonde girl masquerading as a chef casing the neighborhood."

"Oh, I know where Pascal lives. And Lavine lived next door."

"What?"

"Pascal lives across the street from the Audubon Zoo. And Lavine lived in his garage apartment. I didn't know New Orleans had a zoo. I'm not a big fan of zoos. The one and only time I went, this monkey threw his feces at me. Ruined my Christian Dior suit. Can you believe it? *How rude!*"

An annoyed desk clerk walked over. "Miss Lockhart, you have a phone call. You can take it at the front desk."

"Don't go anywhere," I told Ruth. "I'll be right back." On the way to the front desk, the desk clerk reminded me that the front desk was not my personal office and he was not my secretary. How rude!

I stormed back to the table. "Ruth, you didn't see Lydia come into the kitchen this afternoon?"

"What?"

"You heard me! That call was from Jacko. I was right. He said Lydia found out Chef Pascal had left the restaurant early. She called Jacko to come get her. She'd found out where Pascal lived by bribing the sous chef. I can't believe you didn't see her."

"She could have come in, but if she was in one of her bizarre costumes, her own father wouldn't have recognized her. Where is she now?"

"Jacko's on his way back to work. When he left her she was up in a pecan tree across the street from Pascal's house."

"Well, at least, we know where she is," Rip said.

"In some pecan tree near the Audubon Zoo? That's a big help. Ruth, stay here in case she comes back."

Rip and I jumped from the table before Ruth could argue. The concierge was giving a woman directions to the French Quarter. After his third attempt, I pulled the stupid woman aside and pointed, "It's over there." I pointed to the east. "You can't miss it."

"Please, how do I get to the Audubon Zoo?" I asked the concierge.

"It's actually in Audubon Park down St. Charles Street about three miles. The easiest way is to take the St. Charles Streetcar. The St. Charles line is the oldest, continuously operating streetcar in the world, dating back to 1835. It's also the very first passenger railroad in the country."

I thanked him and told him I'd be back later for the rest of his history lesson. "Where's the closest stop."

"Right outside the hotel. It should be along any minute."

Two minutes later Rip and I were rolling down St. Charles. Giant oak trees lined both sides of the street, making a sultry day a little more pleasant. Now that I knew Lydia was safe, as safe as that pig-headed girl can be, I was able to breathe easier. Had I not been on a case, I would have loved strolling the neighborhood with Dixon. Seemed like our lives were one big continually operating case. Why couldn't Dixon and I have stayed at the Hotel Monteleone, or some place on Bourbon Street, or even in a tent? Why did I have to suggest we visit Rip? Would we ever be able to have a vacation, tie the knot, have breakfast on Sunday morning without being interrupted by a bullet whizzing through our window? Would Ruth, Lydia, and my mother ever leave us alone? It's like Dixon said, "It's what we do, hon." Why was he not sitting here next to me rather than Rip Thigbee, Finder of Lost Souls? Maybe that's what I am, a perpetually lost soul.

"Sydney, are you okay?"

"Just peachy."

We got off the streetcar at Exposition and St. Charles. The Audubon Zoo grounds appeared to cover a huge area, and across the street were at least a dozen cottage-style houses. Within two minutes, we spotted five with garage apartments. "I should have gotten more information before I took off," I said. Just then I heard the clatter and clank of the streetcar. "We're going to split up. You look for Lydia and Pascal."

"I don't know what Pascal looks like."

"Medium build, slim, dark hair, pencil mustache, and the telltale sign, a young girl dressed as a chef trailing him. Also, remember to look upward while you're checking out garage apartments. Lydia might still be in a pecan tree."

"Where are you going?"

"I taking this streetcar to the *Times-Picayune* to find out more about Frank's body. If you find Lydia, bring her back whatever it takes."

"That will be kinda difficult. All I have is a gun."

CHAPTER THIRTY-THREE

I walked into the newsroom and found Calvin Logan at his desk pounding away on his typewriter with lightning speed. A cigarette dangled between his lips and another one sat smoking in an ashtray. "Mr. Logan, I'm glad I found you here."

"Where else would I be? I spend more time here than at my apartment. In fact, sometimes I forget where I live. I'm glad you came by. I went to the Pontchartrain a few times looking for you, but you weren't there."

"You were looking for me?"

"I make a point to befriend as many detectives as I can. They're great sources of information. I hear your boyfriend is still in jail."

"He is. I need some information if you are willing to share?"

"You bettcha. Let's get out of here so we can talk. I'm in desperate need of a bottle of beer." He grabbed his notebook, a folded newspaper, plucked both cigarettes, and we left.

"My usual haunt is River Room, but if I bring a gorgeous dame like you in there, you'll have every reporter in the city sitting at our table. Here, this place is quiet and no one will bother us."

I easily understood why we'd be left alone. Davy's Dive lived up to its name. It was almost empty, which I'm sure was due to the smell—that of a bus station restroom after rush hour. Calvin noticed my wrinkled nose and said, "You'll get used to it after a few minutes. What will you have?"

"A cola."

"That's no fun."

"I'm just now sobering up after imbibing earlier in the day."

"A woman after my own heart." He brought our drinks back, a bottle of beer, a cola, and two highball glasses with amber liquid.

"Bourbon shots. I get nervous sitting with someone in a bar who's not drinking." He handed one to me. "Cheers!"

What the hell? We clanked glasses. "Mind if I go first, Mr. Logan?"

"Be my guest, and please call me Calvin."

"What do you have on Frank Threadgill's resurrected body?"

"Not much. The cops don't know shit. All I got from them was that some vandals were out for a night of ghoulish fun."

"That doesn't sound like ghoulish fun to me. Although I've never done it, prying open a tomb and extracting a body from its coffin in a public cemetery must not be easy. How was his body mutilated?" I pressed.

"Cops wouldn't tell me."

"Sounds like someone hated Frank Threadgill enough to go to a lot of trouble to get revenge even after he died."

"I have a different theory. Did you see my photos in the newspaper?"

"I've been sort of busy."

He unfolded the newspaper he'd brought with him. "Take a look. See anything unusual?"

"He's stripped to the waist."

"What the photo doesn't show is that he was stripped period. All his clothes were thrown off to the side. I thought they might have been looking for something."

"Something that was buried with him, in one of his pockets? But they could have checked those without removing his clothes."

"Maybe they were being thorough."

"Did you know that Frank Threadgill wasn't his real name? It was Karl Wilner."

"That's news to me. Maybe someone wanted to keep his true identity hidden."

"By mutilating his body and making him unrecognizable?"

"But, look again. His face was untouched." He pointed to the photo.

"Why do you think they couldn't just wait and let the body deteriorate naturally?"

"Maybe they couldn't risk it. They feared that something would come to light causing the body to be exhumed."

"Where's the body now?"

"At the coroner's."

I wasn't sure how much to tell Calvin Logan. Most of what I learned from Garrison, I had to keep under my hat and definitely off the record, but I could start with the Klan. "What do you know about the local Klan?"

"Ah, nice bunch of fellows. I'd like to put them all on a ship and sink it in the Gulf. They were involved in some pretty nasty violence back in the thirties. Every now and then they do something despicable just to let the law-abiding citizens know they're still around. Last year they held a public rally in Jackson Square. They almost caused a riot. The police broke it up and sent everyone home. I haven't heard much from them since. Why do you ask?"

"Threadgill, or Wilner was a member."

"How did you find out?" Logan flipped open his notebook. I covered it with my hand.

"I can't tell you much. I'd be in a hell of a lot of trouble if I did."

"Hey, that's not fair."

"I know it's not, but once I solve this case, and I will solve it, I'll reveal a lot more. I can't jeopardize the investigation. I'm afraid Dixon will be arraigned. But when this is all over, the story is yours, and I promise it will be a big one."

"You've got to give me more than that, Miss Lockhart."

I spent the next several minutes giving him enough information from the story I'd heard from Elliott Ivy and Walt Garrison, without mentioning their names. I did tell him about the attempt on my life and how I believed it was connected with the recent murders.

The dull look in his eyes I'd seen earlier had morphed into a devilish spark. He called for another round of drinks, replacing my cola with a beer.

"Did you know Detective Bergeron is a Klan member?"

He downed his shot. I swear I could feel his adrenaline

pumping. "No, I didn't. If you didn't have a boyfriend, I'd kiss you. This is so much better than reporting on brawls on Bourbon Street and purse snatchings in the French Market. I'm glad I ran into you, but you could easily give a guy a complex. I live here, and you blow into town a few days ago and hand me a story I've been waiting for my entire career."

"You don't even know the details."

He raised his bottle. "Here's to the details."

"Listen, Calvin, you cannot leak any of this. If it gets out too early . . ."

"I know. I know. You can trust me."

"Good, because I need your help. You're from here. You can get information easier than I can. Right now I'm working with my zany cousin, a twelve-year-old girl whom I have no control over, and a rookie detective who's lived in New Orleans for less than a month. Of those three, I'd put my money on the twelve-year-old. Mildred Threadgill was murdered in our room at the Pontchartrain Hotel. Lavine Rose, a maid at the hotel, was also murdered. I'm not sure where, most likely in the hotel, but her body was found at Threadgill Appliances, wrapped in a burlap sack. She was thrown into the Mississippi River."

"I know that part, remember. The cops arrested your guy. But how did the girl's body get from the store into the river?"

"Dixon was at the store when he saw the guys put the body in the trunk and take it to the river. I later found out they were the appliance store's foreman, who was murdered yesterday, and a guy named Bugger who's in the hospital after getting hit by a car while I was chasing him."

"Damn, if you ever need a job, I'm sure I can get you on at the newspaper. How's your Dixon man holding up?"

"He's tough, but I have a feeling he's putting on a good front for my sake. Calvin, I can't let him down. How well do you know the coroner?"

"Well enough. He's always been willing to provide me with information when he can."

"I want to see the body."

"When?"

"As soon as possible. Do you think he's still there?"

"Let's go find out."

"Tell the coroner I'm your new trainee. I still do some reporting for the *Austin Statesman*. I still have my press pass."

"Woman after my own heart."

WE CAUGHT THE CORONER AS he was locking his door to leave. "Bad timing, Logan. I'm sure you want something. Come back in the morning." His gruff manner didn't bother Calvin.

"Come on, Joe. Just a few minutes. I'm trying to impress my new reporter. Don't make me look bad."

Joe turned. "You're a woman."

"I told you, Miss . . . Jones. This guy is sharp."

"You're a riot, Logan. Okay, five minutes."

The morgue felt like a meat locker and smelled like a butcher shop.

"We need information on Frank Threadgill. Anything you can give us?"

"The man died of a heart attack. His body was removed from his casket and acid thrown on it. What more do you expect me to know?"

"Acid?" I said.

"Yep."

"But you're positive he couldn't have died from anything else?" I asked.

Joe looked me up and down and frowned. He finally said, "When he died I took tissue samples and sent them out for analysis just to be thorough. But there's no doubt in my mind it was a heart attack. I'm surprised it hadn't happened sooner. He had major blockages in his arteries. I spoke with Threadgill's doctor when I signed the death certificate. The guy did not have long to live. Death was quick, which was no surprise. His doctor said Frank was taking nitroglycerin tablets. When he died he was out. His vial was empty."

"That's odd, don't you think?" Calvin said.

"I thought so too, but his doctor said Frank wasn't diligent about taking them. He didn't take his medical condition seriously. He let his prescription run out a couple of times before."

"So the tissue samples didn't show anything?" I asked.

"They came back last week, but I haven't had time to look at them. We've had two murders and a suspicious death. A hobo was found near the train tracks. The cops weren't sure if it was an accident or foul play. I'll take a look at them on Monday morning."

"Any chance you can do it sooner?" Calvin said.

"You're asking for a lot of favors," he said.

"It's important. I'll make it up to you. A steak dinner."

"I'm not making any promises. In case you didn't know, this is the weekend."

"If you wanted a Monday through Friday job, Joe, you would be working in a bank."

"Anything else you want before I go home?"

"Yeah, can we see the body?" Calvin asked.

"Two steak dinners." After much grumbling, Joe pulled open the drawer and rolled out Frank Threadgill's body. "I'll warn you. It's pretty ugly. The body was embalmed, but this being New Orleans, and with our high water table, decomposition is much faster." He flipped off the sheet. Threadgill's burned skin from the neck down looked more like charred, yet soggy tree bark. His face had been spared the acid, but mold had started breaking the skin. I bent over and scanned the body closely.

"What are you looking for?" the coroner asked.

"Any marks on the skin," I said. "Like a tattoo or birthmark."

"You can see for yourselves. The acid burned deep. Any marks on the body are gone."

"His face wasn't touched," I said. "Why would someone do that?"

"My job involves the what. I examine the body and report my results. It's the cops who figure out the why. I have to admit, though, this entire thing is odd even for New Orleans."

"What kind of acid was used?" I asked.

"Probably hydrochloric or sulfuric by the looks of it, a high concentration. You can see the severe chemical burns."

"Where could someone get ahold of a high concentration?" I asked.

"It's readily available from an apothecary or maybe even a parfumeur."

"How much would it take to do this damage?"

"Eight ounces would do it."

"Are there any apothecaries in New Orleans?"

"Are you kidding? You must not be from here. Go to the French Quarter and throw a stone and you'll hit one."

"Pick one."

"I'll do better than that. I'll give you three. My favorite, Ringlee's Parfumeur, is on Chartres Street right off St. Louis. There's one on Iberville right before you get to the river. Can't remember the name. And somewhere off Royal west of St. Philip Street is a place called Mademoiselle Marjou."

"One more thing. Did the police ask you about the acid?"

"No."

CHAPTER THIRTY-FOUR

Calvin Logan and I stepped outside. I took a deep cleansing breath, but the morgue odor penetrated my clothes. Calvin lit up. "What are you thinking?"

"According to Rip Thigbee, Mildred Threadgill got a phone message telling her that Frank will not take something to his tomb. Take what to his tomb? Perhaps someone else knew that Frank wasn't who he said he was and didn't want his true identity known, which a birthmark or tattoo would reveal."

"That makes sense," Calvin said. "Who's Rip Thigbee?"

"The local detective I told you about. His agency is called Finder of Lost Souls."

"You're kidding me. That place is for real?"

"For me, everything started there. He helped me on a previous case. Dixon and I stopped by to say hi right after we arrived. His girlfriend/receptionist was frantic because he was supposedly missing. Long story. Anyway, when we returned to the hotel, we found Mildred Threadgill's body in our room."

"Damn. Think the cops know that Frank Threadgill wasn't his real name?"

"Good question. I'm not the person to ask them."

"Surely, Detective Bergeron sees the connection with what happened to Threadgill's body and the murder of his wife and Lavine Rose. This should lend doubt about your boyfriend's guilt."

"He might be pursuing other leads, but I doubt it. Dixon shouldn't have been arrested in the first place. We were together at the cemetery attendant's building when Mildred Threadgill was murdered. I was inside talking to the attendant. Dixon was just outside the door, smoking a cigarette, but the guy claims he didn't see Dixon."

"You think he was lying?"

"I don't know, but I'm damn sure going to find out. Let's see if our luck holds."

I WAS DELIGHTED THE POLICE put a twenty-four hour watch on the cemetery. A light was on in the cemetery register's office. Calvin waited in his car while I went in to talk to the attendant. He was dozing in a chair. A half-eaten sandwich and a thermos sat at his elbow on a table. He almost fell over when I walked in. He gained his balance and looked around as if he didn't know where he was.

"I hope you're not the only one surveilling the cemetery."

He rubbed the sleep from his eyes. "I'm earning time and a half," he said. "Hey, wait. The police were here asking about you and that fellow you were with a few days ago."

"You saw him?"

"Yeah, he was standing outside when I was showing you where Threadgill was buried."

"The police told me you didn't see him," I said.

"I told them about you coming in and that there was a man with you, but that I didn't get a good look at him."

"Did they ask if you could identify him?

"No."

"I pulled my wallet out of my bag and slipped out Dixon's photo and showed him."

"Yes, that could possibly be him from what I saw. Why?"

"Because he's been arrested for murder, which was committed at the exact time we were here. You were able to give me an alibi, but not my friend."

"Oh, no. I had no idea." He rubbed his hand across his forehead. "I'm so sorry. They just asked me if a woman and man came here on Wednesday morning asking about Frank Threadgill's tomb. I said yes. The detective asked me for a description. I told them what you looked like, but that I couldn't see the man that well."

"That's all?"

"Yes, then they left. They couldn't have been here more than a couple of minutes."

"With all that's happened, maybe your memory was jarred. You might want to tell the police this."

"I really didn't see much. I can't help you. Hey, you weren't the one who disturbed Threadgill's tomb were you?"

"My friend was in jail when it happened. Would I be here asking questions if I had tried to get to Threadgill's body?" I couldn't keep my irritation down. The last thing I wanted to do is threaten the guy.

"I got work to do." He grabbed a flashlight and left.

I managed a thank you and bit my tongue from saying anything else.

"Any luck?" Calvin said.

"I can't believe this," I said. "Bergeron told me the attendant didn't see Dixon, but he did. He told Bergeron a guy was standing outside, but he didn't get a good look at him, so Bergeron didn't pursue it. I'm sure the attendant is hiding something, but when I pressed him, he clammed up and then asked me if I was the one who disturbed the tomb. With Bergeron being a member of the Klan, he must have known Frank. I had a suspicion that Dixon was set up, but I didn't believe it. Now, I'm certain."

"What are you going to do? Dealing with corruption in a police force is like fighting with the devil when you can't see him."

"Maybe it's not the entire force, but Bergeron will regret ever having laid eyes on me once I prove Dixon's innocence. Is there any way you can find dirt on Bergeron?"

"I never liked the guy, but I had no reason to think of him as corrupt. Finding if he'd ever done anything improper or illegal will take weeks or months, if ever."

"He's in the Klan. If that gets out, it could ruin him."

"Wake up, Miss Lockhart. I don't know about prejudices in Texas, but Louisiana is the deep south and racism is not often frowned upon, even with cops, especially the cops."

"I have to solve this case. And trust me, I will find the killer, and when I do, you'll have to report it too. Everything, even the corruption if there is any."

"I'll do what I can."

"Can you check out those apothecaries Joe mentioned? See if anyone has been in recently to buy a cup of acid."

"I will. I'll check out Bergeron too, but I have to be careful. If this thing blows up in my face, I may want the name of that newspaper you work for in Texas because my job will be over. I was not big fan of the New Orleans Police Department, but I relied on them for crime news."

The look on my face must have spoken volumes.

"I realize how that sounded," Calvin Logan said after a long silence. "Like I said, I'll do what I can. I don't think it's a good idea that you come into the newspaper office. Call instead. Tell the switchboard operator you are my sister, Sonya. The operator is known to listen in on conversations when she's not busy—a little vicarious entertainment. Here's my home phone number too."

"If you need me, call Rip Thigbee's."

I WALKED BACK TO THE HOTEL, hoping the fresh air would clear my mind. It was difficult to concentrate with Lydia sitting up in a tree somewhere spying on a possible killer. A block from the hotel I looked up to see Rip step off the streetcar. "Find her?" I called.

"Nope. I scanned every tree near the zoo. I think word spread through the squirrel community about some guy who was up to no good. I got plunked with a few pecans." He rubbed his neck. "And I'm going to have a stiff neck in the morning."

"Damn, Jacko should never have left her alone. What if something's happened to her? Go back to Pat O'Brien's and get Jacko to show you exactly where the house is. I have no choice but to go to the police."

"That's not necessary, Sydney. You call yourself a detective. You couldn't even find me." I looked up to see Lydia, sitting on the front steps of the hotel, sipping a cola. I pulled her to me and wrapped my arms around her. "I'm sorry. I was worried sick."

"Humph."

"I know you can take care of yourself. You've proven that many times, but this case involves three murders. At least one of those murders was committed here at the hotel, maybe two. I can't have you going off on your own even in this hotel. Whoever is doing this is desperately covering their tracks. Probably killing those who know too much."

"Pascal, the chef."

"How can you be sure?"

"He supposedly left work early today, but he didn't go home. I found his house, but he never showed up."

"Yes, I gathered that. Jacko mentioned you sitting in a tree across from Pascal's house. How long were you up there?"

"All afternoon and into the evening."

"Without a bathroom break?"

"One, thanks to the thick bushes near my stakeout location. But, I'm starving. I take it I missed Palmer. Oh well. The theater can get by without me until we solve this case."

"Lydia LaBeau! You were no more staking out Pascal's place than the man in the moon. That was an excuse not to go back to Austin."

"Would I do that? I'm not the conniving type like Ruth."

"That's where you're wrong. Ruth is predictable and painfully honest. You, on the other hand, are sneaky and sly. Palmer hasn't arrived yet because of bad weather. As soon as he does, you're getting on that plane." She turned and walked away.

"Where are you going?"

"Up to the room to clean up."

"You've got Spanish moss in your hair."

"Moss I can deal with. Leaves and bark in my pants are not acceptable. You can order me the fried chicken that's on the menu. I've heard it is excellent."

"If you can hang around in voodoo shops and Bourbon Street bars, you can order your own fried chicken."

CHAPTER THIRTY-FIVE

I tried to come up with reasonable excuses not to tell Dixon what I'd discovered since the last time I saw him. But I needed his strength. I hope he still had it. This time he took the news much better than I expected.

"Keep focused, hon. Find the killer, everything else will fall into place. Don't worry about me. But I want someone with you the entire time. Rip or Ruth, or that newspaper reporter."

"Calvin Logan."

"If he's willing to help, take advantage of it. This case has a lot of puzzle pieces. Don't worry about Bergeron. Stay out of his way. And above all, don't discuss the case with him if he contacts you. Like I said before, bring me the latest and I'll try to figure things out. It keeps me from going stir crazy. We have a few minutes. Have you heard from Greg Stower?"

"Not yet, but I've been all over the place. His wife said he was on a fishing trip, but she'd try to locate him. He might have tried to call. I'll let you know as soon as I hear anything."

We went over the facts again. On the way out, Dixon said, "Make good use of your team."

I laughed. "Is that what you call them?"

Team member Lydia, dressed in her voodoo queen costume was waiting for me at the front desk. She was sucking on a lollypop and chatting with Sergeant Jim.

"What are you doing, Lydia? I told you to stay at the hotel."

"You mean today too? I thought that was for yesterday only."

"Why? Why did I ever think you'd listen to me? Let's go."

"I do listen to you. I just don't follow instructions well. How's Dixon?"

"He's fine. He has faith in me. I wish I did. He's taking it much better than me when I was in jail in Palacios. Let's go. I have my work cut out for me."

"I'm glad Dixon's being optimistic."

"Actually, I'm concerned. He's almost too optimistic."

"That's a man for you. Acting tough to keep the woman hopeful."

"What the hell have you been reading?"

"It's that magazine, *Psychology Today*. Ruth left it in the room."

"You're smarter than any of that crap in the magazine. I didn't think you liked lollypops."

"I don't. Sergeant Jim gave it to me, and I was being nice. This thing is disgusting." She tossed her lollypop in the bushes. "I'm hungry."

"You're always hungry."

"I digest fast and I'm a growing girl."

Twenty minutes later, Lydia and I downed our coffee and two plates of beignets. "Feeling better?"

"Much. Thank you."

"You're covered in powdered sugar. Come on. I'm determined that last night will be Dixon's last behind bars. Let's see if Ruth turned up anything."

I OPENED THE DOOR TO OUR room. On the floor was an envelope that had been slipped under the door.

Lydia read the note. "It's from Lily Morton. She wants you to come down to guest services as soon as you can."

I slipped my gun from my shoulder holster and stuck it in my boot. "Let's take the stairs."

"We don't have much choice. Have you noticed the last couple of days that the elevator guy slides right on past the seventh floor?"

"It's probably a mechanical problem."

"Nope. This floor is now referred to as Murderer's Row."

"You're a hoot, Lydia."

"I'm serious. Most of the rooms on this floor are now empty. How old do you have to be to carry a gun?"

"Much older than twelve."

"That doesn't answer my question."

"How about this? You're nowhere near the legal age."

"I heard that in most states a parent or legal guardian could sign for their child to possess a firearm."

"That applies to hunting rifles and shotguns, not pistols." I wasn't sure that was true, but I needed to reroute Lydia's train of thought.

"Guess what? Sergeant Jim said that in Louisiana, parents or guardians don't have to sign for their children to possess a gun."

"I'm neither your parent nor guardian, so get that idea out of your head."

"If I'm going to help you with your cases, I'm going to need protection."

"Lydia, I've never asked for your help with our cases. You just show up." I made a mental note to warn Serge about this weapon conversation the first chance I got.

The door to the alcove where Lily Morton worked was closed. I knocked, but no one answered. I drew my gun and eased it open. Lily Morton was sitting in her chair, the phone receiver in her lap. In my experience, and I've gained a lot in the last few days, the blood that soaked her blouse was caused by a fatal stab of a knife.

I closed the door and wiped my prints off the doorknob. I grabbed Lydia by the arm. "Don't say a word," I whispered. "Let's go." We ran up the stairs to our room.

"What's going on, Sydney?"

"Lily Morton was stabbed. I'm afraid she's dead. The cops will be all over this place in a matter of minutes. I don't want to end up in jail with Dixon. I need to get out of this hotel."

"We can take the stairs and go out the back door near the kitchen."

"No, we'll go out the front door like nothing's happened. If Lily's been dead more than an hour, I might be okay. The switchboard operator would realize soon that Lily's phone was off the hook, so it won't be long before her body is discovered. I have the best possible alibi. I was at the police station. Besides, the doorman, concierge, and desk clerks saw us come in through the front door. They can vouch for me, but then again with Bergeron, that's not saying much. He discounted a witness who provided Dixon with an alibi. Bergeron's not interested in motives, and I can't trust him."

"Where to now?"

"You're going to show me where Pascal lives. If anyone asks, we're going to the zoo."

"I hate zoos."

"So does Ruth."

"I may have to rethink that."

"You're an odd child."

All was quiet in the lobby. Lydia and I climbed aboard the streetcar and took two seats at the end.

"I think Pascal's taken off," she said.

"You might be right. Hopefully Ruth might have learned something by now. She was in the kitchen filling in for Pascal."

Lydia rolled her eyes.

"This is our stop," Lydia said. "Pascal's house is two blocks away. Are we breaking and entering?"

"You can't be serious."

"Well?"

"I'll decide when we get there."

We stood across the street from Pascal's house. He lived in a modest wood cottage that looked like one you could buy from the Sears & Roebuck Catalog. The garage apartment was detached from the house and set back from the street. Bougainvillea grew along the front of the house, various other shrubs grew along the west side. Oak trees shaded the entire lot. It was the kind of place I could see Dixon and me occupying.

"That's my stakeout tree over there." Lydia pointed across the street. "Two mockingbird families live there. They weren't too happy when a blue jay couple showed up checking the tree out for a potential nest."

"Blue jays can be a pain."

"Tell me about it. The male dive bombed me a few times. An old couple lives in the house on the left. They sat on the porch all afternoon drinking wine, complaining about the heat. The house on the other side is for rent. Several days of newspapers are piled in the yard and the grass is a foot tall."

"Good. Let's check out the rental house and then make our way toward the garage where Lavine lived. You're my daughter if anyone asks. We're looking for a place to rent."

We walked up to the front porch and peered through the windows of the house for rent, then walked around the back. There was a line of tall hedges between Pascal's house and the neighbors on the other side. We would not be seen snooping around. "Let's see if we can get into the garage apartment first."

It was evident the police had been there. Fingerprint dust covered all the solid surfaces. Other than that, there wasn't much to see. Lavine had few possessions. "Looks like her stuff has been cleared out." There were no clothes in the closet or in the dresser. No photos, books, magazines; no jewelry box, no cosmetics of any kind. A faded yellow bathrobe hung on a hook on the bathroom door. Soap had dried in the dish. There was a towel on the floor. It smelled of mildew. "Sad," I said. "There's nothing here that can tell us anything about her, except that she didn't have much of a life. If Pascal was the boyfriend that caused her so much grief, I can empathize with the woman."

"There's a bottle of orange juice and an overripe banana in the ice box," Lydia said. "That's it."

"Pascal's house is next."

Pascal had planted a neat herb garden in his back yard. The basil grew in profusion, giving off a scent that made me think of lasagna.

His house was locked, but Lydia found a key in a pot of geraniums. I knocked, waited, then peered through the window and went in. The first thing I noticed was the aroma of baked chicken. Lydia noticed it too.

"He was just here," Lydia said.

I did a quick check of the house. The kitchen counters were crumb-free. The oven was slightly warm. In the bathroom, water droplets still clung to the shower tile. The towel hanging on the hook on the back of the door was damp. In the bedroom, the sheets were thrown to the side.

"Look in here," Lydia said. "The ice box is full of food—full bottle of milk, a plate of sliced chicken, dish of butter." She lifted the lid on a bowl. "Potato salad. There's a head of lettuce, some tomatoes, cucumbers, onions, and peaches in the crisper. Three cans of funny beer." She read the label. "From Mexico. What's this?" She unwrapped a wedge of cheese. "Eww, smelly." The cupboard held a loaf of bread, jar of peanut butter, jar of fig preserves, can of coffee, bottle of olive oil, and a bottle of white wine vinegar. The kitchen drawers were filled with the usual silverware, a couple of strainers, a whisk, an egg beater, and a larger-than-normal assortment of sharp and shiny knives. A shelf contained several cookbooks. I pulled one down. It was written in French and well-used, judging by the food stains on the cover.

"He's still around," I said. "He must have returned last night, or this morning. There's still some coffee in the pot. It's cold, but smells fairly fresh. This is puzzling."

"What were you expecting?"

"I expected him to be gone. I expected him to be the killer. Are you sure he wasn't here? Maybe you missed something sitting in that tree."

"I didn't. I even walked around the back. I never saw him come or go."

"Maybe he came home while you were on your bathroom break. Check his bedroom. I'll look in the other one." I found a desk and chair in the second bedroom. An old armoire took up most of the west wall. I tried the double door but it was locked. I turned the chair over, ran my hand along the bottom, pulled up the chair cushion, looked under the desk—no luck. There were no pictures on the wall to check behind.

"Just a few man clothes and a pair of dress shoes in here," Lydia called.

"Go back out and see if there's a car in the garage."

I searched the desk drawers. Except for a few utility bills in the first drawer, the others were empty. Lydia came back with a report that an old black Ford occupied the garage.

"Help me with the armoire. I want to push it from the wall. Be careful, it's heavy."

"What are we looking for?"

"A key to this thing."

We managed to scoot it away enough for me to see that there was no key taped to the back. "I'll see if I can pick the lock."

Ten minutes later, I had the contents of a large envelope spread across the kitchen table. It contained newspaper articles from Paris during the war, letters written to Pascal in French and some photographs. I doubted Lydia's French was good enough to translate, but it was worth a try. "Take a look at these. Can you read any of them? The newspapers were from the war."

"Yeah, I could tell by the two-inch headlines and the date. Tada! Look at this." Lydia had the newspaper open to a page showing several individuals, mostly headshots of men and women. She pointed to a photo. "Look at the names." Marcel and Louisa La Duc."

"The guy looks like Pascal. His parents?"

"Probably. From what I can tell, all these people are dead. Maybe victims of the war."

"Keep reading through it while I go through the rest of this stuff."

"This is sad. All these people were found in a barn. They'd been shot and killed by the Germans. Twelve of them. They were part of the French Resistance. I remember Dad telling me about this when I was little. He said these people were heroes. Sydney? What have you got?"

Horror stricken by the sight before me, I held up two photos. Lydia plucked one from my hand.

"That's the couple in the newspaper photo? Looks like they died in a fire. But the article said they were shot."

"Maybe both. Poor Pascal. We need to get out of here before he returns. I'll take another quick look around. Scan the newspapers and see if you can learn anything else, then put everything back in the envelope and put them back in the armoire."

"You don't want to take this?"

"No, we know where it is. I don't want Pascal to know we're on to him until I put some more pieces together."

We left through the back door. "I want to have a look at the car."

"The engine was cold. It hadn't been driven in a while. A fine layer of dust had settled over it. Pascal and Lavine probably rode the streetcar to work." I pulled down the garage door. "There's not much else here."

"Hello? May I help you."

We jerked around to see an elderly lady walking a spaniel. "Oh, you startled me," I said.

"What were you doing in Mr. La Duc's yard?"

"Oh, you caught us," I said, hoping I sounded innocent and embarrassed. "I'm afraid we were snooping. We're interested in this house that's for rent. I was just wondering if the garage went with the house."

"No, dear, that belongs to Mr. La Duc. You can't go wrong with this neighborhood. My husband and I have lived here for almost fifty years. It's peaceful and safe. No ruffians like in some other parts of the city. Where are you from?"

"We're here from Texas. My husband's taken a position in New Orleans. He's a doctor at Charity Hospital. My daughter, Lydia, and I are out looking for a place to rent."

"I'm Doris Irving. My husband, Lou, and I live in that house. This is Pookie."

Lydia walked over. "Is he friendly? Can I pet him?"

"Oh, he'd love that," Mrs. Irving said. "That house has been for rent for a while. The couple who lived there passed away and their children have been trying to rent it for several months." She softened her voice to a whisper. "If you ask me, they are asking too much."

"How much?" I said.

"Two hundred and fifty a month."

"Hmmm, that is a lot. I don't know if Ralph, my husband, would be willing to pay that much. But I love this neighborhood and since it's a safe place, maybe I can talk him into it. I like that it's across from the zoo. Isn't that great, Lydia? She loves the zoo."

I was certain the growl I heard did not come from Pookie. "I love watching the monkeys," Lydia said. "Especially when they are in the market for a mate."

I smiled. "Sorry, she's at that precocious age."

"I understand. Lou and I raised four kids. But I have to tell you." Mrs. Irving's friendliness fell to concern. "Nothing like this has ever happened in the neighborhood, but that young girl who lived in the garage apartment was killed, murdered. You might have read about it in the newspapers."

"I did. That was horrible. You mean *that* was where she lived?"

"Afraid so. The police don't know who did it, but I hope they find out soon. They were here all day asking questions. It was quite disturbing."

"Did you know her?"

"No, I think she was a friend or a relative of Mr. La Duc's. Both of them kept to themselves. They worked at that hotel down the street. I can't imagine what she got herself into that got her killed. Young women these days, working late at night, living all alone. Lou and I got married right out of high school. He is a wonderful provider. I never had to consider getting a job. So sad."

Lydia mumbled something about running her own theater. I pulled her hair. "Can we get a dog like this, mommy?"

"We'll talk later, sweetie." I pulled her hair again, harder this time. I looked up at the garage apartment. "Do you think someone broke into her apartment?"

"No, according to the police, she wasn't killed in the apartment. We were relieved to hear that. I'd hate to think of a murderer lurking in our neighborhood. Rumor has it, she was murdered at the hotel, just like the other woman. What's this world coming to?"

Pookie started barking and tugging at his leash. "Oh, this crazy dog. He sees a squirrel and goes wild. I better go before he pulls my arm from its socket. I hope I didn't scare you from looking into the rental. Like I said, nothing like this has ever happened before in this neighborhood."

"Thanks, Mrs. Irving."

"Bye, Lydia. If your family moves in, I'll let you walk Pookie anytime you want."

Lydia's growl had grown louder. "Say thank you, Lydia." I pinched her on the back.

"Thank you, Mrs. Irving," Lydia said through clenched teeth.

"Pookie looks like a watermelon with toothpicks for legs. He smells like an old dust mop." Lydia said once the woman was gone.

"Don't start. Let's go back to the hotel and hope that I don't get arrested for murder."

CHAPTER THIRTY-SIX

POLICE CARS WERE STILL OUT front of the hotel and two cops were guarding the door. I saw Rip talking to some people who were watching the melee from across the street. He saw us and walked over. "I see you found her," he said.

"It's more like she found me."

"Another murder."

"I know."

"Lily Morton."

"I know that too. I saw her body."

"Me too," said Lydia. "Another stabbing."

"The hotel is swarming with cops. They aren't letting anyone in or out. Last I heard the kitchen staff was all outside in back, guarded by several cops."

"Where's your car?"

"Around the corner."

"Okay, let's go. The cops are probably looking for me. Several hotel employees saw me earlier. That may be good or bad. Have you seen Ruth?"

"Nope. We can go to my office."

We climbed in Rip's car. Lydia in the front seat. I laid low in the back.

"Yoo-hoo."

"We almost got away," Lydia groaned.

"Sydney, where have you been?" Ruth said. "And why are you stretched out in the backseat. There's been another murder—Lily Morton."

"We know. Shut up and get in the car."

Rip took a left away from the hotel and wound back to the French Quarter. "I thought you'd be part of the kitchen crew standing in the back of the hotel."

"I got laid off before this mess happened."

"Did you add too much salt to the mashed potatoes?" Lydia asked.

"Oh, shut up. Anyway, Pascal is back."

"What? When?"

"This morning. He came in after going to the fish market."

"He's there now? Did you talk to him? Ask him where he'd been?"

"Of course, I did." She pulled a cigarette from her case and screwed it into her ebony holder.

"And?"

"He said he was at home yesterday. He twisted his wrist when he fell off his bicycle. He was afraid it was broken, but it was just a bad sprain. He was pretty useless in the kitchen, but he was shouting orders at everyone."

"He was not at home," Lydia said.

"I'm just telling you what he told me. His faced was bruised and his wrist was wrapped up. He could hardly move it."

"Did you see Lily Morton this morning when you were in the kitchen before you got *laid off?*"

"Yes, she clocked in around eight. Do you know what time she was killed?"

"Lydia and I got back around ten after seeing Dixon. We found that Lily had left a note under our door telling me that she needed to talk to me. So, she was killed between eight and ten."

Ruth leaned over to me and whispered, "Do you really have to salt the potatoes?"

At Rip's office, I had him call the newspaper and ask for Calvin. When he answered, Rip handed me the phone."

"Where are you?"

"At Rip's office."

"I was down at the police station. The cops are looking for you."

"I figured that. Is it safe for you to talk?"

"Right now it is, but I might have to hang up without warning. This is serious. As far as I can tell, they aren't interested in anyone else. You were seen at the hotel this morning. They searched your room. No matter what you do, you can't go back there. I don't know much more than that. What are you going to do?"

"You mean after my head stops spinning?"

"I know this is bad. Stay out of sight. Oh, I got some information on the apothecary shops. I went in to Mademoiselle Marjou's place. It was not the type of place where someone comes in and asks nosy questions, so I told her I needed some kind of acid to remove the rust off of my son's bicycle chain and asked what kind I should buy. She said hydrochloric would work. I asked for a bottle. She was out. Her shop was broken into about a week ago and her supply was stolen along with a few other chemicals I'd never heard of. Mademoiselle Marjou didn't even bother to call the police because they were useless she said. I had a feeling Mademoiselle didn't want the cops anywhere around her place. Judging by the heavy sweet, smoky aroma, I'd say she had just smoked a reefer."

"Broken into about a week ago. According to Betsy, that was about the first time Frank's tomb was disturbed. Good work, Calvin."

"Where will you be if I need to reach you?"

"I'll be at Rip Thigbee's apartment. It's upstairs above his office, next door to the House of Voodoo."

"I'm going back to the police station and make a nuisance of myself. Stay hidden."

Ruth, Rip, Lydia, and I crammed into Rip's tiny apartment and got down to business. "Pascal is behind this, I'm sure," I said. "I don't know why yet. He had the opportunity to kill Mildred, Lavine, and Lily. I'm not sure about Vinny Zimmer. Pascal immigrated to the United States about the same time as Frank Threadgill. That collection of newspaper articles, letters, and photographs he keeps hidden in his house fueled his resentment over what happened in France during the war.

"Ruth, think, is there anything Pascal might have said that can shed some light on this?'

"He said hardly anything this morning, except to shout orders at everyone. At first I thought it was because he wasn't able to work, but he was shaking with anger. Chefs have a reputation for being dramatic so I figured this was just the normal Pascal. But the line cook said that if Pascal didn't back off, he was going to quit. He said that Pascal had been hell to work with the last couple of weeks. He was so frustrated while he was telling me this, he almost dropped a full pot of boiling water."

"Jacko and I can tail the guy," Lydia said.

"Lydia, you don't know much about this Jacko fellow," Rip said.

"That's true," Ruth added. "You're just a child."

Lydia stood up. I swear I saw steam coming from her ears. "I know what I need to know." Lydia said. "I've already told Sydney all about him. I know Jacko's tough. He's a big, dumb, nice guy who's bored with serving drunks all day and night. I know he'll do whatever I ask him to do. I know I can trust him, otherwise I wouldn't have accepted his help. And I stopped being a child the day my mother died." She folded her arms across her chest and sat down.

Ruth opened her mouth, closed it, and had the grace to turn pink.

This was a side of Lydia I rarely saw. Losing her temper was out of character. I needed to get her back home to Austin fast.

"Forget Jacko for now," I said. Maybe we can use him later. Lydia, you and Rip go back to the hotel and see what's going on."

I waited until I heard the door slam downstairs and got ready to leave.

"I didn't know that about her mother," Ruth said. "That explains a lot, but I still don't like her."

I got up and looked out on the street. A taxi sat at the end of the block. "I'm leaving."

"Where are you going?"

"Where I can't be found. Where I can get to the bottom of this quickly. I want you to stay here and wait for Rip and Lydia to return and for Calvin Logan from the newspaper to call."

"Oh, sure, everyone else gets to do the important and fun stuff, while I sit around playing receptionist."

"It might not be fun, Ruth, but it's extremely important. If you get bored go down to the voodoo shop. Leave the door open so you can hear the phone ring."

"You're not going to tell me where you're going?"

"No, in case some bad guys come here and threaten to torture you unless you tell them where I am. This way you don't have to lie."

"As if lying was something I couldn't do well, as if lying was something that bothered me, as if not knowing where you are would keep them from torturing me."

"Good point."

CHAPTER THIRTY-SEVEN

I had to wait down the street and around the corner for about half an hour before the Irvings stopped piddling in their front yard. Finally, Mr. Irving went inside and Mrs. Irving and Pookie went for a walk. I went around to the back of Pascal's house. When I was certain no one was around, I dug the key out of the flower pot, and went inside. I locked the door behind me and made myself at home. Because of the most recent murder, chances were the Pontchartrain's kitchen would be closed for a while and Pascal could return any minute. When he did, I wanted to be ready.

I couldn't remember when I last ate, so I made myself a chicken sandwich, scooped up some potato salad, and popped open a can of funny Mexican beer. My gun lay on the table next to my plate. I was thinking about a second beer when I heard Pascal chaining up his bike on the back porch. He unlocked the door and came in.

"Crap! What are you doing in my kitchen?"

"Having lunch. Your roast chicken is incredible. It must be the rosemary from your garden. You'll have to give me the recipe. Would you like a beer? You have two left."

Pascal tossed his keys on the kitchen counter, flopped down in the chair across from me, and nodded toward my gun. "Are you going to shoot me?"

"I hope not."

"Are you here for romance?"

"Nope."

"I should take a knife and slit my throat."

"Second drawer on the left. I recommend the one you use to

filet fish. It appeared to be the sharpest. Someone used a knife to kill Mildred Threadgill, Lavine Rose, and Lily Morton. Was it you?"

"I told you before it was not me. You said it was a steak knife from the restaurant. Anyone in the kitchen, or even in the hotel could have done it. A customer comes in for a meal and takes a knife and goes on a killing spree. I want the killer found. Lavine and Lily were... my friends. So, you and me, Mademoiselle Lockhart, we are on the same paper."

"Page, same page. But we are not on the same page because I think you are lying."

"Phooey. Why would I kill these women?"

"Revenge. Deep hatred. Over what, I'm not sure. Whatever the reason, it lies in here." I picked up the brown envelope I'd placed on the chair next to me, and dumped the contents out on the table. "Are these your parents?"

Pascal exploded, flinging French expletives around like Mardi Gras beads on Fat Tuesday. He tried to grab the photographs, but stopped when he saw I had my gun pointed at him. "You have no right to go through my things."

"You're right I don't, and I feel terrible about your parents, but there is an innocent man in jail accused of crimes you committed. I'm taking you and the contents of this envelope to the police. Unwrap your wrist."

"I need a beer."

"Would you like half of my sandwich?"

"No."

"Potato salad?"

"No."

I took two from the ice box, opened one, and set it in front of him. After a long swallow, he slowly removed the wrapping and laid his hand down in front of me. A hand with fresh red blisters. "You knew."

"I was pretty certain. You must have accidently splashed acid on your hand when you threw it on Frank Threadgill's body. That's why you didn't show up for work."

He pointed to the picture of his parents. "Frank Threadgill did this. My parents were alive when he threw gasoline on them and struck a match."

"How did you get these photographs?"

"Frank Threadgill sent them to me."

"Maybe you should tell me about your time in Paris, Pascal."

"A time I wish not to remember, Mademoiselle Lockhart, but one I can never forget. The story is ugly."

"I'm sorry about your parents. You and your family must have been through a lot during the war. I was in college at the time. Several boys I went to high school with served, one did not come home. Luckily, my brother was too young to be called up. "

Pascal sat across from me at his small kitchen table in his modest cottage in a country that was not his own and began his story.

"It was the summer of 1939. I was nineteen and just moved to Paris to work under Chef Escoffier at the Peninsula Hotel. Tension was heavy between France and Germany, which I'm sure you know. My parents had a dairy farm near Dijon. When Germany invaded France, life changed overnight. The Occupation was choking the life out of our country. For a while we managed to keep going at the restaurant. But our customers were no longer Parisians who were our friends. We were kept in business by the Germans who came to indulge on our food and spit in our faces." He dropped his head in his hands. A few moments later tears fell.

I reached over and took his hand. "I know this is hard, Pascal. But I have to ask. Did your hatred for Frank lead you to kill Mildred Threadgill?"

"I didn't kill anyone, Mademoiselle Sydney. I will tell you more and you will believe me. After a while the owner closed the restaurant. He refused to feed any more Germans. I was out of work and went home to help my parents on the farm. I believed I would soon be able to return to the city I loved, that the war would be over in a few months. We were French Jews. We were horrified when we learned what Germany was doing to its own Jewish people. Frank Threadgill—Karl Wilner was his real name—was a Nazi officer who was stationed near Dijon. We began hearing news about what was happening with the Jews in Germany, the concentration camps, the torture and starvation. People were fleeing Germany, Poland, and Austria. Wilner made periodic raids of the farms in the area, searching for German Jews. The family who owned the farm near ours was brutally murdered when they were caught hiding a Jewish family. Wilner and his men moved into their nice home and took everything their farm produced. He took over our dairy farm too, and my parents were forced to work for the Germans. One evening my parents went to a secret meeting and decided to join the French Resistance. Knowing the risk they were taking, they urged me and my sister to leave the country. I refused. My sister agreed to go to boarding school in Switzerland. The situation grew tense and my parents pleaded with me to go to America and they would follow soon. We had cousins living in Trenton, New Jersey who agreed to take in my family. Still, with everything that was happening, my parents believed—and hoped too—that the war would end soon. By that time, I knew it would not. I knew things would get worse, but I ran like a coward. When Wilner found out that I was gone, he took it as a personal insult and life for my parents got much worse. I know this because I received letters from relatives even though in my parents' letters they assured me they were safe. Then one day, I got an envelope with these photographs. Wilner sent them. I did not know how he found out where I was, probably from the letters I sent home. When I saw the photographs, at first I didn't know who they were. Then I recognized my mother's shoes." He held up his blistered hand. "The most terrible pain I've ever felt. I can't imagine what my parents felt when they burned to death. This is what Wilner did to them to punish me." Pascal slammed his fist down on the photos. "I swore I'd find him and kill him, but the bastard died of a heart attack. His heart dishing out its own punishment and denying me the pleasure of killing him."

"How did both of you end up in New Orleans?"

"I followed him here. Before that, I left Trenton and moved to New York City. I got accepted to the New York City Culinary school and soon found a position as a chef at the Roosevelt Hotel. I was doing well, had worked my way up to head chef, but I could not leave the past alone. It haunted me. One day a little more than a year ago, I found myself face to face with the devil. Wilner came into the restaurant. Imagine the shock. I thought I was seeing things, that my hatred had caused my mind to fail me. But it was him. He was dining with some people and when he rose to go to the men's room, I followed him and waited by the door. When he came out, I stepped in front of him. He recognized me immediately. The look on his face. He knew I held his freedom in my hands. I took the photos, letters, and newspaper articles to the American Embassy, but after weeks, they were unable to identify him or locate him. The guy was a war criminal, and even with all this, there was not enough proof. Then I got word he fled to New Orleans. What a perfect place for a French chef to find work, no?"

"What did you plan to do when you got here?"

"Get revenge for what he did to my family. I wanted to kill him, but Pascal is not a killer."

"So you just waited until Wilner died, broke into Mademoiselle Marjou's apothecary shop, stole her supply of hydrochloric acid, removed Frank from his coffin, and then threw acid on his dead body? That was your plan?"

"I had no plan until he died. Then I got the idea to burn his body, but I knew a fire at night in the cemetery would bring the police. So I used acid."

"So that's all you're guilty of? Throwing acid on a dead body?"

"I know you do not believe me, but I cannot help that."

"Who helped you?"

"No one."

"Moving the heavy slab from the tomb, prying open the coffin, stripping him of his clothes couldn't have been easy. That must have taken time."

"I tried a couple of times, but was always interrupted."

"Right, you needed someone as a lookout and to help you remove the lid. Who was it?"

"No one of importance."

"The police might think otherwise. When I show them the contents of this envelope and tell them about how you injured your wrist, I'm sure they will put out a warrant for your arrest. Not just for removing Threadgill's body from its coffin and pouring acid on it, but for murdering at least three people, maybe four. You hated Frank Threadgill, maybe your hatred extended to his wife, Mildred. Did you kill your girlfriend, Lavine, because she found out you killed Mildred? Lily Morton knew also that you killed Lavine." I wasn't able to fit Vinny Zimmer into this scenario, but maybe I didn't need to.

Pascal jammed his fists into his eyes. His shoulders shook and this time the tears came in a flood. My heart told me that Pascal wasn't a killer, but I had to push him; I had to know the truth.

"Lavine was not my girlfriend, she was my sister. I did not kill her. If I am arrested the police will not care about evidence, they will put me in jail and I will never come out. There will be no fair trial for Pascal, a French Jew who came to this country because he was a coward."

Seeing how Detective Bergeron conducted his swift investigations, which landed Dixon in jail, I knew Pascal was right.

"If you didn't kill those people, who did?"

"I do not know."

"Who helped you open the vault?"

"I told you it was not important."

"Was it Lavine? And then after she was killed you found someone else to help."

Pascal shook his head.

"You have to tell me everything now, or I'm calling the police."

"I found a man to help. I paid him money. If he talks he will be arrested too."

"The cemetery attendant."

Pascal nodded. "I am a fool. He caught me the first time I was at the tomb."

I lifted the receiver off the hook.

"No, no please, do not call the police. I do not know why any of these people were killed. I do not know who killed them."

"You must have some idea why Lavine was killed. She knew what you were planning to do with Frank's body."

"I did it for her. I wanted her to see that he was dead. I

wanted her to see his skin burned off his bones like what he did to our parents. It was all a waste of time and trouble because little Lavine was killed before she could see anything. She died taking all her agony to the grave."

"So, that was you who called the Threadgills and told Mildred Threadgill that her husband was not going to take them to his grave. Take what?"

"His sins! He was not taking his sins to the grave! He died of a heart attack. Very little suffering. It was not enough. What he did to my family. What he did to my sister. She did not stay in Switzerland. We got word she was coming home, but she never showed up. The train she was on was stopped by the Germans. That's all we knew. We tried to find her, but it was no good. I did not even know she was alive until after the war. I got a letter from my uncle. Lavine had been in a concentration camp. I do not know how she survived. She was so little, but her will was strong. My uncle found her. She stayed with him and his family, but she didn't speak for the first year.

They feared her mind was gone, then she seemed to get better. But one day, they found her outside, standing by the well. She had cut her wrists. They got to her in time. After two more attempts to kill herself, my uncle sent her to a sanitarium. She stayed there for a few months. She was finally released. She wasn't any better, nightmares, and depression. Lavine kept to herself. Then, my uncle told me it might be best if she left France. The memories, too much.

So she came to live with me in New York. When I followed Wilner to New Orleans, she stayed with the cousins. I told her I was moving because I'd found a job. But then she showed up a few months ago. I got her the job at the hotel. I thought if I could keep her near, I could watch over her. She didn't go out much, but I worried she'd run into Wilner and she did. She saw him in the market. It was like opening old wounds. Knowing what Wilner did to our parents haunted her every minute. When Mildred Threadgill was murdered, I was sure Lavine did it. But then she was also murdered. I think Lavine was murdered because she saw the person who killed Mildred. It had to have been Walt Garrison who did this."

"You know Garrison?"

"I made a point to find out as much about Wilner as I could. I saw them together a couple of times. I knew Garrison was the German who bought Wilner's appliance store. I'm sure he is another Nazi who found refuge in this country."

"Why would he kill Mildred?"

"Maybe she knew something about him and he had to silence her. Lavine saw him do it and he killed her too."

"That is a plausible theory, but it's not true. You were at the warehouse the day Lavine's body was taken away by Garrison's foreman Vinny Zimmer and a guy named Bugger. Bugger saw you there. He knows you work at the Pontchartrain because he came to the hotel to see me. We went outside to the park across the street to talk. You walked out of the hotel and he recognized you. Here's how I see it. You killed Lavine, took her body to the warehouse, then when you realized you were seen, you killed Vinny and you would have killed Bugger too, but he was hit by a car. He survived."

"I killed no one!"

"I will have no problem getting Bugger to talk to the police."

"Wait! I found my sister dead. I was out in the hotel garden smoking a cigarette when I saw her body by the dumpster. She was lying there. The look on her face. Her eyes opened. She was gone."

"Why didn't you call the police?"

"I was going to. But then I had a better idea. I took her to the warehouse. I wanted Garrison to be blamed. I wanted someone to pay, pay for what happened to my family, pay for Lavine's murder."

"So, Walt Garrison being German, would do just fine to blame?"

"He was a Nazi!"

"Are you sure, Pascal? Let's go. I'm sure the police would love to hear this story. And I am eager to get the charges against my partner dropped as soon as possible."

"The police will not believe it. There is no proof. It is this Bugger guy's word against mine that I was at the warehouse.

He is a thug."

"Someone in the kitchen will remember that you left the restaurant that afternoon."

"My kitchen staff knows that I go to the fish monger every afternoon."

"But that day you didn't. The fish monger can substantiate that. I heard you fussing at him for bringing you unacceptable fish because you didn't show up at the dock at your usual time and he had to deliver what was left. So with Bugger seeing you at the warehouse and the fish monger knowing you didn't come to the dock, that's enough to throw doubt on your story. You could have killed Lavine, taken her body to the warehouse and been back in less than an hour."

"Mademoiselle Sydney, you know I would not do that. You know I did not kill my little sister. Why would I? I loved her. I can see it in your eyes that you believe Pascal."

"What I don't understand is why you stuck around the warehouse."

"I wanted to see Garrison arrested."

"There's an innocent man in jail for killing Mildred Threadgill and for killing your sister, Pascal."

"Are you going to turn me in to the police?"

I wanted nothing more than to call the police and have him hauled away. Lucky for Pascal, I knew that the evidence was weak and I didn't trust Detective Bergeron. And he was right. I did believe him. I'd discuss this with Jake Noles.

"Go back to work. If you disappear or I find out you lied in any way, I'm going to the police. In the meantime, you're going to help me. I can't go back to the hotel. I'm going to stay in the garage apartment for now. You will not tell anyone, understand? I'm taking this envelope for insurance. Do not bother coming into the apartment and looking for it. It will not be there."

I WENT BACK TO RIP'S APARTMENT. Ruth was still there. In many ways she was so annoying, but I always knew deep down I could count on her. "Did Calvin Logan call?"

"A few minutes ago. He said to call him at the newspaper office as soon as you returned. What did you find out?"

"Tell you in a second." The switchboard operator sent my call to Calvin's desk.

"This is Sonya," I said.

"Hey, sis, glad you called. Want me to come by your place?"

"Sounds good."

"Be there in a few minutes."

"I'll be upstairs."

"Calvin's coming by," I said to Ruth. "Keep your fingers crossed that he found out something that can help with this mess." I looked at Ruth's left wrist. "What's that?"

"A voodoo good fortune charm. Frida Mae highly recommended it for getting rid of bad luck. Here, I bought one for you too. It has to be worn on your left wrist."

She slipped it on me. It was made of twine with a tiny charm hanging down. "There's a dagger on the charm. It's symbolic."

"I don't think I need symbols of knives in my life right down."

"Don't be silly. This dagger will cut all evil from your life. Don't take it off until this trouble goes away. Keep it on even when you bathe."

"Did she give you anything that could speed things up?"

"I asked her that. She said to be patient."

"Not an option now."

Next, I called Jake Noles.

"Mr. Dixon said you'd call," Noles said.

"Mr. Noles, Dixon has been in jail for three days. He told me you were going to put pressure on the prosecutor to charge Dixon or let him go. That's seems awful risky."

"It is, but as his attorney I'm obligated to do so. Mr. Dixon has pled not-guilty. Even though he has a clean record he can be held for seventy-two hours before he's allowed to go before the magistrate. I should know something in the morning. Their case is flimsy."

"There's something else you should know." I told him about my meeting with Pascal and about the cemetery attendant being able to give Dixon an alibi for not killing Mildred Threadgill.

"That's exactly what is needed, Miss Lockhart, another suspect. In most cases I'd recommend that you and I go to the police with the evidence you found. In this case, with you being involved, it's not a good idea."

"I agree. I don't trust them, but I will bring them the evidence if Dixon is charged."

"I don't want him to be charged. I'll talk to the DA and see if I can stall things."

"In the meantime, I'm staying on the case."

"I know it wasn't what you wanted to hear, but without a solid alibi for Dixon, it's the best I can do. Whatever you do, be careful, Miss Lockhart. You're playing with fire."

"I will, Mr. Noles, but you said it yourself, the case is flimsy. Surely, Dixon's background as a police officer gives him credibility."

"Not in this situation."

"What do you mean?"

"Being a detective from another state is a mark against him and you. The Louisiana authorities do not like it when an outsider comes in to investigate a case."

"Dixon and I didn't come here to investigate a case. We came here for a vacation."

"Miss Lockhart, you were here investigating a case a few weeks ago. And now you're back with you partner."

"Are you serious?"

"Extremely."

"The murders took place in Texas and . . . oh no."

"And one took place here. You don't think the cops know all about that?"

"But there shouldn't be any animosity toward me. I got the killer to confess."

"And she was extradited to Texas. That still chafes."

"So that's what this is all about? Me tracking a killer to New Orleans and her extradition to Texas?"

"It's not so much as tracking the killer here, it's that you, being a woman did the tracking. You got her to confess before the cops even had a chance to get involved. You made the New Orleans police look bad. So, here you are. You're back in New Orleans causing more trouble. That's not me talking, but the authorities. And being a suspect in Vinny Zimmer's murder you may not have a chance to find more solid evidence. I recommend giving me Mr. La Duc's envelope and hope for the best. Throwing in a few prayers while you are at it wouldn't hurt. You know where to find me."

I hung up. My lungs seemed to stop working. The ringing in my ears was enough to cause me to hyperventilate.

"Sydney, are you all right?" Ruth asked.

"How could I be so stupid? You heard half that conversation. I'm sure you can figure out the other half. We don't have much time, Ruth. I've got to deliver a killer to the police in the morning, or Dixon and I both may never see Texas again."

I heard the street door open. Calvin walked in and I introduced him to Ruth.

"I found out a few things about Bergeron. It's not much. He was called on the carpet a couple of months ago for acting too quickly on a case. It's not that the perpetrators weren't guilty, but he acted too hastily to get the arrest. With the crime rate so high in New Orleans, I'm sure he was under pressure. It's a catch twenty-two situation. Poor judgement is about all he could be guilty of. I'll keep looking. How about you?"

"I'm afraid what I discovered won't make a rat's ass difference." I told him what I'd learned from Noles.

"I thought your name sounded familiar," Calvin said. "I wasn't the one who worked the story about the killer who was extradited to Texas, but it made the front page for at least a week."

"I never thought that case would come back and bite me."

"You're in a pickle. What are you going to do?"

"Find out who killed these people."

"How? You haven't had much luck yet."

"I've discovered another suspect. He had motive for killing Mildred Threadgill and Vinny Zimmer, but not Lavine Rose. And he paid the cemetery attendant to help remove the lid of Frank's vault."

"How did you find out?"

"This has to be off the record, at least for now." I briefed him on my conversation with Pascal. I did not want to go into too much detail.

"It would be so easy to turn over my evidence to Noles, but

I'm not sure I should right now. I think Pascal La Duc is telling the truth. As much as I'd love to turn him in, I can't implicate someone else unless I'm absolutely sure they're responsible for the murders. And in the meantime, I stand a good chance of being arrested."

"You run the risk of this La Duc guy doing a runner."

"I took his envelope of photos. He'll stick around."

"Let's hope. Maybe you should have another go with the guy in the cemetery and try to shake it up. Disturbing a dead body is a criminal offense."

"I'll keep that card in my pocket for now. It's his word against mine and Pascal's."

"Speaking of the incident in the cemetery," Ruth said. "Frida Mae told me that when the story hit the paper that a body had been removed from its coffin and stripped of its clothes, a flock of customers came in wanting everything from gris-gris to voodoo dolls to potions that would appease unhappy spirits from wandering the city. Some wanted potions to do just the opposite."

"When things like that happen, it brings out the crazies," Calvin said. "It might result in a rash of tombs being vandalized. The House of Voodoo might even have to hire more help. Gotta get back to the office. Stay in touch."

Calvin left. The feeling of moving forward quickly left the room with him. I slumped back into the chair. Every part of my body ached. Muscles in my shoulders, back, and neck hadn't relaxed since Wednesday morning when Dixon and I found Mildred Threadgill stabbed to death in our room. The past few days felt like a year.

"Syd?" Ruth said. "Don't worry, this will all work out, you'll see. I'll go see Dixon. Give him the latest."

"I'm not sure if that's such a good idea either. Let Noles handle it. If you show up at the police station requesting a visit, they might haul you in too."

"I know how to handle the cops," Ruth said.

I was in no mood to argue. Ruth could handle the cops. All she had to do was start talking. After a few minutes, they'd easily assume she was a nut case.

The door downstairs slammed again, Rip and Lydia bounded up the stairs. "We have news, Sydney," Lydia said. "It's not good. The cops are looking for you."

"That's not news, that's the story of my life."

"They've taken over our room in the hotel. If we return, you'll surely be arrested."

"I figured that much. Are you sure you weren't followed on your way here?"

"Pretty sure," Lydia said.

"We ran into Elliot Ivy outside the hotel," Rip said. "He came looking for you. I didn't tell him where you were, but that I'd let you know."

"What did he want?"

"He wouldn't say, but he wants you to call him at his office."

"I need to leave here. I don't feel safe staying in one place too long. And I don't trust Frida Mae."

"She's okay," Rip said.

"Maybe, but she doesn't like the cops nosing around. She might tell them anything to get rid of them. Ruth, I think you're safe to go back to the hotel. Lydia and I will be in Pascal's garage apartment where Lavine was living. I'll be in touch soon. Call if you need to contact me, but don't come by. Lavine's phone number is in the book. Rip, can you drive us? Stop by a grocery store so we can pick up some items first?" I tore off a sheet of his notebook paper and we left.

I'D MADE OUT MY LIST FIRST and had given the paper to Lydia to make hers. I shouldn't have bothered. Who was the adult here? Bread, peanut butter, jelly—all good—three Baby Ruth bars, five Twinkies, two cans of oyster stew, two bags of Fritos, hot dogs and buns, mustard, can of chili, wedge of cheese, three cans of Spam, a bottle of chocolate syrup, and a box of Cheerios. "I've never seen you eat this stuff," I said.

"I'm full of surprises. This is what I eat at home."

"No wonder you don't grow." I took the pencil from her hand and scratched out everything but the hot dog fixings and Cheerios.

"Wait, I thought you didn't eat anything named after a dog."

226 | KATHLEEN KASKA

"I just said that to irritate Ruth."

"Fine, but I don't plan to be in Lavine's apartment for more than a day or so. Your list could feed an army."

"That is all for one day. Whatever I don't eat we can leave it for the next tenant."

"That would work since the shelf life on most of those foods extends into the next century."

"Or we could just give it to the birds."

"Why, what have they ever done to you?"

"What you wrote down is boring. Eggs, milk, bread—okay, I do need bread for the PB&Js—meat, orange juice, coffee, bananas, potatoes, lettuce."

Rip parked in the grocery store lot. We gave him the list. "Be back as soon as I can."

"Oh," Lydia said, "Pick up a jar of mayonnaise."

I looked at her.

"It's for the Spam."

"When we get back to Austin, I'm going to teach you how to cook."

"Why? When I'm at your house, you cook. When I'm at the Grangers' house, Caroline cooks. When I'm at the theater, the production company and actors feed me."

"What if I'm not around anymore?"

"Have you ever been to the dog pound to get a dog?" she asked.

"That's where I got Monroe."

"You found a poodle at the dog pound?"

"I know, I was lucky."

"Okay, you saw little Monroe sitting there. A lost puppy with tears in her eyes. Those eyes locked on you and you were a goner. You knew you had to have her. Take care of her. It was meant to be."

"Lydia, I've never thought of you as a lost dog I had to rescue."

"I know. But when I saw you that night in the costume room of the theater, I knew at that moment you needed me. So, remember that if you ever get any more bright ideas about going away somewhere, you can't survive without me." She held up her pinky finger. I hooked mine to hers. Silence filled the car, except for the choking sound of my swallowing back tears.

Rip loaded the groceries into the backseat. "Just made it before the store closed. I went next door and bought this for you, Syd. And this one's for you, Lydia." He handed each of us a brown bag. In mine was a pint of gin, in Lydia's was a package of chocolate kisses.

CHAPTER THIRTY-NINE

To make sure we weren't seen going into the garage apartment, I made Rip park in the alley. He handed me his car keys. "I'll walk back. You keep my car in case you need it."

Once we got upstairs I closed all the blinds to block out as much light as possible. If Mrs. Irving noticed activity inside and knocked on the door, I'd tell her Pascal allowed us to stay here until the place next door became available. But I wasn't too worried about Mrs. Irving. I told Lydia how to make the hot dogs and heat the chili. Over a glass of warm gin, I called Greg Stower.

"Miss Lockhart, I've been trying to call you at the hotel, but I received an odd response. They said you were still staying there, but that they doubted you'd be back for a long while."

"That's because the situation here has grown much worse. Did you find out anything on Frank Threadgill or Karl Wilner?

"The CIA is interested in him, but the agent I spoke to wouldn't tell me much. I called in a favor and he loosened his lips a bit. Seems several other war criminals are in New Orleans and the CIA is about to bust them."

"When?"

"Soon, real soon. He wouldn't be more specific than that, but I have a feeling it might be tonight. Say the word and I'll take off a couple of days and come down there right away."

"Thanks, Mr. Stower. I'll keep that in mind, but I hope that won't be necessary. How about the name Walt Garrison?"

"I did mention that name, but the agent clammed up. He said we were even on the favors. Miss Lockhart, if Dixon's still in jail, you should not consider tackling this situation by yourself.

The agent I spoke to wanted to know why I was inquiring about Karl Wilner. I had to level with him. I told him I'd heard about it because a friend of mine was involved. He wanted a name. I gave him Ralph's name. I had no choice."

"I understand, Mr. Stower."

"Thanks for your help." I hung up before he could respond.

Lydia was stabbing the hot dogs with a fork. "How do I know they're done?"

The pot bubbled over and the skin had split open. "They're done."

"Do you want mustard?'

"Yes. No chili."

"What did the guy say?"

"The CIA plans to bust Frank's Nazi group probably tonight."

"Serge told me about the CIA. He thinks they are a bunch of criminals themselves."

I need to have a long talk with Serge concerning his opinions about Frenchmen and the CIA. I took my notebook from my bag, and over hot dogs and Fritos, I read over everything I'd written. I was no closer to solving the case than I was yesterday.

"Don't look so down," Lydia said. "I know you're worried about Dixon, but you'll work things out. You always do." She had mustard smeared on her face and down the front of her shirt. It was the only indication of her age. How could a motherless twelve-year-old be so wise? Was she really twelve? Maybe she was a midget passing herself off as a child. Maybe she's not real and I just imagined her. Maybe I'm losing my mind. The mind-losing part was not a new thought, but I fear the thought was quickly becoming a reality. I pushed my plate aside and hugged her. Surprisingly, she didn't object.

We did the dishes and cleaned up the kitchen in silence. The phone conversation with Stower unsettled me. At this point I didn't know which avenue to pursue. I wanted, needed to, toss ideas around with Dixon, but that was no longer possible. I wouldn't make it past the front steps of the police station before I was arrested. I kept thinking that if the situation were reversed and I was the one in jail, he'd have had me out by now.

"What are you thinking about?" Lydia asked.

"I'm thinking I want to be at that CIA bust. I'm sure it will take place at the appliance store tonight."

"It's a good thing we have Rip's car. We should leave now and get there early. Find a safe place to hide and watch who comes and goes."

"I hope you're not planning on climbing a tree."

"I will if necessary."

"I shudder to think of what happened the last time I was at Threadgill Appliance Store."

"So, you're not going?"

"I'm not even sure if I should pursue this, but I don't have much else to go on."

"Let's go."

"You're staying here."

"You need me. If things get nasty, I'm your getaway driver."

"You don't know how to drive."

"I'm a quick learner."

I PARKED THE CAR SEVERAL blocks away on an unpaved road bordered by a thick stand of trees. Several rundown houses sat on the opposite side. We rolled down the windows. A duet of crickets and bullfrogs sang from somewhere within the brush. The appliance store shone in the glow of a dim streetlight planted a half a block away. No cars anywhere around. "We might be here a while."

"What else do we have to do?"

"Tell me about your mom." For a moment, I didn't think Lydia was going to answer.

Finally, she said, "She died when I was six."

"I'm so sorry, Lydia."

"Don't be. I don't remember her. She left us soon after I was born. Serge told me she was never cut out to be a mother. Her name was Susan. Serge showed me a picture of her once. She looked like that blonde actress Turner somebody."

"Lana Turner?"

"Yes. Except for the blonde hair, I look nothing like my mother."

"How did she die?"

"Serge told me she got sick. I don't believe him."

"Why?"

Lydia shrugged.

"Maybe he was protecting you."

"Serge was protecting himself. I don't even think the picture he showed me was her. Look!" Lydia pointed. "There's a car pulling into the warehouse lot."

We watched three men get out and walk inside from the back loading dock. Soon two more cars pulled up, and four more guys went inside. Then I saw Ivy step from his car. He looked around, pulled his jacket collar up, and went inside.

"Recognize any of them?" Lydia said.

"The guy who just got out of his car is Elliott Ivy. I don't know the others. You know, it feels like we've come a long way from one disturbed tomb in a cemetery. Mildred Threadgill, dead in our hotel room, Dixon getting arrested, me being chloroformed and taken to the swamp, but in reality, it's only been less than a week. Less than a week, four murders and I'm on the lam. I'd love to get inside that building and hear what's going on."

Two more cars pulled up. Walt Garrison got out of one and Detective Bergeron the other.

"There's your favorite detective," Lydia said.

"I noticed. The tall guy with the mustache is Walt Garrison."

"Shush," Lydia whispered. "Someone's walking up behind us." We sank down further in the seat. I reached over and put my hand on the key still in the ignition. Footsteps grew louder, but the voices shushed. Out of the corner of my eye I saw five men scurry across the street in front of the car. Three carried pistols and the other two rifles. Before I could swallow, they were in the warehouse lot where they separated and surrounded the building. Lydia crawled out the window. She disappeared under the cover of the trees as quickly as a wood spider sliding beneath a rotting log. Every cuss word I knew crowded my mouth urgent to escape. I dared not open the door and turn on the dome light. I made my exit through the passenger window too, not as gracefully as my little arachnid though. "Lydia," I hissed.

"Over here."

"What the hell do you think you're doing?"

"You want to get closer and this is the only way without being seen. Once those armed men get inside, things are going to start happening. We don't want to be in the car and miss the action."

Two minutes later the doors of the building exploded open, and a dozen men walked out with their hands in the air. CIA agents followed. The prisoners were loaded into two wagons and were driven off.

CHAPTER FORTY

I stayed up most of the night, unable to keep the manic raid scene from dancing through my head. The CIA's discovery of the Foreign Americans for Justice might be significant to Dixon's release, but I couldn't count on it. I mulled over my options. I could go to the police with Pascal's envelope or wait to see if the prosecutor charged Dixon with murder. I finally fell asleep around six, but woke up two hours later, having made my decision. I'd contact Jake Noles and have him accompany me to the police station with Pascal's envelope, but first I'd make a quick call, at least I hoped it would be quick, although that depended on who answered.

"Collect call from a Miss Sydney Lockhart, will you accept?"

"Sydney, you have two jobs. I assume you still freelance for the *Austin American?* And unless your insane venture into the world of private detecting is emptying your bank account, you should be able to pay for your own phone calls. Do I have to remind you you're almost thirty?"

"Ma'am, will you accept the charges?" the operator said.

"Do I have a choice?"

"Mom!"

"Okay, I accept."

"Mom, I could be calling from the hospital for all you know."

"You sound healthy to me. Is that little urchin, Lydia, with you? I swear. Where do you meet these odd people? She had the nerve to lie to me about a bogus flu epidemic in Austin."

"Well, can you blame her? You tried to take over her theater production. By the way, what makes you think you can play Madame Butterfly?" If there was any time in my life when I should have bitten my tongue, this was it. Reasoning with my mother was harder than reasoning with a Tasmanian devil. "Listen, Mom, I'm sort of short on time, and as you reminded me, you are paying for the call. Is Dad at home?"

"Why is it you never call just to talk to me?"

The answer to that question was too obvious to bother with. After a pause, Dad finally answered.

"Sydney, how are things in Austin?"

"Is Mom listening?"

"Good to hear it. What's up?" He lowered his voice. "You called at a good time. The timer just went off. She has to pull a cake out of the oven."

"She baked a cake? Never mind. I don't have a lot of time."

"Still in New Orleans?" he whispered.

"Yes."

"Do I have a son-in-law yet?"

My long, exasperating sigh answered that question.

"Please tell me that you and Dixon are at least still engaged."

"We are. The reason we haven't married yet is that he's in jail."

"Of course he is. Why else would you call?"

"Dad, please, you're beginning to sound like Mom."

"God help me. What's Dixon done? Knowing him it had to have been something as benign as spitting on the street."

"Dad, we're in New Orleans. They drink on the street."

"Oh, right."

"Dixon's been arrested for murder."

"I'm sure he had a good reason."

"He's innocent! Dad, please hear me out." I went over my options as succinctly and clearly as possible. "When I woke up this morning, I was sure of what I'd do."

"Then go with it."

"You don't know what I decided."

"You're my daughter. You're smart, reasonable, and brave. But then again, you're also your mother's daughter. You plan to march into the police station with the evidence you've found and demand they release your guy, right?"

"Sort of."

"My choice too."

"But that might mean the arrest of another innocent person."

"You over think things, Syd. Remember, first things first. Get Dixon out of jail. If the innocent person is arrested, you and Dixon can deal with it then. Who is the innocent person you're trying to protect?"

"A French chef named Pascal La Duc. It's not funny, Dad."

"Of course it's not. Sorry. Oh, thank goodness! Your mother burned the cake. I was afraid I'd have to eat it. If I don't hear from you by tonight, I'll assume you've gotten yourself arrested."

Dawn brought with it a distant scent of rain. Clouds hung low in the east and a slight breeze blew in across the Gulf, chasing the sticky humidity from the city. I made a pot of coffee, woke Lydia and told her my plan—a plan she did not like.

"Don't argue with me, Lydia. You're going back to the hotel and tell Ruth to call Palmer to come get you as soon as possible. I might be in jail before noon."

"I'm sure I can come up with a better plan than that. You need me here."

"Lydia, please. I'm going to take a shower. Make yourself breakfast: Cheerios, hot dogs, or Spam, or whatever. I want to be out of here before Mrs. Irving sees us.

I came out of the bathroom and found Lydia dressed in her pirate outfit. She pointed to the newspaper on the kitchen table.

"I've already read the paper," I said. "There's nothing in it about the raid. Come on, we need to leave.

"You might want to wait."

"Lydia, I'm not going over this again."

"I guess you didn't see the story on page three." She held up the newspaper. The headline read, "Heart Attack Victim Poisoned."

I rushed Lydia out, put her on the streetcar back to the hotel and went back inside the apartment. I poured myself another coffee, finished off Lydia's Spam, and picked up the phone to call Calvin.

"Did you read the morning paper?"

"Silly question."

"Sorry, I'm at my wit's end. What do you know about Threadgill's poisoning?"

"I didn't cover the story, but after I found out about Frank, I roused Joe with a phone call. Those tissue results on Threadgill showed there was a high concentration of arsenic in Frank Threadgill's stomach. He most likely ingested it with his last meal. The reason Joe didn't suspect arsenic is because it usually takes a few hours to kill a person even with a large dose."

"Wouldn't Frank have noticed if his food was laced with a large amount?"

"We're not talking normal circumstance here. Frank was already in bad shape. Joe said it wouldn't take much to kill him. He said that death from arsenic poisoning could resemble a fatal heart attack."

"So, Mildred Threadgill poisoned her husband?"

"No surprise. From what you told me, she hated the guy."

"She certainly had a motive. But why was she murdered? The dominoes started to fall when Frank's tomb was disturbed. The murders have to be linked to the Ivy family. But why were Mildred Threadgill, then Lily Morton, and maybe Lavine Rose, all murdered at the hotel? And then there's Vinny Zimmer murdered in a house in the Ninth Ward after disposing of Lavine's body."

"I can't answer those questions. But the good thing is that the police know this. That's good news for your boyfriend. I'm headed over to the police station. Word's out that the Threadgill Appliance Store was raided last night."

"That's another reason I called you."

"You know about it?"

"I watched it happen."

"Does this have anything to do with the big secret you couldn't tell me concerning Threadgill being a member of the Klan?"

"It does."

"And do you know a few members of the New Orleans Police Department were arrested in the raid, including your favorite, Detective Bergeron."

I swallowed the hot coffee too quickly and lost my breath for a moment. "Let's meet later." I slammed down the phone, grabbed my bag, and left.

On the way to Jake Noles' house, my thoughts turned to the Ivys. The murders were linked to them, but Pascal was still the primary suspect. And another suspect would surely shed additional doubt on Dixon's guilt and get him released. My moment of elation plummeted. My gut feeling about Pascal's innocence was stronger than ever. I'm sure he didn't murder the three women, but he had a good reason to kill Vinny. I had Pascal's envelope in my bag. Could I sacrifice one innocent man for another, even though one was my fiancé? Dad was right. First things first. These thoughts rolled around in my mind as I rang the lawyer's doorbell. His wife answered and informed me that her husband had just left in a hurry for the police station.

Rain started to fall. I didn't bother with the car since it was near impossible to find a parking place around the police station. I sprinted the five blocks to Royal Street. By the time I reached the station, I was soaked and out of breath. I grabbed hold of the ornate wrought-iron gate that opened to the building's small courtyard. Why hadn't I noticed this artistic gate before? Why am I noticing it now? What was wrong with me? I felt as if I were Alice entering the looking glass. I wasn't sure what I'd find inside, but unlike Alice, I feared it wouldn't be pleasant. I feared I'd never come out. Stalling only caused me to hyperventilate. I closed my eyes and breathed deeply. My knees started to buckle. Someone grabbed my arms and pulled me up.

"You look a little rattled, hon."

I looked up to see Ralph Dixon, a disheveled Ralph Dixon, suit jacket draped over his shoulder, tie loosened, and a four day growth hiding the dimple in his chin. Rain dripped from the brim of his fedora. Behind him, a dire-looking man stood holding an umbrella—Jake Noles no doubt. "Does she need a paper bag?" he said.

"She'll be fine." Dixon took me in his arms.

"Thank you, Mr. Noles," I said.

"Once I saw the morning paper, I called the district attorney,"

Noles said. "No DA in his right mind would refuse to release this man."

"I would love to see Detective Bergeron sitting in jail," I said. "I heard about the raid last night and the arrests."

Dixon and Noles exchanged a brief glance.

"Thanks, Mr. Noles," Dixon said. "Sydney and I will be around to see you later today."

"Make it tomorrow. Busy day today." Noles, hesitated, tipped his hat, and left.

"Is there anything else I should know?" I asked.

"Come on. I want to get cleaned up. I'll tell you about it on the way to the hotel. I assume my clothes are still there somewhere."

CHAPTER FORTY-ONE

We were in the third room at the Pontchartrain, or at least I was, since we'd checked into the hotel on Tuesday evening. This was another upgrade. Ruth would be pleased that we were given the room Tennessee Williams stayed in when he wrote Streetcar except for the fact that Lydia was now staying with Ruth. Dixon walked out of the bathroom looking like he did on our first morning here. Hair wet, towel wrapped around his waist—Adonis returned.

"It's been a hell of a week," he said. He wrapped me in his arms again and we stayed that way for a long time.

"Guess what?" I said. "Palmer called while you were in the shower. He's arranged to get a four-seater to fly Ruth and Lydia back to Texas. He'll be here in a couple of hours."

"You mean I'll have you all to myself?"

"You will. Now kiss me."

"Gladly. Have you been eating Spam?

DIXON AND I HOPPED THE STREETCAR to the French Quarter. The rain had turned to a drizzle and a line was beginning to form at Café Du Monde. We were ushered to a tiny table squeezed between two others. I didn't care. The beignets and coffee smelled like heaven.

"You and I have some unfinished business, and I'm not talking about solving a murder. When we get back to the hotel, I'll call the office and see what's happening in Austin. If there's not much on the books, let's stay a few more days."

"Good idea. We'll let the cops handle the murder cases. We are no longer on the job. We still don't know who killed Frank,

Mildred, Lavine, Lily, or Vinny." I told him all about Pascal and the intense grudge he held against Threadgill or Wilner. "But it's not our problem either. You're free and that's all that matters. I wash my hands of this entire saga. I could use another coffee." I signaled the waiter.

"Make that two. Tomorrow morning, we go to the courthouse, get married, wrap up things with Jake Noles, and spend the day touring the city. Lunch at Camellia Grill, dinner at Commander's Palace. Tonight we find a jazz club. How does that sound?"

"Wonderful."

We sipped our coffee. Made small talk. Smiled at the family seated at a table next to us. Another mild rain shower drifted through, here and gone in minutes, taking with it my feelings of anxiety. I drained my fourth cup of coffee and plunked my cup on the table. "Who are we kidding? We have a few murders to solve."

Dixon laughed and looked at his watch. "That only took two minutes. Let's make sure Ruth and Lydia are gone, and begin in the morning, but tell me more about this chef."

"My gut feeling is that Pascal isn't a killer, but the hatred he felt for Threadgill over what he did to Pascal's parents might cause anyone to kill, especially after that hatred has built up over the years. Is it possible we have more than one killer here?"

"It's possible, but in my experience, when there is a string of murders in a few days, it's usually the work of a desperate person."

"I wonder if Elliot Ivy is still in jail. I have a feeling he isn't. I have a stronger feeling, he knew the raid was going to happen, so did Walt Garrison. I also want to check on Bugger in the hospital."

Dixon borrowed a pencil from a passing waiter and made notes on the back of our bill. "Anyone else?" he said.

"I'm curious about Frank Threadgill's poisoning."

"The first murder."

That's as far as we got in our discussion when I spotted a motley crew standing in line. Much to the annoyance of the people in line in front of them, we pulled up more chairs and Lydia, Ruth, and Rip joined us. We told them of our illusory plans to let the cops handle the murders because we were determined to have a vacation. The only one who didn't believe us was Lydia, but she kept her mouth shut. Bless her.

"Well, I'm ready to get back to Dallas," Ruth said. "I have business to take care of."

"It must take you at least a week to count your money," Lydia said.

"My money goes to a lot of worthy causes, young lady. You think I'm so shallow. I'll have you know that I donated blood to my half-sister, Marcella, when she needed an infusion a few months ago."

"Transfusion," Lydia said.

"Whatever. You have powdered sugar all down the front of your black pirate jacket, young lady. Who in their right mind wears a pirate jacket in this heat anyway?"

"Who in their right mind wears a Chanel suit and Ferragamo heels on cobblestone streets?" Lydia volleyed.

"I'd love to listen to more fashion tips, but I have to get back to the office." Rip smiled. "At this point, I don't care who killed those people. I know that sounds heartless, but investigating live people is beyond my ability. I'm going to stick to searching for souls. You know where to find me, Syd. Next time you're in town, we'll take the cemetery tours. Nice to see you again, Ruth. And nice to meet you Lydia and Mr. Dixon."

I watched the big guy walk away and wondered if I'd ever see him again.

"Are you two packed and ready to go?" I asked.

"We are," Ruth said. "I hate to leave you, Syd, but New Orleans is not for me. Come, young lady. Palmer will be at the hotel soon."

"I think I'll just walk home," Lydia said.

"Your sarcasm is so lame," Ruth said.

Lydia reached in her pocket and pulled out her gris gris. "I don't need this anymore, Syd. You take it just in case."

"She's got her wristband with a good fortune charm," Ruth said. "She doesn't need that bag of putrid animal remains. At least I don't have to smell it on the plane. Call me when you get back, Syd. Palmer and I will come to Austin. Dixon, you haven't had a chance to get to know Palmer."

"I'm looking forward to it," he said. "See you soon. Have a safe flight."

Ruth and Lydia left the café arguing over which amulet was more potent, a gris gris or a wristband with a voodoo charm.

"I really think those two like each other," Dixon said.

"In a sadistic sort of way."

DIXON AND I STROLLED THROUGH the French Quarter and around Jackson Square. The rain had stopped and steam rose from the pavement. Water dripped from the flower baskets hanging from the balconies. Jasmine, emitting its sweet, sensual fragrance, grew in profusion over archways and arbors that led into private courtyards. A sign attached to a wrought iron gate of another courtyard read, *Lasissez le bon temps rouler.* "Do you think it's part of the city's heritage? This feeling of letting the good times roll?"

"It's a party city, no doubt about that."

Dixon rolled up his shirt sleeves, removed his tie and stuffed it into his coat pocket. Eventually we made it to the riverfront where the steamship the Delta Queen was docked. Its gleaming white exterior, trimmed in bright red, provided luxury transport up the Mississippi all the way to Cincinnati.

"Did you know it was taken out of service during the war and used as a transport for the wounded from ocean ships to San Francisco Bay hospitals?" Dixon said. "It was painted battleship gray during its time of military service."

"How did you manage to stay out of the military?"

"By the start of the war I'd just finished college and had enrolled in the police academy. When I realized I'd be drafted, I decided to enlist rather than wait around for the notice to arrive in the mail. I failed my medical exam."

"You?"

"They detected a heart murmur."

"You're kidding."

"Don't worry. Those things usually are not serious and often go away. Do you want me to go for a physical before we tie the knot?"

"No, I'll take you the way you are."

"Are you sure? You look puzzled."

"I was just thinking about Frank Threadgill changing his name and entering the country illegally after the war. Everything Pascal told me about him. What he did to Pascal's parents and then taking refuge in the country he was fighting against."

"You still believe Pascal is not the killer?"

"I do, but I've been misled before."

"We all have, but your intuition has always been strong. You were the one who realized that it was Rita Fredricks who killed those people in Hot Springs."

"Yes, but I was fooled by your sister Nora. I mean Loretta."

"That was my fault. I should have told you about her. In that sense, I was fooled by her too. I never thought she'd show up in my life."

"I don't think it was a coincidence."

"Neither do I. We don't have to worry about her now. After hearing what you've told me, I agree with you about Pascal. I can't see him killing his sister. He has no motive, at least not that we know of. But I'm not sure about the other murders."

"Whoever killed Mildred, Lavine, Lily, and Vinny had to have poisoned Frank. It had to be someone close to him to slip the arsenic into his food. Pascal had motive to kill Frank, but how could he have poisoned him? His got his revenge by throwing acid on Frank's body."

"We'll take a closer look at the Ivys. Enough about the case. Those beignets are long gone. If we're going to party tonight, we need to fortify ourselves. Let's enjoy the day. Tomorrow morning we'll start with Pascal, and then the Ivys. I haven't taken you to Felix's Oyster Bar yet. The word I got when I was incarcerated was that it's the best place in town for oysters."

"You had culinary discussions in jail?"

"Most of my cellmates were one-nighters arrested for drunkenness, but a couple of guys were doing a few weeks for petty crimes. All they talked about was what they were going to eat when they got out. I took notes. How about if I take you dancing tonight?"

"We've never done that. I didn't know you could dance."

"There's a lot you don't know about me, hon."

"I'm in. Let's go."

A short time later, we took two stools at the counter across from a gilt-framed mirror that covered the back wall. "I want everything on the menu," Dixon said. "I don't ever want to see another cold cheese sandwich again. How about two Oyster Po'boys and two draft beers?"

"Sounds great. I don't know how you stood it. Four days in that awful place. You held up nicely. I still can't believe you were arrested in the first place. At least Detective Bergeron will get a taste of his own medicine."

"He was just doing his job."

"No, he wasn't. Didn't Noles tell you about Bergeron's intention of getting back at me for when I was here investigating the last case?"

"Forget it, Sydney. Look." He pointed to the mirror. "We're two people in love who are here to get married tomorrow."

"You know, I've been thinking. I'd planned to wear street clothes, but I think I'd like something a bit nicer."

"What changed your mind?"

"Lydia. When we were in the costume shop looking for clothes for her, she found a used wedding dress and chided me for not making the most of the occasion."

"I don't recommend wearing a used wedding dress. There's surely a bad story attached to it."

"I agree, but it got me thinking. It's a special day. Not having a big church wedding doesn't make it any less important. There's a boutique across from the hotel."

"Let's have another beer and go shop," Dixon said.

"Another beer, yes, but you can't go with me to buy a dress. You can't see it until the wedding day. Actually, you're not supposed to see it until I walk down the aisle, but since there is no aisle, and we're going to the courthouse together, we have to adjust the tradition."

We walked back to the hotel. Dixon went up to the room and I went into the boutique. Five minutes later, I was ready to walk out with a dress box containing a cinnamon colored polka dot strapless tea-length tulle dress and a pair of ivory heels, when a black cocktail dress caught my eye. I tried it on. It fit. I'd wear it tonight. Sometimes the best decisions are those made quickly.

Dixon and I lounged in our room for a couple of hours and then took a taxi to the Bourbon House where Red Allen was playing. I'd never heard of the guy, but Dixon assured me that Allen was one of the best jazz trumpeters in the business. We were lucky to get a table.

"I didn't know you were into jazz."

"I heard some great jazz when I was here with my buddies."

"How did you know about Red Allen?"

"I asked the concierge at the hotel."

CHAPTER FORTY-TWO

Dixon was right. He can dance, and dance we did. The Bourbon House was packed and after a few turnarounds on a too-crowded dance floor, we left and found a place where a local band was playing Dixieland jazz. We closed the club down and fell into bed after two. Waking up this morning, I realized that last night was the first time Dixon and I threw caution to the wind and kicked up our heels. It's not that we weren't interested in having a good time, it was that we rarely had a chance. We've always had fun together, but with it came the need to rush out to take care of business. As much as I'd like to believe this was not our case, I couldn't let it go. The killer was still out there. What if another innocent person was arrested?

All these thoughts ran through my head while Dixon lay snoozing beside me. He was usually the first to wake up, so I had the privilege of ordering room service and picking up our clothes from the floor. I hung my black cocktail dress in the closet and sneaked a peek at the dress I'd be married in today. I took the box to the bathroom, closed the door, and slipped on the tulle dress. Even with my eyes puffy from last night's partying, I looked stunning. The color looked perfect with my red hair. We'd have to get our picture taken. I'm not sure why I've always resisted getting married. And I'm not sure why I told myself I would not have a big, glamorous wedding. Yes, I do know. It was my need to rebel against my mother. I took a good look at myself in the mirror. "Sydney, when are you going to grow up? Rebelling against your mother when you were a teenager was cool. You're almost thirty, maybe it's time to stop."

"Are you alone in there?" Dixon called. "Are you walking and talking in your sleep?"

"Be out in a minute. I'm trying on my dress again."

"Having second thoughts about it?"

"No, it's perfect. I wanted to be sure. I think you'll like it."

"I know I will. Now come out of the bathroom."

I put the dress back in the box and threw on my robe. Dixon held up the sheet and I crawled in bed beside him. "I think we should take this bed home."

"I'll have them wrap it up."

Our continental breakfast arrived and we went over the list Dixon made and discussed our plan for today. We agreed that whatever progress we made, we'd knock it off by 3:00. That would give us time to return to the hotel, change into our wedding clothes, and make it to the courthouse before closing.

"I'm going downstairs to get a newspaper," Dixon said. "Back in a minute."

"Okay, I'll call the office and the Grangers." I was happy to hear that things in Austin were running as smoothly as could be expected with the electricity still out. The rest of the office furniture was to be delivered tomorrow. Billy finished painting yesterday. Phoebe's organizing our files. We've even had a few walk-in cases, none more serious than stolen patio furniture and a couple of cheating husbands. Speaking of which, Lawrence Earl Nash of the missing person case finally surfaced. Seems he'd been staying with yet another girlfriend and he came home after the girlfriend threw him out. Imagine his surprise when he discovered Mrs. Nash had changed the locks and filed for divorce.

I talked to Carolyn Granger. Monroe and Mealworm were enjoying their time with the Grangers, at least Monroe was; Mealworm enjoyed nothing, except Dixon. Finally, I called Serge at the Next to Nothing Theater to see how the play was coming along. Serge said everything was on schedule and that Lydia was doing a fine job with the production.

"Anyone missing us?" Dixon said, tossing a newspaper onto the bed.

"No, I'm not sure if we should be pleased about that. I worry about Lydia, though. She was gone for three days, and her own father didn't even realize she wasn't around."

"She's a survivor."

"True, but she deserves more."

"No objections there. She's welcome to stay with us as much as she wants, and the Grangers feel the same way. I agree that living in an apartment above the theater is no place for a young girl, but it is her home."

"Her education is so sporadic. She'll be in high school in a few years."

"We'll have a talk with Serge when we get back. What are you thinking about? You've got that sly smile on your face."

"Do I? I realized how much alike you and my dad are. With both of you, life is simple and straightforward. I couldn't have handled all that time in jail. One night in the Palacios jail was enough even with the police chief's wife catering to me."

"Oh, Emma Fogmore. I wonder if she won the election and is now police chief of Palacios?"

"It would definitely be to the town's benefit."

"We'll have to visit one day."

"Not anytime soon. Oh, Billy had some questions for you about charges for the Nash case. I told him you'd call. There's still no electricity in the office. An inspector is coming in today to check the electrical lines, not just in our office, but the entire Scarborough Building."

"Good. I'll give Billy a call now. I also want to call Marcella and thank her for finding Jake Noles. And thank Greg Stower for his help."

"Anything in the newspapers?"

"A lot. Fortunately, my name is not mentioned. Seems the police are stumped over the murders. I'll let you read it. Try on your dress again. Make sure it's perfect. I'll go downstairs to make the calls."

Dixon left.

I showered and dressed. I wrapped my hair into a twist to keep it off my neck. I heard Dixon come in. "Back already?" I called. "That was quick. I'm almost done in here. Dixon?"

I opened the bathroom door. I'll never learn.

"You're a difficult person to keep up with, dear. If I wasn't

MURDER AT THE PONCHARTRAIN | 249

such an old lady, I'd have gotten me a pair of roller skates."

Dixon's always telling me to keep my gun with me at all times when we're on a case. What would it take for me to remember that? "Mrs. Ivy?"

CHAPTER FORTY-THREE

Alma Ivy scanned the room. "Nice suite, but no surprise in a posh hotel like this one." Her eyes locked onto mine. The hand holding the pistol didn't shake. Her aim didn't waver. The woman looked as calm as a Sunday morning. "You didn't expect me?"

"How did you know which room we were in?"

"Are you serious?" She had the nerve to laugh. "I have my ways."

"Someone at the hotel?"

"Your questions will not help you. We have some matters to settle."

"Is that gun really necessary?"

"Absolutely."

I poured myself more coffee. "I'd offer you some, but there's not enough. What matters are you talking about?"

"You're a smart one. I was afraid you'd figure it out sooner or later. I tried really hard to get rid of you nicely, but you wouldn't take a hint, so I have to speed things up. I hate to do this, but it's necessary."

"You're going to shoot me?"

"You leave me no choice."

"Dixon is downstairs, and he'll be up any minute."

"I saw him. There was a line at the lobby phone. He's reading the newspaper and won't be up for a while. He's so nice looking. You two make a cute couple. I'm glad he's out of jail. That works to my advantage. Another murder, yours, and he'll be back behind bars and things will be back to normal for me."

"You won't get away with it. Dixon has no motive for killing me."

"What do I care about motive? What do the police care about motive? And I will get away with it. I have so far."

"A gun is a lot noisier than a knife."

"That's not your concern."

"You're a fool, Mrs. Ivy, if you think you'll leave this hotel after shooting me. The other murders will catch up to you."

"Don't look so smug. Who would expect an old lady to kill those people, especially her own daughter and niece?"

"You've got a point there. I'm sure you had a good reason."

"Sadly, I did. My nosy daughter had been snooping in her boss's office after work on Monday. She found a file she had no business looking at."

"Yes, I know. Mildred found out her husband was a Nazi."

"Clever girl. Mildred came to me. She wanted to go to the authorities."

"And you were against that?"

"Of course I was. I couldn't let her tell the authorities that her husband was a war criminal. If she turned Frank in he'd talk, and I would be deported or worse. My husband and I came to this country after the first war. We couldn't get visas because of the work we were forced to do with the German government. We tried immigrating as refugees, but that didn't work. We finally managed under different identities. After that, it was so easy. Everything went well. We settled here and started a new life. Then, a year ago Frank Threadgill showed up."

"He knew you?"

"Oh, yes, he knew us well. He was my cousin."

"Your cousin? You let you daughter marry her close relative?"
"She agreed to it?"

"She didn't know Frank was a relative."

"Why in God's name would you do that to her?"

"It was Frank's idea. You're thinking about Mildred and Frank having children. That wasn't going to happen. Frank's war injuries would have prevented that. Besides I was, at first, against the marriage, but Frank convinced me it would provide camouflage."

"What a disgusting thing to do."

"True, but it was necessary. There's more to it, but it's not important. Oh, don't look down your nose at me. You know nothing about me or my life."

"I know enough. Whatever justification you feel you had, you're still a cold-blooded killer. Your daughter's cold-blooded killer."

"That was unfortunate."

"And you feel no remorse?" For the first time since the macabre conversation started, I noticed a tad of emotion show on her face.

"You call me cold-blooded, but you don't know what my life has been like. I didn't want to kill my daughter. I warned Mildred to leave it alone, but she refused. She was never the type to think things through. Always quick to act without considering the consequences. I knew she'd keep digging and find out about my husband's and my past, which would ruin us. If she would have just kept her mouth shut, she could have continued living in that big house. My own daughter accused us of being traitors."

"I didn't know Mildred, except that she appeared to be an unhappy, troubled woman who dabbled in voodoo. I judged her based on that. That was wrong. It sounds to me like she was trying to do the right thing. Mildred had more backbone and integrity than I gave her credit for."

"Integrity means nothing when you're trying to survive. You weren't in Germany during the first war. After years of turmoil, your heart hardens and you make decisions that change you forever. Endurance is all that matters. My husband was a chemical engineer. The German government forced him to work on nerve gas, which was killing him. If we were deported back to Germany, we'd be shot. Mildred never understood what we went through. Mildred had everything she ever needed, everything she ever wanted."

"Except a happy marriage."

"So, what if Frank wasn't the best husband? He provided for her, and what did she do? To deal with her little problems, she goes to see that crazy voodoo woman for spells and charms, trying to punish Frank after he's already dead. She told me she was going to get that crazy ghost detective to investigate further into what Frank had going. I hadn't plan to kill her. I tried to reason with her, but I saw the hatred in her eyes. Looking at me as if I were a piece of dirt. *She* hating *me*. Hating me for surviving when she had it so easy. When I told her she was making a big mistake, she laughed. She said I was the big mistake and she'd make sure I paid for what I'd done. She flew out of my house in a rage. I followed her to Thigbee's office and then to the hotel. I couldn't imagine why she was going there, except maybe to tell Lily what had happened. I followed her in through the kitchen door and saw her run up the stairs. I found her in your hotel room. She started screaming at me. She grabbed the knife from the breakfast tray and came after me. We fought. I pushed her and she fell on the knife."

"What about Lavine Rose? You killed her too, then Lily, then Vinny Zimmer."

"None of this was planned, but once I started down that road, I had to continue. I wasn't sure Lavine Rose saw me. She was at the end of the hall when I came out of the hotel room. I returned to the hotel later that afternoon. I waited outside the back of the hotel, trying to decide what to do. She came out for a cigarette and started sobbing. I guess giving Mildred the key to your room, made poor Miss Rose feel responsible for Mildred's murder. I had the opportunity. I had to kill her."

"Then you tried to set-up Pascal La Duc."

"Who in the hell is he?"

"The chef at this hotel. You put the steak knife in his locker."

"When I came downstairs I didn't realize the knife was still in my hand. I had to get rid of it and I stuck it in an open locker. I didn't think anyone saw me."

"But your niece did."

"Lily had the nerve to try to blackmail me. She told me she saw me going up the stairs after Mildred and was going to tell the police if I didn't pay her $25,000. It would have been her word against mine, but I couldn't chance that either. It's amazing how no one pays attention to an old woman. It's almost like we are invisible. I went into that kitchen three times, once following

Mildred, then back down to the kitchen to get rid of the knife, and finally to shut up my niece. No one saw me except Lily, and that's because she knew me. All the other people working went about their work like the peons they are. Rushing around as if their lives depended on serving their betters. Then all I had to do was to get the file out of Garrison's office."

"And that's where Vinny Zimmer came in."

"I knew him from when Frank owned the store. I can recognize a greedy, shameless leech when I see one. I told him I'd give him two hundred dollars to get me the file. I knew he'd feast his eyes on what was inside, but that didn't bother me. Sure enough he called, and I had another blackmailer to get rid of. I arranged to meet him at some shack by the river. I walked in. He had a gun pointed at me. I asked him to show me the file. It was lying on the table. I threw the money at his feet. It only took one glance and I pulled the gun from my pocket and shot him before he could blink. None of this would have happened if Mildred hadn't rushed to the hotel to see two private detectives. Then I read in the newspaper that Mr. Dixon had been arrested for the murders I'd committed. What luck. Now you're the only one I have to deal with."

"That's not true. You have Walt Garrison to deal with and the other members of the FAJ. After the raid on the appliance store some of those guys will be glad to spill the beans, if they haven't already, and your name will come up."

"That does concern me somewhat, but you see, all it takes is thinking several steps ahead, like playing chess."

"Aren't you curious about the missing money from the sale of the store?"

"There was no missing money. Frank contacted us about having to leave New York City because someone recognized him from when he lived in Germany. We told him to come here. We told him about the appliance store. When Frank sold the store, he gave the money to me in case the authorities caught up to him and found out he was a war criminal. Frank and I talked about what we would do if that happened. We would use the money to disappear if things got bad."

"What about your family?"

"My family doesn't need me. Mildred had both houses. She was not exactly destitute. Then Frank died of a heart attack. With my husband dead and Frank out of the picture, I had time to consider my options. The governmental authorities were on to him, but not me. You see, I know how to cover my trail. I'm just a poor widow who had no idea her husband and son-in-law were war criminals. I did not plan to kill anyone. I was trying to survive."

"That story sounds good, Mrs. Ivy. Except for the part about Frank dying of a heart attack. I think you poisoned him. He was at your house, sitting at your table when he died. You poisoned him so that there would be no link to you and the past because of Frank's involvement with the Nazis."

"Nothing can be proven." She snickered.

I walked to the window. Ribbons of light shone through the blinds. I looked out on the street below. "It's starting to rain again."

"Stalling will do you no good either. But, have it your way. I didn't want to have to do this here, but I will."

I thought of Pascal's envelope with proof that Frank was a Nazi. I understood his frustration over Frank's untimely death. He would never have to stand trial for the atrocities he'd committed. Pascal would not see justice done. There was nothing in the articles and letters Pascal collected that implicated Alma Ivy and her husband, but she didn't know that. "Before you pull that trigger, there's something that might interest you. There's someone else who knows about you and your cousin's past." A stretch of the truth, but it was my last hope. "He's the reason Frank fled New York City. And he followed Frank here."

I had her attention, but for only a couple of seconds. Her frown smoothed and turned in to a grin. "Nice try." She pointed the gun. "If that's the case, I will deal with that too."

"What about your son? You forgot about him."

"My son has nothing to do with this."

"Elliott has been working with Garrison investigating Frank Threadgill. He knows Frank is really Karl Wilner. He knows Frank was a war criminal here in the country illegally. It's only a matter of time until your son links all of this to you."

"You lie!"

"You'll have to kill him too. Maybe when he comes over for Sunday dinner. That would be a good opportunity, don't you think? I don't recommend another poisoning though. That's too risky." At that point I realized I'd gone too far. I saw her finger tighten on the trigger. I heard the click of the doorknob. I saw the handle turn. Mrs. Ivy jerked around and fired.

"Dixon!" I dove and knocked Mrs. Ivy to the floor and slammed my knee deep into her spine. I plucked the gun from her hand and jabbed the barrel into the base of her skull. I looked up to see Dixon, my Dixon, sprawled on the floor in the doorway. Blood sprayed the door—a stream running down his side and soaking the carpet.

CHAPTER FORTY-FOUR

Y ou're insane. Get back in bed."

"I have a wedding to attend." Dixon reached for his slacks.

"The license doesn't expire for another several days." I pushed him back down. "You heard the doctor. You were lucky, but he wants you to spend the night in the hospital. One day longer will not make any difference. Besides, if you ever expect me to exchange wedding vows with you, you have some serious explaining to do."

"It was Bergeron's idea."

"You lied to me."

"I was hoping you wouldn't notice that." Dixon smiled.

"Those dimples will not work this time." He took hold of my hand and pulled me toward him. "That won't work either." I jerked my hand away.

The door opened and Bergeron walked in. "Hey, should you two be doing that? You have a hole in your arm, Mr. Dixon."

"My fiancée's not happy with me," Dixon said. "I'm afraid she wouldn't listen to anything I have to say. Maybe she'll listen to you."

Detective Bergeron stepped back into the hall and brought in another chair. "Sit, Miss Lockhart, this will take a while."

Bergeron finished his story, leaving me dumbfounded. I looked at Dixon. He knew I was buying none of this. He knew he was in deep shit.

"So, you see, Miss Lockhart, your boyfriend made the right decision."

I picked up my bag. "You're wrong, Detective. The decision he made was unforgiveable." I left the hospital.

I didn't know how I got to Pat O'Brien's. I wasn't sure how long I'd been there. If the three empty Hurricane glasses in front of me were any indication, it had been a while.

"Want to order something to eat, Miss Sydney?" Jacko said. He placed a menu on the bar. "It's on the house."

"That's nice of you. But I'm not hungry."

"You need to get something in your stomach if you're going to sit here the rest of the day and drown your sorrows. You want my advice?"

"You can take your advice and shove it, Jacko. Do your job." I held up my empty glass. He didn't argue. I watched the light rum, dark rum, and assorted fruit juices fill the glass. I watched the grenadine turn the concoction pink. I watched the maraschino cherry land in the liquid splashing drops onto the bar. It wasn't until Jacko slammed a glass over the top of the silver shaker and began mixing my drink, that my head began to swim. "Maybe I should eat. How's the gumbo?"

"The best. Hey, Broussard," Jacko called to the cook. "Bring the lady a bowl of gumbo and some garlic bread. You're going to be okay, Miss Lockhart. You'll see." He set my drink in front of me. I reached for it. He slid it to the side and said, "Ain't for you."

"You're going to kill me, hon." I turned to see Dixon, pale and sweating, sitting next to me. He swigged down half the drink. "Double that gumbo order, Broussard," he said.

I stood to leave. He caught me as I stumbled. "Do not touch me."

"Sit down, Sydney."

"Do not call me Sydney."

"If I order you another drink, will you sit down? Please? After all, I talked my way out of the hospital, ignoring the warning that I'd end back up there with bigger problems if I left."

"You lied to me."

"I did. I'm sorry. I wish I could promise you I'd never lie to you again, but that would be a lie. I'd lie, cheat, and steal to keep you safe. I'd sell my soul to the devil if it meant protecting you. If anything bad ever happened to you, I'd slit my throat. And if you don't forgive me and marry me, I'll slit my throat right here because life will not be worth a goddamn piece of shit without you."

Jacko held up the bar knife. "It's up to you, Miss Lockhart."

"Hey, lady." A woman sitting on the other side of me said, "If you don't want him, I'll be glad to take him off your hands." She leaned over and whispered. "He's just a man, honey. Take it from me, they are the weaker sex. They're just doing the best they can. Don't be stupid."

Tears slid down my face. "I don't know. I just don't know."

"Hon, Bergeron had me over a barrel. After that first night in jail, he realized that I was not the one who killed Lavine Rose or anyone. In fact I'm pretty sure he knew it all along. From the last case you investigated here, he knew you were good. He knew we were a really good team. He couldn't have us blowing his operation since he was so close to arresting those Nazis in Frank Threadgill's group."

"It was a federal case."

"True, but Bergeron wanted some credit for uncovering the Nazi war criminals in his city. He needed the accolades. He knew Mildred Threadgill's murder was the link."

"That's disgusting."

"It is, but his career was on the line for several screw-ups. He wanted to keep me in jail to send a message to the killer that the cops didn't have a clue what was going on."

"And what if things did not work out like he planned?"

"I know. At first I refused to go along with his plan, but he threatened to throw you in jail too."

"You should have let him. He had no real evidence against us. That would have come out in court."

"You don't understand, Syd. This federal case is bigger than both of us. Bergeron has connections. I'm convinced we would have stayed in jail a long time. I'm also convinced, he would have found something that would have stuck. Planted evidence against us. He didn't come out and say it, but the implication was there. If it was just me, I wouldn't have gone along with it, no matter what."

"You thought I was not capable of handling this?"

"On the contrary, I knew you could handle it, but I needed

you on the outside. I needed you to solve the case."

"But I didn't! Instead we both came close to being murdered! You closer than me."

"Yes, I know. I honestly thought that once Noles got me released, I'd be back on the case. I let my guard down. That's something that will be hard to live with. The only thing worse is not having you."

Before I knew it, I was blubbering. Dixon's one good arm wrapped around me. Our gumbo arrived. I was suddenly hungrier than I'd ever been in my life. We ate in silence.

Dixon scraped his bowl clean and pushed it aside. "I love you more than life, hon. It would be a shame to let that breathtaking dress you bought yesterday go to waste. What do you call that color anyway?"

"You—"

"Peeked." Dixon threw some cash on the bar. "I'm about to pass out. Let's go. I need you to help me back to the hotel."

"Good luck with that."

"Please."

Jacko was staring at me with anticipation. The woman next to me poked me in the ribs. "Could you two please leave us alone? I'd like a private word with this man." I turned to Dixon. "I need to know I can trust you."

"Truthfully, Syd, if I had it to do over again, I would have made the same choice. You can trust me where it counts. Let me ask you this, you're smart, intuitive, would you have fallen for a guy you couldn't trust?"

"That's not fair."

"Answer the question, hon. What we do, it's never going to be easy. Could you see yourself with a nine-to-five sort of guy? Someone who comes home from the office, changes clothes, and goes outside to mow the lawn? Someone who goes to the country club and plays golf on Saturday? And you. Why did you quit teaching? Why did you refuse to write fluff articles for the newspaper? Neither one of us wants that traditional life. Am I right? But here's the most important question. Are you upset with me because I went along with Bergeron's plan without telling you, or are you reluctant to get married?"

That last question felt like a slap in the face. Dixon could read me like a book. Finally, I said, "I'm not reluctant, I'm scared."

"Me too."

"Really?"

"A little. There's one thing I'm sure of, I will never doubt you."

I stuck my hand in my pocket for a tissue. Then I felt it. On the way to the hospital after Dixon had been shot, I put Lydia's gris gris in my pocket. At that moment I knew everything would be okay. "You know, that day we met at the Arlington Hotel?"

"How could I forget? I thought you'd just murdered a man."

"I remember, and you were torn, asking yourself how you could fall for a woman who'd slashed a guy's throat?"

"I never seriously thought you were guilty."

"You did. But I forgave you. Anyway, that very night there was a full moon coming up over Central Avenue, and for the first time in my life, I realized that the reason I could never see the man in the moon before was because I was looking at it wrong. In my mind, I was thinking 'man on the moon.' Like someone had carved an etching on the surface. But that night I realized that the man was inside looking out, and suddenly I saw him. It was you."

"I have no idea what you just said. But does that mean you still want to get married?"

"I think so."

"That's good enough for me. I don't think I'll need that knife, Jacko."

"Oh, after we're married, promise me you'll do your own laundry."

BACK AT THE HOTEL, I PUT Dixon to bed. He fell asleep before I could get his shoes off. I went downstairs to use the lobby phone. I had a pocket full of nickels and long list of people to call. "Collect call to George Lockhart." I gave the number to the operator. It rang three times, before I changed my mind and I hung up. I missed my dad, but I didn't need his advice this time. I called the office and told Phoebe we'd be back in a few days. I called Lydia at the theater, but she couldn't come to the phone. The trap door was still not working right, and Danny Pistow was threatening to quit the production again. I called the Grangers. Everything was fine with the dog and cat. Calvin was next. I gave him as much information as I could and promised to touch base with him as soon as I could catch my breathe. He'd been needling his contacts at the police station and had enough news to keep him busy for a while. My last call was to Walt Garrison. He wasn't happy to hear from me until I told him about the evidence I'd discovered that might help him with his case against the men the CIA arrested. After I hung up, I stood in the phone booth until someone knocked on the window.

There was on more thing I needed to do. I walked into the kitchen. "What's tonight's special, Chef Pascal?"

"Mademoiselle Sydney." He walked over and gave me a kiss on the cheek. "I need a break." He reached for a bottle of wine from his locker and grabbed two glasses. We went outside.

"I read in the newspaper what happened. I do not understand everything, though. The story said that old woman had lost her mind, but it doesn't make sense to me. I still feel cheated. My poor sister is dead and Frank Threadgill went unpunished for what he did to my parents."

"I'm sorry, Pascal. You've been through a lot."

"Are you leaving us?"

"Yes, it's time to go home."

"You will come back to see Pascal?"

"I will."

"Do me a favor. When you return, please stay at this hotel anyway."

It was good to hear him laugh, but I knew he was feeling pain. "I want to give you this before I leave." I handed him his envelope and a piece of paper with a name and phone number.

"Who is this?"

"Walt Garrison, a man who might provide you with an outlet to deal with your feeling of helplessness and to put what happened to your family to rest. I told him you'd be calling. He will tell you what the police didn't. I hope it helps."

He uncorked the wine. "I was saving this for a special lady. Unless your boyfriend is waiting, we will drink to friends, oui?"

"Yes. My boyfriend is upstairs asleep." I sipped the wine. "Good stuff. I just have one more question to ask you. You found the knife that killed Mildred Threadgill and removed it from your locker, didn't you?"

"Pascal is no fool. You would have done the same thing if someone tried to hang a frame around your neck."

I couldn't help but chuckle.

"You laugh at Pascal's English."

I leaned over and gave him a kiss on the cheek. "Your English is perfect."

When Pascal and I finished the bottle, I went upstairs and fell asleep next to the man I'd chosen to marry.

THERE WERE TWO COUPLES AT the court house before us, so we took a seat and waited. "Are you nervous?" I asked.

"I hadn't thought about it until now."

"You have all the paperwork?"

"Right here." Dixon pulled out an envelope with everything we needed to get married.

Finally, it was our turn. Dixon took my hand and we stood in front of the counter. He handed the paperwork to the clerk. Then she looked down her nose at us. "Where have you been? I almost gave up on you coming back. In fact, I wish you wouldn't have. I lost a five dollar bet with the judge that you'd not be back, but then, it's not too late." She set a wooden sign on the counter in front. Carved on the sign was the word "closed."

I pointed to the clock on the wall. "It's only three fifteen."

"We're closing early. The judge's daughter has a recital this afternoon. Come back tomorrow."

Dixon and I stared at one another. "Do you want to come back tomorrow?"

"No."

"Me neither."

"We can get married anywhere."

"We'll just sneak out of the office one day and head to the courthouse in Austin. But promise me you'll wear that dress."

"Won't Billy and Phoebe wonder about that? I usually wear slacks and cowboys boots."

"We'll have to tell them. We'll need them as witnesses."

"You're right. You'll have to promise me something. If I wear the dress, you'll have to wear black cowboy boots."

"It's a deal."

"So, we're leaving in the morning?"

"Yes."

He pulled a piece of paper from his pocket.

"What's that?"

"Billy sent this telegram yesterday. In all the commotion, I forgot about it." Dixon read it, folded it, and put it back in his pocket. The crease in his brow deepened.

"Oops. What is it?"

"The fire in our office."

"What about it?"

"It was arson."

THE END

WITH THANKS TO

To editor Vicki Julian.
To the many readers who read the early drafts.
To publisher Maureen Carroll who is a delight to work with.

And a special thanks to all my readers who
eagerly await the next Sydney Lockhart mystery.

ABOUT THE AUTHOR

Kathleen Kaska is the author of the awarding-winning mystery series: the Sydney Lockhart Mystery Series set in the 1950s and the Kate Caraway Animal-Rights Mystery Series. Her first two Lockhart mysteries, *Murder at the Arlington* and *Murder at the Luther*, were selected as bonus books for the Pulpwood Queen Book Group, the country's largest book group. She also writes mystery trivia. *The Sherlock Holmes Quiz Book* was

published by Rowman & Littlefield. Her Holmes short story, "The Adventure at Old Basingstoke," appears in Sherlock Holmes of Baking Street, a Belanger Books anthology. She is the founder of The Dogs in the Nighttime, the Sherlock Holmes Society of Anacortes, Washington, a scion of The Baker Street Irregulars.

When she is not writing, she spends much of her time with her husband, traveling the back roads and byways around the country, looking for new venues for her mysteries, and bird watching along the Texas coast and beyond. Her passion for birds led to *The Man Who Saved the Whooping Crane: The Robert Porter Allen Story* (University Press of Florida). Her collection of blog posts for Cave Art Press was published under the title, *Do You Have a Catharsis Handy? Five-Minute Writing Tips.* Catharsis was the winner of the Chanticleer International Book Award in the nonfiction Instruction and Insights category.

Check out her popular blog series, "Growing Up Catholic in a Small Texas Town." www.kathleenkaska.com

Follow her on: Twitter, Facebook, and Instagram.

https://twitter.com/KKaskaAuthor
http://www.facebook.com/kathleenkaska
https://www.instagram.com/kathleenkaska/

Other BOOKS you might enjoy
FROM Anamcara Press LLC

ISBN: 9781941237-82-3
$21.95

ISBN: 9781941237-85-4
$21.95

ISBN: 9781941237-38-0
$18.95

ISBN: 9781941237-33-5
$20.99

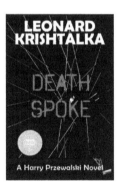

ISBN: 9781941237-30-4
$21.99

ISBN: 9781941237-32-8
$21.95

Available wherever books are sold and at:
anamcara-press.com

Thank you for being a reader! Anamcara Press publishes select works and brings writers & artists together in collaborations in order to serve community and the planet.
Your comments are always welcome!

Anamcara Press
anamcara-press.com